Fool's gold : a western story

11/2013

CC
2w.

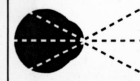

This Large Print Book carries the
Seal of Approval of N.A.V.H.

FOOL'S GOLD

A WESTERN STORY

KEN HODGSON

WHEELER PUBLISHING
A part of Gale, Cengage Learning

GALE
CENGAGE Learning·

Detroit • New York • San Francisco • New Haven, Conn • Waterville, Maine • London

GALE
CENGAGE Learning®

LIBRARY OF CONGRESS CATALOGING-IN-PUBLICATION DATA

Hodgson, Ken.
  Fool's gold : a western story / by Ken Hodgson.
    pages ; cm. — (Wheeler Publishing large print western)
  ISBN-13: 978-1-4104-5814-8 (softcover)
  ISBN-10: 1-4104-5814-8 (softcover)
    1. Gold mines and mining—Fiction. 2. Blue Mountains (Or. and
Wash.)—Fiction. 3. Oregon—Fiction. 4. Large type books. I. Title.
PS3558.O34346F66 2013
813'.6—dc23   2013003463

Published in 2013 by arrangement with Golden West Literary Agency.

Printed in the United States of America
1 2 3 4 5   17 16 15 14 13

This book is for Johnny D. Boggs

*Raro simil hominibus bonam fortunam
bonamque mentem dari . . .*
[It is rare for men to be possessed of
good fortune and good sense at
the same time . . .]

Livy
Annales, XXX, 42

*quid non mortalia pectora cogis,
auri sacra fames?*
[hunger for accursed gold, what mortal
heart do you not drive?]

Vergil
Æneid, III, 1.56

All you need in life is ignorance and
confidence, and then success is sure.

Mark Twain
in a letter to Mrs. Foote,
December 2, 1887

CHAPTER ONE

Jake Crabtree didn't relish the idea of eating his tomcat. He squinted through bloodshot eyes and stared at the purring coal-black excuse of a mouser that was sitting contentedly alongside the cook stove and sadly shook his head. This wasn't going to be easy.

He had named the cat Ulysses, after the best President and general this country ever produced: Ulysses S. Grant. Jake had proudly served under the bombastic and now famous man throughout the wilderness campaign during the waning days of the Civil War.

Now, over a dozen years later, snowed in at a mining shack high in the Blue Mountains of Oregon, he was planning to make a stew out of a perfectly good tomcat named after that noble man.

To Jake's way of thinking there wasn't a lot of choice. He simply had nothing else to eat. The pack rats and mice had gotten into his larder while he was on his usual winter drunk and eaten or destroyed all of his supplies.

"You worthless fur ball. You probably opened the door and told them to bring along their buddies from the looks of things," Jake fumed at Ulysses.

He walked over, plopped down on the edge of his bed, and smacked his head on the rail of the upper bunk, just as he'd done every winter for the past seven spent here on the side of Greenhorn Mountain.

"Damn, I'm gonna have to fix that someday," Jake grumbled.

Painfully Jake surveyed the jumble of empty whiskey bottles that littered the floor of his shack. From the looks of things his drunk had been a decent one. All ten cases he'd stashed away last fall had been drained of their last golden drop.

There wasn't any work he could do on his gold mine while the snow was piled high under the eaves of his cabin. When the harsh winter kept him from working, Jake went into the closest thing to hibernation a human being could muster.

Now he regretted he hadn't made just one more trip to Baker City last fall and laid in a bigger stock of canned goods. Thanks to his worthless tomcat, the pack rats had had a field day with the potatoes, flour, and cornmeal in his pantry while he was enjoying his well-deserved somnolence.

Jake rubbed the back of his throbbing head, then staggered to his feet. Dr. Mac-Nair had given him a bottle of Hollister's patented headache and stomach cure last summer. He finally found it in the back of a wooden blasting powder box he'd nailed to the wall for a shelf. Jake grabbed up the bottle with a shaky hand and uncorked it, sending white tablets flying. He successfully kept a dozen or so in his trembling palm that he quickly popped into his mouth. Doc had told him not to take more than two at a time, but if the bigger dose killed him, at least he would feel better.

Jake washed the acrid-tasting pills down with a dipper of water. When he put the dipper back into the water pail, he noticed a dead mouse had been floating in it for what looked like a *very* long time. Green mold covered the hapless rodent so heavily it had taken him a moment to identify just what it had been before taking its last swim.

"Ulysses stew, yes, siree, that's what ol' Jake's having for dinner and my guess is you're gonna make one mighty stringy and tough meal," he mumbled.

Jake plopped heavily back onto his bed, this time remembering to duck. He reached over to the nightstand and picked up the Bible Slappy Johnson had given him on one of his trips to Baker City. "God-Happy" Slappy was always making the rounds of saloons and whorehouses trying to save souls and give away Bibles.

"You'll get a lot of good out of this," Slappy had told Jake proudly when he accepted the gift.

Slappy had been correct in that assessment. Jake opened the Bible, ripped out one of the onionskin pages, and squinted at it in the dim light that filtered around the covering he'd fastened over his single window.

The page was from the Book of Amos. He saw some words about God's sending a famine and decided that was enough reading. The Old Testament was definitely boring. Perhaps when he got to the new part, the story might pick up.

Jake creased the page in a V and tore it. He grabbed a nearly empty sack of tobacco from the shelf and carefully shook black shreds of Old Rip into the partial page with a quavering hand. One quick lick to moisten the paper and shortly he had it rolled into a very serviceable, if somewhat long, cigarette. He fired it with one of the few sulphur matches left in the box, took a deep puff, and began coughing so hard he was forced to stand up to keep from choking.

"Maybe the New Testament will smoke milder, too," he ventured.

Might as well see how much snow's left outside since I'm already up, Jake thought. Sunlight streaking into his eyes while he was trying to hibernate was something he carefully avoided. Before uncorking his first bottle, he always tacked a piece of rusty tin over the only window to prevent the problem.

The single piece of tin came loose easily. Jake dropped it and the hammer to the cabin floor. He stared through the window, open-mouthed and wide-eyed.

"Well, I'll swan Ulysses, will you look at that. We done had ourselves an early spring!"

Jake had expected to find drifts of snow still piled up to the eaves of his shack. What he saw, however, were open green fields in the clearings below the dense pine and tamarack trees that surrounded his cabin.

Most interesting of all to Jake's situation, a young buck deer stood profiled in the open, his head raised cautiously, looking around. The noise of the falling tin and hammer had put him on alert.

Breathing deeply and trembling more than ever, Jake quietly made his way to the shelf by his bed. He placed the new pair of wire-rimmed eyeglasses he'd gotten last year on his nose, then grabbed up his Winchester. That deer would make a lot bigger meal than a lazy tomcat.

He jacked the lever as quietly as he could and leveled the rifle at the deer through the windowpane. That pane of glass had been packed all the way from Boise, but right now it didn't seem important.

His hands shook badly, but worst of all he saw two deer. He blinked and tried to make his eyes focus, but there was no way around the fact that every time he looked, Jake saw two fuzzy deer standing maybe two hundred feet away. With his left hand he raised the spectacles on his bony nose. There was only one deer now, but his eyesight was so poor Jake knew he didn't stand a prayer of hitting within twenty feet of it.

"Dad-blast that eye doctor," Jake mumbled, letting the glasses slip down on his nose again. "Ulysses, you'd better hope like hell I shoot the right one."

The deer on the left appeared slightly clearer. He leveled the Winchester's sights to point shakily at the deer's shoulder, and fired. The deafening explosion and flying shards of glass caused Ulysses to jump on the bed and scoot under the covers.

Jake watched disgustedly as the deer bolted and ran into a clump of trees, totally unscathed.

"When I see that eye doctor again I'm gonna shoot him. He'll be in real trouble because now I'll know to aim at the doctor on my right!"

He stuck his head through the jagged glass opening that just moments before had framed the only pane of glass for miles. Jake was agreeably surprised how warm the weather was and wondered deeply in what month he'd sobered up. The snows usually didn't melt this completely until some time in May.

"Dad-gum it, Ulysses, if that doctor who sold me these spec's had known his ass from his elbow, I wouldn't have to cook you up. If it's any consolation, I plan on shooting that son-of-a-gun the next time I'm in Baker City."

The water had just come to a roily boil when Jake tossed in some salt and added a couple of pithy onions that had only been partly eaten by varmints. Then he slowly walked to the bed where Ulysses was now sitting on his haunches, purring and attentively watching the goings on with wide, intelligent, and trusting green eyes.

The sleek tomcat jumped affectionately into his master's arms and began nuzzling Jake's beard with his chin, purring up a storm.

"Dang it all, cat, you could at least scratch me or bite me," Jake moaned, staring sadly at the butcher knife clutched in his hand.

Carrying the purring Ulysses cradled in the crook of his arm, Jake walked the few steps to his cook stove with leaden feet. The knife handle felt sweaty in his grip. He took a long moment to watch the roiling water in the stew pot, then sighed as he drew back the butcher knife.

CHAPTER TWO

"Jake!" a familiar voice boomed through the opening where his window had been. "Jake Crabtree, are you in there or did you go and wake up dead this year?"

Startled, Jake quickly hid the butcher knife under a dirty dishtowel. "Well, I'll swan, iffen it ain't Whort Pigg."

The weathered wood door to the small mine shack flew open and Jake's eyes squinted against the unaccustomed sunlight. His old friend, Whorton Pigg, stood close and his features were clear. Anything more than a few feet away was a blur. From the round black hat worn by another man still mounted on a horse he figured it was John Two Trees, Whort's Indian wrangler on his Silver Spur Ranch. Interestingly enough, there looked to be an extra saddled horse alongside Whort's and the one John Two Trees sat astride.

"Whort, you and ol' John are a sight for

sore eyes," Jake said.

Whort backed up a step and stared at Jake Crabtree. "Well, I'd say you're just a sight."

Jake shot a glance downward and surveyed the once-white pair of long johns he'd been wearing since fall. He had to agree that Whort had a point. Some cleaning might be in order.

"You and Doc have always been real fanatical about bathing. Take a bath every week or two and you're takin' a chance with your health. I keep telling you I never even get the sniffles during the wintertime."

"I don't doubt why it works thataway," Whort replied. "The Grim Reaper would have to pinch his nose shut to haul you off."

Jake rolled his crimson eyes to the floor. "Whort, you wouldn't have any grub with you? The pack rats kinda overran ol' Ulysses and ate me outta house and home."

"John and I have a few biscuits and some jerky. We could add it to that pot of stew I saw you fixin'. Just what were you planning to cook up, anyway?"

"Oh, I was going rabbit hunting in a bit," Jake replied with a hint of hesitation. "The things are thicker'n fleas on a Missouri hound this time of year . . . just what time of year might this be, anyway?"

Whort Pigg simply shook his head. Jake,

Gage MacNair, and he had been in the War Between the States together. That was now over twelve years ago. Shaken by the brutality of war, the young men had come West together at the war's end. Following the Oregon Trail westward, they eventually settled in the Powder River Basin in eastern Oregon near the town of Baker City.

Since that time, Whorton Pigg had become the owner of the Silver Spur Ranch, a few miles southwest of Baker City. He also had acquired a beautiful wife, Jenny, who had yet to bear him any offspring.

Gage MacNair, the gregarious Scotsman with flame-red hair, had obtained a medical degree and maintained a booming practice in an upstairs office next to the Gold Dome Hotel on the main street of Baker City.

At the thought of Doc, as most everyone called him these days, Whort's lips pursed. He didn't want to give Jake the sad news, but knew that he must.

"It's only the twentieth of April. We had a Chinook blow in and melt most of the snow. About Doc, he's ailin' bad."

Jake's arms dropped to his sides, sending Ulysses jumping for safety. "What do you mean ailin'?"

"He's got a cancer in his stomach. He won't make it many more days. I reckon

19

he's in a lot of pain for all the whiskey he drinks would make you seem like a piker. He asks if you might come see him . . . before it's too late."

"Yeah . . . uh . . . sure," Jake stammered. "Is Henrietta down at the ranch?"

Henrietta was Jake's mule. He always wintered her at the Silver Spur. The ranch sat in a valley at a much lower elevation and received less snow than fell at the mine. There also was someone at the ranch sober enough to feed her some hay on occasion.

"She wintered a bunch better than you did from the looks of things," Whort commented.

"Dad-gum it all, Whort, I'm powerful sorry to hear about Doc. I run the witch sticks over our claims last fall and I've finally got the Mother Lode pinned down. Just a few feet of drilling and blasting in this one spot and we'll hit it richer than the Comstock. Doc's been grubstaking me all these years. He's in for half."

Whort clucked his tongue. "Reckon all the gold in the world ain't worth much when you're getting ready to shake hands with Saint Peter."

The rancher felt a lump building in his throat. He turned and walked out into the crisp clean air and took a deep breath.

Whort never could understand the lure of prospecting for gold and what it did to people's thinking. To his way of looking at life, a piece of God's good earth with water, cattle, and a wife who didn't nag too much was better than any gold mine. Jake, however, was always one to go chasing after rainbows.

John Two Trees had tied the horses and sat leaning stoically against a bare Tamarack tree. "I'll stay out here. Smells better."

Whort nodded in agreement. He fished through a saddlebag until he found the canvas sack containing the jerky and sourdough biscuits Jenny had baked early that morning, then traipsed back into the rank closeness of the cabin.

Jake grasped the grub sack like a drowning man would a life preserver, confirming Whort's suspicions that the miner wasn't planning on hunting down any rabbits. "Here you go, ol' cat."

Ulysses snatched the proffered strip of jerky and ran out the door with his prize. Jake added the rest of the meat to the stew pot. Gnawing hunger allowed him to wait only a few minutes before ladling a bowl full.

"Better grab some," Jake said, daubing a biscuit.

Whort's nose wrinkled. "That's OK," he said quickly. "John and me ate a mighty big breakfast before coming up here to fetch you."

Jake wolfed down the biscuit. He picked up the bowl, using both hands, and slurped it dry. Twin streams of the impromptu stew trickled down the sides of his brown beard. "You boys just don't know how much ol' Ulysses and me appreciate your dropping by with some chow."

Whort shot a knowing eye after where the black tomcat had gone. "I imagine the *rabbit's* grateful. Now I reckon we oughta quit lollygagging around and head for the ranch. In the morning we'll take the wagon into town and visit Doc. You can get scrubbed up tonight. Doc's sick enough without causing him more grief. Besides that, Jenny's frying up steaks with potatoes and onions for supper tonight. You know how rascally women are about a man cleaning himself up before coming to the dinner table."

Jake winced, then nodded his head knowingly. A meal cooked by female hands was possibly worth taking a bath for. There was only one other thing in this wide world where a woman was an outright necessity. That could be rented easily for a silver dollar. Once he struck a rich vein, he'd have plenty of dollars and absolutely no need of a wife that could turn mean quicker than a pet bear.

"One more bowl of this good stew and the rest of them biscuits and I'll be ready," Jake said.

The sudden realization of his old friend and benefactor being near death struck Jake like a falling boulder. If that vein of gold turned out to be a little deeper than expected, he might be forced to get a job.

Whort read the distress in Jake's pained expression. "Don't fret. We'll get to Baker City in plenty of time for you to say farewell to Doc."

"Yeah," Jake answered, his mind a jumble of anguished thoughts. "That'll be good."

After a long hot soak in the copper bathtub Jake had to admit he felt better. He took a straight razor to his whiskers and scraped his face clean, leaving a handlebar mustache.

Most interesting of all, those wire-rimmed glasses that had failed him so miserably earlier today now seemed to work just fine. Everything he focused on was crystal clear and there was only one of whatever it was.

"I'd guess those spec's just needed a little getting used to," he mumbled to himself.

"Sure saved me the task of plugging that eye doctor."

Jake dried, then slipped into a new pair of white long johns and a pair of clean denim pants and a boiled shirt. He not only felt like a new man, he looked the part.

Nobody on the face of God's earth could butter-fry a steak better than Jenny Pigg, Jake thought, as he carved a huge forkful off his second one. The lithe brunette had even cut slices into the meat and poked in cloves of wild garlic, just the way he liked his steaks cooked.

"It's good to see a man with an appetite," Jenny remarked.

"Jake ain't one to be overly picky about his grub," Whort said. Then added quickly: "No disrespect meant to your good cooking, darlin'."

"This is a great steak," Jake said, talking with his mouth full. "I got plumb down to living on stems and pieces before the snow went. The pack rats done near cleaned me out."

Jenny said: "Why, that's such a shame. Perhaps you should consider getting a good cat."

"Done got one, ma'am. I call him Ulysses, but I can't say he's a good one." Then to change the subject Jake added: "We'll most likely make a strike this year. Then I can afford to lay in enough supplies to feed the rats, too."

"I would sincerely like to see you strike gold, Jake. Whort has told me how hard you work at that mine."

"A man must earn his keep by the sweat of his brow," Jake said, causing Whort to roll his eyes. "By the way, what's for dessert?"

"Rhubarb and cherry pies, and I whipped up some vanilla snow ice cream to top it with. I do hope you would like a big slice."

Jake answered with a vulpine grin. It was times like these that made females downright tolerable.

CHAPTER THREE

Hoarfrost glistened like powdered diamonds on pine and spruce tree needles. The newborn sun had yet to clear the mountains and the bright blue Oregon sky offered no warmth when John Two Trees hitched a pair of dapple horses to Whort's freight wagon.

Always one to enjoy the moment, Jake Crabtree was luxuriating in a delightful, breakfast prepared by a woman. Now on his second plateful of bacon, eggs over easy, and corn dodgers, he appeared perfectly happy to spend the day at the kitchen table.

Whort fidgeted with his empty coffee cup. "Jake, did you grow roots to that chair or are we gonna head to town while we're still young?"

"Don't go rushing the man," Jenny chided. "From the looks of him he's been half starved to death. A few good meals will put some color in his cheeks."

A wife like her might not be too bad to have

around, Jake thought. Then he realized it wouldn't take long before she would be after him to do something distasteful, like get a job. "Don't go getting your underwear in a bunch. I'm just gathering up my strength. Mining's a mighty rough business and saps a body something terrible."

Whort shook his head. He had yet to meet another man who could talk more about nothing than Crabtree. If he kept quiet, Jake might eventually finish eating.

"More coffee, Jake?" Jenny asked sweetly when Jake wiped the last speck of egg yolk from his plate with a dodger and popped it into his mouth.

Whort knew what the answer would be and spoke before Jake finished chewing. "Thanks, hon, but we need to get on the road. When we're in town, I'll pick up those things you've been needing from the general store."

His wife understood and placed the coffee pot back on the cook stove.

Jake's sad eyes followed her every movement. "Reckon you're right, Whort. Takin' care of business always comes first in my book, too."

The wagon groaned to a halt in front of the Gold Dome Hotel. The drive into town had been done in stony silence. Both men had been lost in memories of bygone times and dreaded seeing their old companion on his deathbed.

As the pair climbed down, a freckle-faced boy with grease-plastered black hair, ran over hawking the local newspaper: *The Baker City Bedrock.*

Jake tossed the grinning kid a silver half-dime. "Reckon I oughta get caught up on the news. Who knows what all has gone on since the last time I was in town."

Whort nodded. *The Second Coming could have happened and you likely wouldn't have noticed.*

Jake folded the newspaper, stuck it into his back pocket, and followed his friend to the steps that ran up alongside the red brick hotel to Doc's office and residence.

A metal sign engraved with gold letters and fastened to the railing announced:

GAGE MACNAIR, M.D.
OFFICE UPSTAIRS

The men hesitated long enough to check out a fluffy white cloud that floated motionless in the still, blue heavens. They sighed in unison, then trudged up the steps.

Whort rapped softly. There was a heavy

clump of approaching footsteps. The knob turned, and the door cracked open.

"Glad you finally made it. He ain't got much longer," a harsh and gravelly female voice grumbled as the entryway swung wide.

Lanny Payton glowered at the two men. A smile had never been known to cross the portly, gray-haired woman's face during the five years she'd worked as Doc's nurse.

"Well, we're here now," Whort said. "And I've brought Jake Crabtree along."

Lanny swept her dark, emotionless eyes over Jake as if she were checking out a disease. "Yeah, I know him. He's the shiftless miner that good man lying in there has been handing out money to."

Jake's mustache wiggled. "I'd prefer the term business partner, but whatever snaps your corset."

The elderly nurse snorted, stepped aside, and ushered them in with a curt wave. The pungent smells of a doctor's office were overwhelming. Chloroform, potassium permanganate, and other noxious potions blended together to form what the men knew as miasma, or bad air that was responsible for causing all manner of disease. If any place on earth could be said to reek of death, they were standing in it.

"The doctor's in his bedroom," Lanny

said gravely plodding through an opening into a shadow-filled room.

Sobered by the harsh reality of their surroundings, Whort and Jake followed her wordlessly. Along the wainscot wall, underneath a shuttered window, a cadaverous figure lay on a double brass bed, covered to his neck by a single sheet. On an oak nightstand sat two empty whiskey bottles and a nearly full container of laudanum.

Lanny went to the stove, opened it, and tossed in a couple of sticks of wood. "Light hurts his eyes. That's why I keep it dark," she proclaimed. "And he gets cold easy. I'm always stoking the fire. Next thing you know, he's sweatin'. Lord only knows what I've been through."

The sunken eyes of the bedridden man fluttered open. "Lan . . . Lanny, who's here?"

The nurse strode over and stood protectively by the bed. "It's Whort Pigg and that Jake Crabtree man."

Gage MacNair made an abortive attempt to raise his head from the pillow. The effort exhausted him and it was several minutes before he could wheeze: "Jake . . . you've made it. Thanks, Whort, for fetching him. Come closer. There's something I need to ask."

Jake was already beside the bed. He realized sadly Doc was blind. "I'm right here, old friend. All you've gotta do is tell me what you need done."

"About our mine . . . have you found gold yet?"

"Uh . . . no . . . but I'll have the vein opened right soon."

"Won't do me much good. There's something more important."

"Tell me what it is."

"Remember that flat spot in the meadow that overlooks the valley, where all the wildflowers grow?"

"Sure do," Jake said. "The prettiest spot in the Blue Mountains."

"I think so, too. I've grown tired of being around people. Bury me there."

Jake's eyes widened. "Why I'd reckon Whort and I can do that for you."

A faint rattle that sounded like gurgling water escaped Doc's lips. "That's the most good I'll ever get out of that mine. Did you ever give it a name?"

"Had to. The clerk wouldn't record the claims until I did. I called it the Merry Widow."

Doc tried to laugh. "One thing about you, Jake, you've got imagination."

"We're gonna hit it big. The witch sticks

31

have it pinned down."

"Hope you're right about that."

"Sure as God made little green apples."

Another deeper, more ominous rattle issued from the doctor's mouth. "Whort, you and Jake listen up. There's something else I have to tell you. . . ."

Jake bent down and leaned closely with his ear.

Doctor Gage MacNair wheezed deeply, then his body grew limp.

Lanny pushed Jake aside, pulled down the sheet, and stuck a stethoscope on the doctor's chest. Her eyes were moist when she looked up. "He's gone," she said.

Jake kept his eyes focused on Doc as if he was waiting for him to wake up and finish his statement. "That's a pity. I wonder what it was he wanted to say?"

Lanny clucked her tongue. "We'll never know. I suppose all that's left to do is send for Woody Ash. Doctor MacNair made all of the arrangements before. . . ."

Whort sighed. "Jake and me will go fetch him, if he's in town."

Woody Ash was Baker City's sole undertaker. When people stayed healthy and there was no need of his services, Woody scoured the hills, prospecting for gold.

"He is," Lanny said firmly. "Came by

yesterday to pay his respects."

Jake flashed a fiery look and started to speak when Whort stepped over and placed a hand on his shoulder. "Let's go see that his wishes are carried out."

The two gazed one last time at their departed friend, then turned and walked through the examining room. Both were relieved when they were outside and could breathe fresh air.

"I sure hanker to know what ol' Doc wanted to tell us there at the last," Whort said on their way down the stairs. "A man's dying wish is something to be heeded."

"We'll ask around. Woody might know."

Whort brightened. "You might be onto something. Lanny did say Doc had made arrangements with him."

The Ash Undertaking Parlor and Cabinet Shop was housed in a small, whitewashed clapboard beside Bowman's Livery Stable. A lean-to kept the ornate black and polished silver hearse protected from the elements.

Woody was fitting a lid onto a tiny coffin when Whort and Jake entered. The mortician looked up and went to meet them. Said to be the tallest man in Oregon, Woody stood over seven feet tall with his boots on, yet was skinny as a pole. His bony face twisted into a semblance of a smile.

"Howdy, boys. Glad to see someone drop by. I always hate buildin' coffins for babies, but Lord only knows there's need of them on occasion."

"Doc MacNair's passed on," Whort said stoically.

The undertaker swallowed. "I'm sorry to hear that, but can't say it's any surprise. I'll send for Harry . . . he's my helper . . . and we'll pick him up."

"Obliged," Jake said. "Doc wants to be planted up at the mine, you know."

"Oh my goodness, yes, I do. I'll get word out to the parson and his flock. Tomorrow afternoon would be a wonderful time for the service."

"Tomorrow!" Whort spouted.

"Yes, sir," Woody answered firmly. "The procession could leave here around eight. Figure an hour or so to dig the hole and a little time for the preacher to say the words. Folks would be home in time for supper."

Whort stared at his boots. He'd told Jenny he would be back at the ranch tonight. Considering the circumstances, however, she would understand. "Reckon you know best."

Woody forced a slight smile. "He was an admirable man. Baker City has truly lost one of its greatest citizens."

"Amen to that," Jake said. "By the way, Woody, Doc was fixing to tell us something mighty important just before he went. Did he leave you any instructions or tell you anything that we oughta know about?"

"Oh, my goodness, why, no. He just picked out his coffin. It was my very best, too. Cherry wood with a red velvet lining. I had a leaded-glass window put in just like he asked. I'd be happy to show it to you."

"Reckon we'll see it tomorrow," Whort said quickly. "You sure he didn't tell you nothing more?"

"Just what you already know . . . that he wished to be buried at the mine. When folks get ready to pass on, sometimes their mind wanders."

Jake ran his tongue along the bottom of his mustache. "That's probably all it was. Eight o'clock in the morning, you say?"

"Yes, sir. We'll leave from the Presbyterian Church."

Whort shot a brief, sad glance at the tiny, half-finished coffin before turning toward the door. "We'll see you then."

For the second time in one day both men were glad to be outside and in the fresh air. They walked side-by-side down the dirt street. Neither knew their destination.

Whort broke the frigid silence. "I never

thought much on having to bury a baby. That tiny coffin was an awful thing to behold."

It took Jake a moment to get his voice to work. "That it was. And I need a drink."

The Belle of Baker Saloon was just across the street. The rough-looking bartender placed two empty shot glasses on the long oak bar.

"Rye whiskey," Whort snorted. "Bring us the good stuff. And leave the bottle."

Cushman Pierce, the silver-haired minister, dressed appropriately in a coal-black suit, led the funeral procession driving a spring buggy. By his side, a somber Lanny Payton kept daubing at her eyes with a white handkerchief.

Woody Ash had placed bundles of billowy white ostrich feathers on the corners of his hearse. A slight breeze caused them to flutter like spring butterflies.

All told, nearly a hundred citizens of Baker City followed the polished funeral coach as it headed into the Blue Mountains where they would lay the town doctor to eternal rest.

Jake Crabtree reined the wagon into the back of the line. Whort sat humped up with his slouch hat pulled low. He suffered from

36

a terrible hangover and was glad to let Jake drive. At least, Whort had remembered to send an order to the general store and have Jenny's supplies laid in.

How Jake could be spry as a kitten was a total mystery. He'd drunk more whiskey than Whort had, yet this morning at the Gold Dome Hotel Jake had wolfed down two huge plates of flapjacks and teased the young waitress unmercifully. Whort had only managed to force two cups of black coffee into his churning innards while he sat there, listening to Jake ramble and envied Doc.

When the funeral procession drew to a halt, Whort had begun to believe he might live through the day. The rancher slipped out his gold pocket watch and flipped open the cover. It was ten past one in the afternoon. With luck, he'd be home before sunset.

Jake set the brake and hitched it firmly. When Jake jumped down from the wagon, Ulysses ran to greet him with a high-pitched screech that reminded Whort his healing still had a ways to go.

"Sure was a nice drive up here, wasn't it," Jake said happily. "Doc should be appreciative to be planted on such a fine day as this."

Whort hadn't noticed the weather. Now that he thought on the matter, he decided his friend was correct in his observations. The temperature had risen at least into the sixties. Overhead, the orange orb of a warm sun hung in an azure sky. Only the occasional trilling of a bird and the soft rustle of a breeze through the pine trees broke the still calm.

Jake placed his hands on his hips and surveyed the verdant valley from their lofty viewpoint on the side of Greenhorn Mountain, while Whort climbed slowly down from the freight wagon.

"It's an easy task to figure out why Doc would want to spend eternity here," Jake commented. "I'd reckon God was having a good day when he made this place."

Whort clucked his tongue. "Ain't enough grass to run cattle on."

Jake walked to the wagon and grabbed up a long-handled shovel that he tossed to Whort. Then he turned and began struggling with something black and heavy.

When Whort saw what it was, a burning lump rose in his throat like brimstone. Sometime last night, while he was lost in a whiskey fog, Jake had gone and taken down Doc's metal office sign. The one that read:

"Thought this would make a right fitting headboard for his resting place," Jake announced proudly.

Whort struggled in vain to say something without choking up. He quickly gave up on the task and with teary eyes trudged over to help with the grave digging.

While the men struggled with pick and shovel at their task, the womenfolk set out a splendid dinner on wooden tables hauled in for that purpose. White linen table cloths were soon burdened with heaping plates of fried chicken, mountains of mashed potatoes, huge bowls of cream gravy, and fresh-baked bread along with a tempting assortment of pies and cakes.

Jake had decided early on to make certain none of the ladies strained themselves carrying plates of food and so stayed behind. He was gnawing the last succulent bite of meat from a chicken leg when, from the gravesite, men suddenly began shouting and running wildly about.

Woody Ash, who appeared to be leading the charge, came running toward Jake, his eyes wide. "My God, look at this!" he yelled loudly. "It's pure quill. I've never seen anything like it in all my born days!"

"Now calm down," Jake said as the under-taker skidded to a halt. "It's just a grave. Reckon you've seen plenty of those before. Are we getting ready to plant Doc or what?"

"He'll keep!" Woody proclaimed loudly. He shoved a glittering rock in Jake's startled face. "We've struck gold!"

CHAPTER FOUR

Jake cocked his head in bafflement and stared questioningly at the rock grasped in the undertaker's huge hand. He had dug into some similar-looking stuff the first year he'd prospected here, only he had believed it to be fool's gold.

"Woody, are you sure that's gold?" Jake asked skeptically.

The undertaker blinked. "Are you telling me you've been prospecting up here all of these years and don't know gold when you see it?"

A truthful answer in front of all of these people would have caused Jake untold embarrassment. "Kinda pale, ain't it?"

Woody looked dumbstruck. "Why, my goodness, I thought you'd know. That's the silver mixed in with it. Around these parts, a lot of gold is light-colored."

"Well, I'll be a monkey's uncle," Jake said absently. He reached over and snatched the rock from Woody's hand. It wasn't a very large chunk, yet it hefted like it was made of lead. "Sure is durn heavy."

T. Greene Moss came shuffling over at an angle, working his two canes as fast as he could, a fire of excitement burning in his rheumy eyes. The wizened miner with a bushy white beard had been in on the big California Gold Rush of 'Forty-Nine. A couple of years ago his pelvis had been broken in a cave-in leaving him so stooped and crippled that he could only move in a sideways direction, like a sand crab. The old man had worked in dozens of gold mines. If anyone here would know gold ore when he saw it, T. Greene Moss was the man.

Jake turned and held out the specimen for the old miner's scrutiny.

The flame in T. Greene's watery eyes intensified. "Jumpin' Jehoshaphat!" he boomed. "Rich as anything I've ever set eyes on, an' I'm here to tell you, I've seen a bunch of high-grade in my time. That chunk alone's worth a couple hundred bucks."

Two hundred dollars. Jake was addled by the situation. His witch sticks hadn't crossed or bobbed up and down when he'd crossed that spot before. Now that T. Greene Moss had verified gold, Jake began to lose faith in his witch sticks and came to realize he owned a rich mine.

"I've been telling everybody for years I was going to strike it rich," Jake said firmly.

"Oh, my word, oh, me, oh, goodness gracious," Woody Ash was so excited that all he could do was babble. "We found gold. There's gold on Greenhorn Mountain. I've got to file a claim. I have to move fast."

"Hold your taters," Jake said before the lanky undertaker could run off. "I've done got two claims filed here. They're all recorded nice and legal down in the courthouse and have been for years. This strike's on our claims." He looked toward the distant coffin. "Now let's show the man some respect and get on with the service."

Cushman Pierce charged in and stared at the chunk of ore. "The good Lord's known for patience." The preacher surveyed the verdant mountainside with feverish eyes. "There's got to be more veins up here. It's a good thing we brought some diggin' tools, 'cause the funeral will have to wait. I'm goin' prospecting."

"Count me in," Woody said. "I'll partner with the preacher, that way we can cover twice as much ground."

"Amen, brother," Cushman said as he joined Woody who was already in a dead run for a pick and shovel.

43

"Dad-gum it all!" T. Greene Moss shouted. "We've got ourselves a jenny-wine fer real gold rush."

Jake could only shake his head in amazement as he watched the old miner go sidling down the slope working his canes faster than a man running from a charging bull. T. Greene, Jake decided, could move plenty fast when the spirit moved him.

"What about Doc?" Jake yelled at the milling crowd. "We all came up here to give him a good send-off."

"No time for that now," Willard Hammer, the blacksmith, answered over his shoulder, running for his horse.

Jake Crabtree watched in awe as everyone in the funeral party went berserk with gold fever. Womenfolk ran beside their men to jump on wagons, pushing and shoving aside anyone who slowed their progress.

Lanny Payton elbowed one man from the seat of Woody's funeral hearse, then sent another sprawling with a hard kick to his forehead when he tried to climb aboard. Using some very unlady-like words and the crack of a whip, she cursed the horses into a run. Before traveling a hundred yards, Lanny tried to take the hearse between some trees where the opening was too narrow and got jammed up. The jolt from the sudden stop caused Lanny to sail through the air and land on her derrière. The panicked horses broke their traces and headed toward Baker City.

The nurse quickly jumped up, unscathed, and ran through the thicket of trees yelling: "Gold! We found gold."

Jake sighed as the last of the stragglers charged off into the dense forest. Interestingly enough, no one had gone uphill. Most had decided the ore ran downhill for some reason. Briefly Jake wondered just exactly where his claim lines were, then decided a surveyor could establish those later, after he was wealthy. He certainly had laid claim to the source of the rich ore that had driven everyone nutty as a peach orchard boar.

Believing he was alone, Jake turned his attention to the wooden picnic tables where that delightful-looking dinner was laid out. The mashed potatoes and gravy were cooling off. Fried chicken was fine cold, but since there was no one around to partake, it seemed a shame not to dig in while all of that food was at the peak of perfection.

Jake walked over and picked up a sparkling white China plate with gold trim that he felt befitted the occasion. He heaped it full of mashed potatoes. Using a ladle, he made a crater in the center and filled it to overflowing with cream gravy. Since there was no one around to criticize his manners, he slid a cast iron skillet full of golden fried chicken close, sat down, and dug in.

Jake was bitterly disappointed when his stomach refused to hold any more of this repast, and he had yet to eat any of the pies and cakes. He thought on the matter. It would be a simple task to stash most of this food in his cabin that was luckily only a couple of hundred feet away. Three trips later, Jake believed he had enough food laid away to keep that empty spot in his gut plugged for at least a couple of days.

"Cat," Jake grumbled, tossing Ulysses a chicken bone, "you'd better not go and swear off pack rats just because I'm in a good mood."

Feeling happy and satisfied, he tore another page from the Book of Amos, rolled a smoke, lit it with his last sulphur match, and wandered outside. With his belly full and content, Jake took a puff of his cigarette and looked down the gentle slope to where a ray of sunlight glinted from the leaded-glass window on Doc's coffin. It was time to go inspect his new gold mine and apologize to his friend for the unexpected delay in getting him planted.

Jake walked slowly down to the cherry

wood burying box Woody Ash had been so proud of building. He sighed when he saw Dr. Gage MacNair's sunken and cavernous face staring towards the heavens through that blasted window.

"What in the name of heck do folks want with a coffin that has a peephole in the lid?" Jake mused aloud. "Once they're covered over, I'd expect the view would come to be terrible boring."

"That window's for us."

The voice from the dark shade of a nearby towering pine startled Jake so badly his cigarette fell from his lips when his mouth dropped open. Being around dead people always made him nervous.

Whort Pigg stepped out into the warm, bright sun. "It's so we can take one last look and say good bye to a friend or loved one before going on with the business of living."

"Dag-nab it, Whort," Jake gasped. "You scared me so bad we came near to needing two holes dug. I thought you'd gone to stake some claims."

"Reckon I'll leave the rainbow chasing to you and all them other idiots who are out there marking off mining claims. Besides, I enjoyed the entertainment. I always did wonder just how much grub you could pack away."

"Now, Whort," Jake said, feeling chagrined that his stashing away of food from the funeral dinner had been observed. "You've got Jenny to fix you vittles every day. Living out here like I do, a man gets mighty tired of his own cooking."

Whort's gaze moved to Doc's grave. "Did you really strike it rich?"

Jake ambled over and peered into the depths. He guessed the hole was nearly six feet deep. Woody always stopped digging when his chin was even with the edge. Bright rays of the high afternoon sun glistened off a streak of metal in the bottom that looked to be almost a foot wide.

"Richer than any mine ol' King Solomon ever had," Jake proclaimed. "I knew it was here all along, too, just had a little difficulty pinning it down. We'll simply have to find Doc another resting place somewhere hereabouts. He wouldn't mind. Doc was an understanding sort."

Whort's lips pinched into a thin line. "He was surely a good friend to everyone. A man like him should have gotten a decent send-off."

"Reckon starting a gold rush will cause folks to remember him more so than simply up and dyin'."

Sometimes Jake had a cockeyed way of

looking at things. Whort shook his head sadly. "If you'd pitch in and give me a hand, we oughta drag his coffin out of the sun. Batty as everyone's gone, it might be a while before Gage gets laid away proper."

"Good idea," Jake agreed. "For sure we can't go ahead and use this hole. Now that it's turned into a gold mine, he'd just be in the way." He nodded toward a thick clump of spruce trees downhill that had patches of snow underneath. "Be nice and cool down there."

Whort eyed the thicket, then bent over and grabbed a copper handle on the side of the cherry wood coffin. "I suppose that's the best we can do."

When the heavy coffin had been dragged into place, the two men used their hands to cover it with snow. The gold seekers had carried away all the shovels.

Whort stretched his back and placed his hands on his hips. "He'll keep until things settle down enough to try another funeral. Thankfully I've still got my wagon, so I'm going to head back to the ranch. I'll send John Two Trees up with your mule. Let him know what's going on so I can plan on when to come back."

"Don't fret none. We'll wind up having a good service for ol' Doc yet."

Whort shot one final pensive look at the coffin before turning to leave. "I surely hope so."

As the gray evening metamorphosed into night, cold reclaimed its domain in the rugged Blue Mountains. Jake Crabtree had a comfortable fire crackling in his cook stove and a pot of coffee boiling. Earlier, he'd cleaned up his shack and nailed the piece of tin back over the broken window to keep the heat inside. A single kerosene lamp on the rude table gave off a flickering yellow light.

Jake had felt himself blessed when he found a carton of Lucifer matches and a box of thick, black cigars left behind on a picnic table after the gold colic struck. Building a fire without matches wasn't something he was adept at. A few times the prospector had been forced to leave the lead bullet out of his old Navy Colt and fire into the stove using a double charge of gunpowder. That always blew ashes all over the place and made an awful mess.

Finding the box of cigars had been icing on the cake. They smoked a lot milder than what he had been used to. He bit the end off another and had just started to light it when he heard a banging on the door.

He ambled over and opened up to behold Woody Ash and Cushman Pierce, or at least what was left of them. Both men looked like they had gotten into a fight with a pack of wildcats and came out losers. Their black suits were mud-splattered and hung in tatters.

"Would it be all right if we came in and warmed up?" the preacher asked, his breath blowing frosty white.

"Why, sure," Jake said, stepping aside.

Woody ran to the stove and bent his lanky frame over it. "Thanks, Jake, it's colder than a witch's heart out there."

Cushman Pierce shut the door. "We got us a claim," he announced proudly. "Right below yours and next to one Lanny Payton and T. Green Moss staked. Ours kind of went cattywampus over theirs."

"That caused a little discussion," Woody said. "Never thought an old lady and a cripple on two canes could be so darn' cantankerous."

When Cushman stepped close to the lamp, Jake noticed the preacher sported a black eye.

"I'd reckon that discussion wasn't any too friendly," Jake commented.

"Lanny's a Baptist," Cushman said. "They're always causing problems. Being

51

Christians, however, we eventually came to an understanding."

Woody rubbed his hands together over the warm stove. "We each wound up with a short claim on the same vein. I'm glad old T. Greene's pistol misfired, otherwise there could have been some trouble before we got our boundaries agreed on."

"Amen," the preacher said. "The good Lord abhors violence."

Jake sighed and decided to change the subject. "Coffee's ready."

"A hot cup would be nectar from God," Cushman said.

Jake nodded toward the table. "Well, take a seat and I'll rustle up some supper, too. I reckon you'll want to bunk here tonight."

"We'd appreciate the grub," Woody said. "But we've got to head for town. I notice my hearse jammed into some trees. It's a long walk . . . likely take us till morning."

"What's your rush?" Jake asked.

Cushman Pierce frowned. "We must get our claims filed in the courthouse. Not everyone is going to be so agreeable as Lanny and T. Greene were."

Woody added: "There's people running all over these hills. The first locations hold if there's any dispute later on."

Jake asked with sadness in his voice:

"What about getting poor old Doc laid away?"

The preacher reached into a torn pocket and extracted his Bible. "I'll read some words from the Good Book for him. That's the best we can do for a spell. The ox is in the ditch, you know."

It was news to Jake that, on top of everything else going on, some cow had gotten itself stuck in a ditch. He took a puff on his cigar and wondered what else would go haywire because he'd struck it rich.

CHAPTER FIVE

Isaac Beekman placed a marker in his book with a sigh, then closed it and added it to the jumble on his oak roll-top desk. The novel was Jules Verne's FROM THE EARTH TO THE MOON. The Frenchman had a vivid imagination, but his writing style, Beekman thought, was nowhere near as fine as his own. Some shining day, the name of Beekman would grace the cover of many great and profitable novels. All he had to do was find some editor who recognized true literary genius when he saw it.

He gazed lovingly at his latest manuscript that had been returned with a scathing letter of rejection. Of his eleven completed books, this was by far his greatest work. DUST OVER TEXAS; OR JEREMIAH FOGHORN MAKES GOOD was a heart-warming and worthy story of a newspaperman who braved wild Indians single-handedly to drive a herd of cattle to market.

He needed to raise money to afford medical treatment for his mother-in-law's stuttering. For the sixth time in two days he slid the rejection letter from its envelope and read the words of the stuffed-shirt editor:

After the passage of six years, please feel free to resubmit this book. By then I shall be retired, and there is no love lost on my apprentice.

Milo Z. Nettleman
Slayton Publishing Company
New York City

Isaac mumbled to himself: "That idiot wouldn't know great writing if the book fell off a shelf and hit him on his head."

DUST OVER TEXAS was every bit as good as SETH JONES: OR, CAPTIVES OF THE WILD FRONTIER by Edward Ellis. That novel had sold over four hundred thousand copies. All Isaac Beekman needed was luck. Then he would turn the literary world on its haughty ear.

He added the rejection letter to a drawer that contained over a hundred more, and swiveled his chair around to survey his grimy flatbed press. Making a dreary day to day living by printing a weekly newspaper, *The Baker City Bedrock,* was a terrible waste of his talents.

Florence, his once sweet and lovely wife who had turned into a shrew, would give him no rest until the week's issue had been printed. Then his son, Isaac the Second, could make deliveries to subscribers and hawk copies on the streets. Once that was attended to, he could focus on writing a new novel. This one he decided to submit under a pseudonym.

Beekman forced himself to his feet with a grunt. His waistline had become a testimonial to Florence's good cooking. While her tongue had become razor sharp, his wife's efforts in the kitchen remained superb. The newspaperman tweaked his brown walrus mustache and contemplated this week's edition.

Aside from the town doctor's passing away and some financial trouble plaguing New York City, the news was a total bore. No matter how much he eulogized and embellished Dr. MacNair, it would consume only one column. Creating news where none existed was Isaac Beekman's specialty. The most important thing was to have the reported events happening hundreds, or even thousands, of miles away to prevent the embarrassment of truth rearing its ugly head. Those immense and totally unexplained stone statues on Easter Island had fascinated him for many years. An idea began to form in his mind that could fill an entire page. Perhaps the world-famous archeologist, Anton V. Dutweiller, of Germany, had just unearthed similar statues in Idaho. On second thought, Georgia would be a better choice. Idaho was uncomfortably close to Baker City.

Isaac's pudgy hands were sketching out his imaginary scientist's academic background on a piece of foolscap when the front door burst open. The editor suppressed a frown when he saw Willie Johnson approaching with a wide-eyed expression painted on his pockmarked face. Willie, however, was a good source of local information. Once Isaac had handed over an entire half dollar for sordid details about Preacher Pruett's raid on Molly Spade's "recreation" center. That edition had sold out within hours after it hit the streets.

"Well, spit it out," Beekman grumbled. "I'm a busy man."

Willie gave a yellow-toothed grin. "This here's a dollar story for sure."

"I'll decide that. For the life of me I can't imagine anything happening around Baker City that could possibly be worth a whole dollar."

Willie clucked his tongue loudly, a habit of his that Beekman found annoying. "Well, sir, this is only the biggest thing to hit these parts since that rich gold strike in the Virtue Mine back in 'Sixty-Two."

The newspaperman laid his pen aside. Willie had gotten his undivided attention. The possibilities of a gold discovery in the area were immense. He could run a special edition at a dime a paper and sell every copy. Through his efforts, news of the strike could be made to rage like a summer forest fire. New businesses would be drawn like flies to honey. He might even be able to sell his newspaper business at a tidy profit. Then he could devote full time to writing his great novels.

"Give me the details man. I need facts."

Willie's grin fled. "I want my buck."

"You'll get it, if the story's worth it. I won't know that until you lay it out."

"I want my buck," Willie repeated firmly.

Beekman sighed, then fished a silver Liberty dollar out of the depths of his pants pocket and handed it over with a frown. "If your information's faulty, I expect you to make this up."

"Huh," Willie snorted. "Consider it cheap. I should be up on Greenhorn Mountain staking a claim myself, instead of standin' here jawin' with a tightwad."

"So the strike is on Greenhorn Peak?" Beekman felt a pang of disappointment. He'd hoped the frenzy would hit closer to town.

"The courthouse is packed with folks filing their claims. Why, they say the vein's pure gold, maybe a hundred thousand dollars to the ton."

The editor immediately discounted the figure by ninety percent. Should the reality of the situation call later for some embellishment of the facts, he was prepared for the task. "Who made this strike?"

"Why, it's the durndest thing. They was fixin' to bury Doc up on those claims of Jake Crabtree's when they dug right into the vein."

"The gold was struck while digging a grave?"

"Gol-darn it, that's what I'm a-tellin' you. Ever' blasted soul at the funeral saw the vein. I don't know why I ain't headin' up there myself. A claim anywhere near there would bring more money than you'd pay in a hundred years."

Isaac Beekman felt he'd gotten his money's worth. It would take a personal visit to the site, then he would use his editorial skills to flesh out the facts to his best advantage.

With any luck, he could have the story printed with editions leaving Baker City on tomorrow's stage.

"I will follow up on this purported strike," Beekman said. "Just how might I find the location?"

"Just follow where everyone's headin'. I'd doubt there'll be enough folks left in Baker by tonight to hold a poker game."

The moment Willie left, a smile of satisfaction crossed Beekman's jowls. His coverage of a genuine gold strike would carry his byline across the entire nation, possibly the world.

Carefully he filed his planned story on the Easter Island statues for future use. In his grip he placed pens, nibs, and foolscap, the tools of his trade. His vivid imagination and a few simple facts would take care of the rest.

Digging gold was downright back-breaking work. Jake had spent the entire morning single-jacking a lone dynamite hole into the vein. Not only was quartz terribly hard rock, the confines of the narrow grave made swinging the hammer difficult. Finding gold, he decided, was definitely easier than mining it.

Jake stood upright with effort. Once the

feeling returned to his legs, he climbed the makeshift ladder and left the hole. As he trudged to his cabin, he realized with some surprise no one had shown up to check on his progress. That was too bad. A visitor would give him cause to stop and talk for a spell.

He shooed Ulysses from a wooden case of Giant dynamite and took out a single red stick. Using his pocket knife, Jake sliced it in half and returned the other portion back into the box. Keeping dynamite in his cabin was a necessity; otherwise, it would freeze and pure nitroglycerine leak out and cause problems.

From a roll kept on the shelf above, Jake cut a six-foot piece of fuse. It was longer than he needed, but fuse was cheaper than being blown up. He carefully extracted a blasting cap from a small wooden box. Those things always gave him the heebie-jeebies, especially when it came to crimping them onto the fuse. He slid the open end of the cap onto the fuse, then grimaced when he stuck it into his mouth and bit down. A lot of miners had blown their jaws off from crimping caps with their teeth.

Ulysses trotted closely behind when Jake returned to the mine. He was smoking a cigar, carrying the explosive in one hand

and a broom in the other. "Cat, you'd be advised to go back to the cabin and take a nap. Things are going to get mighty noisy hereabouts."

The tomcat ignored the suggestion and sat on his haunches to keep a curious eye on the proceedings. Jake wondered about his cat's lack of good sense when he climbed back into the grave. He poked the end of the fuse that held the blasting cap into the dynamite. Carefully he folded the supple fuse over alongside the cartridge and stuck it into the blast hole. Using the broom handle, he slid the charge to the bottom with a firm tamp.

"All right, Ulysses," Jake grumbled, "for once in your ornery life, listen up. Either head back to the cabin or get ready to learn how to fly."

The sleek black tomcat responded by purring loudly.

Jake took two long drags on his cigar. "Well, don't say I didn't warn you!"

He touched the end of the cigar to the fuse. A yellow flame shot a couple of inches from the powder center as the fire began to work its way to the blasting cap. Jake scooped up Ulysses as he climbed from the hole. "I'll swan, you addle-brained cat, you're stubborn as a mother-in-law."

The ladder wasn't much, but to keep it from being blown up, Jake pulled it from the shaft. Packing his purring cat and broom, he headed back to the cabin. There was no hurry. Fuse burned at forty-five seconds to the foot. Two and one-half minutes was plenty of time.

The day had warmed agreeably, so Jake left the door open when he went inside and poured a cup of coffee. When dynamite exploded, it left behind a noxious cloud of fumes that gave the worst headache imaginable if a person breathed them. A smart man always took plenty of time to return to work after a blast. Jake figured at least an hour would be prudent.

Then he saw a surrey coming through the trees and pulling to a stop alongside the shaft where the lit fuse was burning closer to the dynamite every second. Jake ran outside, spilling his coffee while waving and yelling at the stranger who was so huge the carriage listed to one side.

"Gol-durn it! Dynamite!" Jake shouted.

The fat man with a huge walrus mustache smiled as he waved and answered: "And a good day to you, too, sir."

A deep boom issued from the shaft as an exploding cloud of smoke and dirt blotted the visitor from view.

CHAPTER SIX

"Tarnation, Ulysses," Jake said, shocked by what had occurred. "The first caller I've had all day and I've gone and blown him up!"

From out of the brown cloud raced a wild-eyed roan horse with a similarly wild-eyed driver bouncing on the buggy seat. Jake was relieved to see the man's hat was still on his head and he appeared undamaged by the experience.

"Whoa, Mabel, whoa, girl!" the fat man called soothingly to the horse that showed no sign of wanting to slow down. With a frown the driver yanked back on the reins. The spooked horse gave up and stood shivering in its traces.

"You all right?" Jake questioned as he approached.

"I must say . . . that was an unusual greeting," the ponderous man said in a surprisingly jovial tone. "I do believe I may have misinterpreted your warning."

"I'm glad you ain't hurt."

The stranger climbed down from the buggy with a grunt and tied the horse to a tree. He brushed dirt from his natty suit, then walked over and extended a pudgy hand. "No damage done, sir. My name is Isaac Beekman, owner of *The Baker City Bedrock.* Who do I have the pleasure of addressing?"

"I'm Jake Crabtree and this here is the Merry Widow Mine."

"Why . . . *excellent* . . . just the gentleman I've traveled all this distance to see."

"Reckon the news has got out," Jake said with reservation. He always felt uneasy around anyone who used big words.

"My good sir!" Beekman boomed proudly. "My understanding is this may well be the grandest thing to happen in Baker County, or should I dare say in the entire state of Oregon?"

Jake said, feeling the soreness in his shoulder: "I've got a pot of coffee on the stove. If you'd like, come inside and sit a spell and get the ringing out of your ears."

"I would be delighted to join you," Beekman said with a sincere smile as he followed the prospector to his cabin.

Jake poured his visitor a steaming cup. "So you want to write about me in your paper?"

Beekman blew on his coffee. "Thousands of people are anxious to hear of your wonderful strike here in an area where none has been made before. Then, with your permission, of course, I would like to examine the vein."

Jake mulled the situation. If there was a downside to talking with this fleshy newspaperman who used bigger words than a stump preacher, he couldn't think of what it might be. Going down in history as an astute and successful prospector seemed like a favorable idea.

"You like pies?" Jake asked. Then he noticed the chair holding the fat man up could barely support his bulk and realized the question had been unnecessary. "I've got a cherry one in the pantry."

"My dear sir," Isaac Beekman replied with a broad smile, "how kind of you to offer. I am totally famished."

In the space of a few short minutes, except for one small slice Jake had managed to slide on his own plate, the entire pie had disappeared into the newsman's maw.

"Delightful, my good sir. Very delightful," Beekman said as he wiped the back of his hand across his mouth. "Now let's get down to the business at hand. Give me something of your background."

Jake always liked to tell how he had become a war hero, personally decorated by now President Grant. By judiciously omitting a few petty details, the story came out a lot more to his liking.

The journalist looked up from his notes. "How glorious, a brave, decorated soldier who was wounded in action makes a success of his life. The reading public will love it . . . simply love it."

Jake considered being tossed from his horse into a thorny blackberry thicket getting wounded. Those vines had scratched him up plenty terrible. "Pain is something all men must learn to deal with."

Beekman was impressed. "A philosopher as well as a brave soldier. Now, tell me how the gold discovery came about. My understanding is the vein was struck accidentally in a grave being dug for Doctor Gage Mac-Nair."

Jake snorted. "It wasn't no gol-durn' accident. I tried to locate his grave so we wouldn't dig into any vein. It was just no use. There's simply too much gold up here to bury a person and not dig into some of the stuff."

The portly reporter kept scribbling while he spoke. "My, this sounds like a fabulous strike. Perhaps it could be compared to the fantastically rich Comstock Lode."

"Strange that you should mention old Pancake," Jake said proudly. "That's what all of his friends call him, you know. All Henry Comstock lives on is pancakes, a mighty boring diet if you ask me."

Beekman lifted his pen and stared at Jake incredulously. "You are actually acquainted with Comstock?"

"Why, I most certainly am. Old Pancake himself was the man who put me onto this place." To Jake's way of thinking this story wasn't a lie. Some years ago he had met a crazy person in Baker City, who claimed to be Henry Comstock. The man had pointed a shaky finger westward. "There's lots of rich mines out there, young fellow. You should go find one."

"What a remarkable coincidence," Beekman said. The journalist suddenly realized he wasn't the only one present capable of devising fiction. "Returning to the business at hand, would it be permissible for me to view this magnificent strike of yours so I may accurately describe it for my readers' edification?"

Jake didn't have a clue what "edification" meant. "I reckon whatever it takes for them to know I struck gold. Sure, let's go take

68

ourselves a gander at what that blast turned up."

The newspaperman swigged the last of his coffee and followed the prospector to where the dynamite blast had nearly finished his writing career. He watched with trepidation when Jake dropped a flimsy wooden ladder into the depths and motioned him over with a beaming smile. There was no question in the journalist's mind: that ladder would never support his bulk.

Jake noticed the reporter's obvious hesitation and agreed. "I'd reckon you can see the vein plenty good from up here."

Isaac Beekman had seen plenty of rich gold ore before, but nothing like what greeted his gaze in the bottom of the hole. His mouth dropped open in amazement. The man who made his living with words was at a loss for something to say. Chunks of white quartz were literally held together with ribbons and masses of soft, glittering gold.

"Sure is a pretty sight, ain't it?" Jake said proudly as he scampered down the ladder to begin pawing through the ore. "Yep, I'd guess you wouldn't be writing anything that would upset a preacher if you said this was one mighty rich gold strike."

"My good man, I have never beheld such

a treasure house."

A feeling of magnanimity surged through Jake's being. This fleshy newspaperman who stood in awe at his accomplishment was going to make him famous. He bent over and grabbed the richest looking piece of high-grade he could find. The hunk probably weighed a solid twenty pounds. Jake tucked the chunk of ore under his arm and climbed from the shaft.

"Here you go, sir. Take this back to town and put it in the window of your newspaper so folks will know Jake Crabtree's struck pay dirt. Consider it a gift for coming to see me."

The startled journalist grabbed the offering with both hands. "Why, thank you. This will certainly dispel any question as to the veracity of your strike. I intend to turn out a special edition of *The Baker City Bedrock* just to give coverage of your fantastic find."

Beekman also planned on displaying the piece of high-grade, at least for a while. Then he'd sell it. The windfall was as unexpected as an acceptance for one of his novels. Flaunting the gold strike at the Merry Widow Mine wouldn't tax his imagination. This was one of the few times in memory when the truth would serve. As a matter of course the newspaperman's esti-

mate of the width of the vein and its rich-
ness might grow beyond what he saw, but
not by much. He surveyed the forested surroundings thoughtfully. "You are no doubt
aware, Mister Crabtree, that a town will
most certainly spring forth on this site?"

Jake's brow creased into a frown. The very
idea of a town being built here was hard to
fathom. "Why, this place ain't all that far
from Baker City. Besides, I've got mining
claims filed on the vein."

"Of course you do, my good sir," Beekman boomed with authority. "A man of
your foresight and ability must see the value
in engaging the services of a surveyor and
laying out streets and lots."

Jake had never considered the idea of a
town, but the benefits could be wonderful.
Having a saloon within walking distance of
his mine was a splendid notion. He twisted
his mustache while imagining how the
streets in his new town would be laid out.
"You're plumb right about the fact there
should be a town here. I'd venture there's
not a town in Oregon called Crabtree."

Beekman tried to conceal his disapproval.
"No, sir, I'm quite certain there isn't. And
while the name does have a certain ring of
charm, perhaps something with an air of
adventure might prove more of a draw." The

71

newspaperman swept his arm along the clear-running brook. "Has this majestic creek been given a name?"

Jake shook his head. "Nope, none that I ever heard of anyway. Doc MacNair always loved this place. That's why he wanted to be slabbed out up here for all eternity."

"Why, how poignant. I believe you have it."

"Doc Creek?"

"Perhaps Slab Creek might be more appropriate to the situation."

Jake thought for a moment. "That does sound like a nice name. I reckon, out of respect for old Doc, who we'll get around to burying shortly, we'll call the town Slab Creek."

Isaac Beekman said: "A most interesting name for a gold rush town. Soon, very soon, my dear Crabtree, the town of Slab Creek shall be wagging on the tips of thousands of tongues."

"I rather like that idea," Jake said with a dreamy expression. "Having my own town right here will save me a lot of running around."

"I must be going." The journalist sighed, and trudged towards his surrey. The walk was a short one, but somewhat uphill and the reporter was wheezing when he untied his horse and climbed aboard. He carefully stashed his prize specimen of gold under the seat. "Thank you for the delicious pie."

"Why, you come around anytime," Jake said.

"I'm certain, sir, not only myself, but multitudes shall do just that. Now I must be off. Soon news of your rich strike will be headed across many states." Beekman cast one final gaze at the mine. "It may be most prudent to post a guard over that treasure you have unearthed. Not everyone has respect for law or another person's property unless they are nudged in that direction by a gun."

Jake smiled and shrugged off the cloud of worry the reporter had raised. He didn't have an enemy in the world and no one would show up to steal any of his gold. There were more important concerns, like figuring out where the main street of Slab Creek would run.

"You have a good trip home, Mister Beekman."

The ponderous newspaperman flicked the reins. The horse was still wild-eyed over nearly getting blown up and quickly trotted down the hill.

Jake waved as he watched the side-heavy buggy disappear into the trees. He decided it would be a day well spent if he finished plotting out his town. A town named Slab Creek. Doc should be downright proud to have been responsible for causing it to come about.

CHAPTER SEVEN

Rincón McCutchan tried to ignore the six-foot-long rattlesnake that was slithering its way down the bar of the Belle of Baker Saloon. The two teamsters leaning their elbows on the counter obviously didn't see it. That was a good sign. He grimaced as the huge reptile passed within inches of the men, then breathed a sigh of relief when it wiggled into the wall and disappeared. He always hated it when something like this happened. It was just so blasted difficult on occasion to figure out whether things were real or not. The doctor back in Colorado had warned him he might start having hallucinations. Rincón realized he needed to pay more attention to his headaches. The only time the spooks came out was when he had one of those splitting headaches that felt like the top of his head was going to explode.

"You're packing around five lead slugs in

your body," the sawbones had said. "I can't take them out without killing you. Those bullets will eventually poison your system as they leak lead. Hallucinations, headaches, and abnormal behavior are all symptoms you'll experience."

The bullets had been a consequence of claim jumping, and it was just too bad that doctor had been correct about his seeing things and those awful headaches. Thank goodness he hadn't noticed any other changes. Perhaps, mused McCutchan, if he came up with enough money, he might be able to find a really good doctor back East, one who could remove those lead slugs. It would be a relief to know everything he saw was really there. In the meanwhile, all he could do was keep searching for a plan to get rich and put up with an occasional spook or two.

"Paper, mister? Buy the special edition and read all about the big gold strike!"

Isaac Beekman's brat of a kid had slipped into the saloon. The boy had a shrill voice that made Rincón's skin crawl. He started to run the irritating urchin off when his brain clicked into gear. *Read all about the big gold strike!*

"I'll take one, sonny," a burly freighter said.

"They're a dime, mister," the brat squawked. "This is a special edition."

The big man gave a snaggle-toothed grin and tossed him a silver coin.

Raising the price of a blasted newspaper a whole nickel galled Rincón, but he needed to know the details to find if there might be a gold mine in his future. "Down here, boy," he growled. "Bring me one of those papers." At twice the normal price, he wasn't going to budge a foot.

The kid with black, grease-plastered hair ran over, laid out a copy of *The Baker City Bedrock* on the oak bar, and extended his palm. Rincón slid in two slugs along with eight pennies so deftly the witless youngster never noticed.

He thought his headache might be coming back and rubbed his temples. One of the benefits of being a bartender was an endless supply of free whiskey. He poured a water glass full of bourbon, then surreptitiously added enough tobacco juice and strong tea to bring the level of the bottle back to where it had been before his pilfering.

Henry Hayes Hedgepath, the skinflint lawyer who owned the joint, had eyes sharper than an eagle's. Until Rincón made his big stake, he needed this job. It would be a wise move not to let whiskey bottles go empty without a corresponding amount of money going into the huge brass cash register that sat underneath a scandalously wonderful portrait of a nude woman. Rincón downed a healthy swallow, then began to read about this so-called rich gold strike. Isaac Beekman had a well-known reputation for tinkering with the truth. Should the gold find be even moderately rich, however, it might warrant Rincón's full attention. He would just have to use a little more caution than he had in the past.

A WONDERFULLY RICH GOLD STRIKE! touted the headline, just as Rincón had expected. The pudgy newsman had to justify that additional nickel. Then he took another drink of whiskey and began to read with renewed interest. Within a few short days the mere mention of Baker County, Oregon will bring forth vision of inexhaustible riches. A veritable spider web of gold veins has recently been unearthed on the south slope of Greenhorn Mountain, west of our fair city. Jake Crabtree, a decorated veteran, who despite having suffered grievous wounds during the war that would have caused a man of lesser courage and determination to become an invalid was the first to discover an exceedingly rich and seemingly endless vein. The writer, having just returned from a first-hand visit, can truthfully state that a veritable treasure house of free gold has been opened by Mr. Crabtree. The glistening yellow metal by which all wealth is measured lay exposed not by mere ounces, but its value must be reckoned in pounds per ton.

Rincón McCutchan folded the newspaper, a thin grin on his lips. He had read enough. Besides, his temples had begun throbbing from the concentration. This gold strike could possibly be his ticket to riches. He slugged down the remaining whiskey in his glass and pondered the situation.

Running up to the vicinity of Greenhorn Peak and staking claims wasn't in his plans. If Rincón were to acquire a rich mine, he would gain title to it over the strenuous objections of the legitimate owner. This time he couldn't afford to be as bold and fearless as he had been in Colorado. His first task would be to get to know Jake Crabtree. A semblance of friendship along with the lubricating properties of some good whiskey could possibly expose the prospector's Achilles' heel. It would be a move that might accomplish Rincón's goals without getting him shot again.

Rincón's head still throbbed despite the whiskey. He pilfered another glassful and drank it down. A warm glow flowed through his lanky body and his muddled thoughts turned crystalline in clarity. Lawyers wound up owning every rich mine Rincón had ever been acquainted with. From conversations he had overheard at the bar, Hedgepath had gained the saloon from a widow lady with three young children to raise. It seemed her husband owed the shyster a small fee, then he had unexpectedly died from lockjaw. Since the widow was unable to pay, Hedgepath had sued and won the only asset the poor lady owned: the Belle of Baker Saloon.

My kind of man, Rincón thought. A partner not hindered by a trace of conscience would be a real asset.

CHAPTER EIGHT

John Two Trees couldn't help but be amazed at just how quickly white men could go crazy. All it took was the finding of that yellow metal called gold and they lost every bit of good sense. Even those who seemed perfectly normal before became crazy at the sight of gold.

As he led Jake Crabtree's mule, Henrietta, alongside the Powder River, John felt happy to be a Nez Percé Indian. They were The People and not affected by loss of their minds upon viewing a yellow rock.

John Two Trees had been educated at an Indian school run by a white missionary. That was how he came to know the ways of the white man and also to read and write their words. He felt lucky to have had his grandfather to teach him the ways of The People. If there were a choice, John would prefer to stay with his tribe. The white man's rules were many and changed like the seasons. The People, on the other hand, lived by laws of the spirits, and no spirit had ever changed a law like white men were so fond of doing.

"Outta the way, Injun," a wild-eyed white man yelled as he approached from behind, driving a freight wagon pulled by four lathered horses.

John Two Trees led Jake's mule into the brush and stopped until the empty wagon rumbled past. White men were always in a hurry. Then, when they reached their destination, they often did nothing. Perhaps the spirits could cure that, too. The People could always hope.

Jake Crabtree was pleased to see John Two Trees walk into Slab Creek, leading his faithful mule. Loading gold ore onto a freight wagon with a long-handled shovel was hard work. Now he had a good excuse to stop and visit, at least for a while. The Indian never had been much for long-windedness.

"I'll be back directly," Jake said to Packy Jackson as he leaned his shovel against the freighter's wagon.

"For two bucks more I'd be obliged to load it by myself," Packy said. There was little doubt in his mind that he'd wind up doing most of the work, anyway.

Jake saw nothing wrong with that idea. "Sure, Packy, I'll be glad to help you out. Just add the two dollars to my tab."

"Yes, sir, Mister Crabtree," the freighter said.

Being called *Mister* was beginning to have a downright charm to it, Jake thought. There were definite rewards for striking gold.

John Two Trees looked sadly at the hole from where the ore had been dug. He recognized this Packy as the man who had run him off the road earlier. The Indian bore the freighter no ill will for his rudeness. Crazy people were to be pitied, or so his grandfather had taught.

Jake walked over beside John Two Trees and nodded to where a circle of lodge poles had been wired together to form a corral. "I'd expect Henrietta's plumb glad to get home."

The Nez Percé led the gentle brown mule inside the enclosure. John Two Trees was glad to see the fence allowed the animal access to the creek for water. Of all the crazy white men he'd known, Jake Crabtree had been the first to lose his mind long before he'd found any of the yellow metal.

"I'd have reckoned on you riding a horse up here," Jake said. "It's a tolerable ways from Whort's ranch."

"Not far," John Two Trees answered.

The Nez Percé was puzzled as to why white men would go to the trouble of putting a saddle on a horse just to travel a few miles. Then John Two Trees remembered to ask: "Mister Whort wonders as to when he should return to bury the medicine man?"

Jake cocked his head. That was a good question. It would be five days tomorrow since the gold had been struck in Doc's grave. Following the newspaperman's suggestion, he'd sent word to have a surveyor come and lay out his town. Perhaps the engineer could plot a nice cemetery some place out of the way where there wasn't any vein, if that was possible. "Tell Whort I'm studying on that. I'll get word to him when I've got a plan."

The Indian kept his stoic expression and thought on the sad situation. The People would never leave one of their dead unhonored. Then he remembered the gold strike and felt sorry for the white men who had lost their way. "I go now." He turned and quickly melted into a thicket of towering spruce.

"Well, I'll swan," Jake said, shaking his head. "That Indian's just in too big of a hurry to appreciate what I've gone and found up here."

Packy Jackson mopped sweat from his brow with a dirty handkerchief. He eyed the heavy wagonload of rich ore that sparkled in the sunlight. There was a solid two tons of high-grade on the wagon. It galled him that he hadn't been lucky enough to locate a rich claim himself. Becoming a wealthy mining magnate was certainly a lot more desirable than freighting.

"Sure is a pretty sight, ain't it?" Jake said, sauntering over while blowing on a steaming cup of coffee. "The best part is, there ain't no end to where that came from."

Packy cast a covetous glance at the vein of gold in the bottom of the shaft. "Looks like you hit the Mother Lode. It won't be long afore you'll be needin' to put up a gallows frame. That ore's headin' straight for China."

Jake cocked his head. He wasn't aware of anyone in these parts who needed hanging.

"Why'd I be going and putting up a gallows for?" Jake asked.

Packy Jackson tried to mask his dismay over the man's lack of knowledge. He wondered how anyone could be smart enough to find a vein of gold and not know how to go about mining it. "Well, some folks call them a head frame. They're a big wood tower over the shaft so you can raise the bucket high enough to dump it into a mine car."

"Oh, yeah, a head frame," Jake said with conviction. "I never heard 'em called a gallows before. Yep, I plan on getting one of those, but until I get paid by the mill, I'm gonna have to keep doing it the hard way. Machinery costs money."

"That it does. Colonel Ruckle, who owns the Virtue, told me he spent two hundred thousand dollars on his mine and mill."

Two hundred thousand dollars. Jake Crabtree could scarcely comprehend that so much money existed. The most he'd ever held in his hand had been a quintuple eagle. Some loudmouth had showed it off in the Powder River Saloon before he visited the red-light district and exchanged his gold piece for a lump on his head. The heft of that huge coin remained clear in Jake's memory. He took a sip of coffee and surveyed the loaded freight wagon with renewed interest.

"Say, Packy," he said, "you've been hauling ore for quite a spell. Do you have any idea as to what this load might fetch?"

Packy swallowed and cast a squinty-eyed look at the glistening wagon load. "Gold is awful hard to eyeball, but I'd be surprised as a politician in heaven if this don't mill out at nigh onto two hundred ounces to the ton."

It was Jake's turn to swallow. "At twenty dollars an ounce that would total over eight thousand bucks."

The freighter shook his head. "Nothing but pure gold brings that much. The bank buys it for a discount and then lops off more for impurities. Then there's the millin' charges and my freight bill. Figger three, maybe five, thousand dollars, give or take a grand. The assayer makes the final decisions."

Jake was stunned, both by the tremendous amount of money he could expect to receive and just how much his cut got whittled down in the process. "Maybe I oughta think about building my own mill right here."

Packy Jackson definitely did not care for the turn this conversation had taken. Freighting ore to a mill was a big part of his business. "Well, first off, you've gotta have a ton of money to build one of the durn' things. Then you've gotta hire men that know how to run it without losin' most of the gold in the process. I'd think a long while on buildin' a mill afore I started waking snakes. I reckon on you gettin' plenty rich without frettin' the milling."

Jake worried his mustache with his tongue and mulled Packy's speech about the pitfalls of owning a mill. Why did everything always have to be so complicated? "Reckon I'll study on the situation for a spell."

"You're a smart man not to go makin' rash decisions."

"I appreciate the advice, Packy." Jake fished a piece of paper from his shirt pocket and handed it to the freighter. "Here's a list of a few things I'd like you to haul back soon as you can. I'm hoping the stores will give me credit until I get my settlement."

Packy Jackson eyed the list and smiled. All Jake had ordered were staples for his cabin and some more explosives. The bill to haul his wants up here would cost more than the supplies. "When folks get a gander at this load of ore, your credit will be good for anything you care to buy."

Jake Crabtree was a happy man when he sipped his coffee and watched the heavy wagon creak off through the trees with his first shipment of ore. There was no doubt in his mind that this would soon be a common occurrence.

The miles slowly dragged by while Packy Jackson's attitude slipped deeper into a funk. Life just wasn't fair. There was several thousand dollars worth of high-grade loaded on his freight wagon and all he would get for his efforts would be a few measly dollars. Jake Crabtree was no different than any other man of wealth. They cared nothing for the poor workers who made them their money. If he became unable to work, all Crabtree would do is hire another freighter. No, life certainly wasn't fair. Packy Jackson would remain a poor man all of his life. *Unless*. The thought of actually stealing was repulsive to him. But rich ore really belonged to God. After all, the Almighty had buried it there in the first place. If he were to stash a little every trip, soon he'd have a tidy retirement laid aside. All he needed to do to keep on the good side of God would be to tithe ten percent.

The only problem was he couldn't sell any for a long while without raising suspicions. Everyone knew he didn't have a claim it could have come from. One nice thing about gold ore was it didn't spoil if you put it back into the ground for a while. Packy made his decision a couple of miles before he came to where the road from the town of Sumpter intersected. There were a couple of hundred people living there, working placer mines along Cracker Creek and Mc-

Cully Forks. The more people there were, the more likely his pilfering of some of God's high-grade might be observed.

He pulled the wagon off the road and into a clump of trees. The tracks wouldn't raise curiosity. Horses needed to rest on occasion and it would be impolite to block the road should anyone else come along.

In the passing of several minutes the wagon had been lightened considerably. The freighter had found a natural depression behind a pile of boulders that would easily hold a ton or two without becoming a suspicious hump. He tossed some dirt on top of the ore, then covered his cache with some dead branches.

Packy Jackson's spirits were high when he headed for Baker City. His depression had flown like a dove. A few more stops on the way back from the Merry Widow Mine and he'd be set for life.

It would be a year or two before he could stake a claim and make his rich strike. That was fine. Even better was the fact that he wasn't actually stealing and God wouldn't hold his actions against him when Gabriel blew his horn.

CHAPTER NINE

T. Greene Moss leaned heavily on his canes and peered into the depths of their new shaft. It had already been sunk over twelve feet deep thanks to money supplied by his partner, Lanny Payton. They had named their claim the Golden Ruckus because of the squabble with the preacher and the undertaker, who had yet to put down the required ten-foot-deep discovery pit, required by law to hold a claim.

The quartz vein wasn't rich, not yet anyway. Actually to see the gold they had to crush the hard ore into powder, then pan it. The thin trail of yellow metal that showed told T. Greene's experienced eye it would assay out at possibly ten dollars per ton, not nearly enough to show a profit. Depth was what they needed. Any idiot knew that gold got richer the deeper a person dug.

"We're gonna hit it for sure," Lanny Payton boomed to T. Greene from the bottom of the shaft. "The vein's getting wider since that last blast."

From where T. Greene stood, it didn't look any different, but his days of climbing down shafts were over. "Sure enough, Lanny. Pretty soon that gold will come in. Then our only problem will be how tuh spend all of our money."

"That's an envious problem," Warm Stove Williams said from beside T. Greene where he stood with his arms folded across his chest, flapping his mittened hands on his heavy peajacket. "Iffen I ever struck it rich, I'd move to Arizona and never be cold ag'in."

Warm Stove Williams had been friends with T. Greene Moss since they had met during the California Gold Rush. For over twenty years Williams had been called Warm Stove because of his inability, no matter how pleasant the weather, to quit shivering from the cold. He had consulted many doctors and had tried many cures. Whiskey that had been steeped in an oak cask with rattlesnake heads and castor oil helped for a while. Then he'd discovered straight whiskey not only worked as well, it tasted a lot better going down. In spite of his malady and old age, Warm Stove managed to make enough money swamping saloons to keep him and his crippled partner in grub along with a small cabin to live in. Lately he'd started shaking so badly he doubted his employment would last much longer. The vein needed to pay off or they might both wind up starving.

T. Greene snorted. "I've knowed you too many years, Warm Stove, tuh not figger that ol' Lucifer won't likely give you a decent toastin' once he gets hold of yer soul. Remember that schoolmarm back in Californey? I'd 'spect she'd buy more coal if the devil ran short."

"Leastwise, I'd finally get warmed up. An' if I didn't make it to the infernal regions, I wouldn't have my ol' friends to keep me company," Williams said.

"All you two galoots ever do is argue," Lanny Payton said as she wheezed her bulk up the ladder. "Here we've gone and found ourselves a gold mine. That should brighten your dark spirits."

The two grizzled, veteran miners surveyed the nurse with knowing eyes when she climbed into the sunlight. They had seen that same rabid look on a thousand faces. Her very essence issued an urgency that could only be sated by gold.

T. Greene said: "Ownin' a mine surely will brighten us, once we hit the pay streak.

Dad-burned gold can be a real woolly bugger tuh pin down fer sure."

"But we're onto it," Lanny proclaimed. "I
seen that shining stuff in the pan with my
own two good eyes. All it has to do is richen
up a tad and our mine will make Crabtree's
seem like a fly in a whirlwind."

"That it will, partner," T. Greene said to
Lanny, then sidled himself around using his
canes until he faced the two burly Dugan
brothers, Seth and Orson, who had been
sitting on a log while Lanny inspected the
vein. "Well, boys, the break's over. Fer the
ten gold dollars a foot you're gettin' paid
tuh sink this shaft, I'd reckon on you wantin' tuh get back to it."

"Yes, sir, we surely do," Seth Dugan said
respectfully to the old man as he and his
brother stood. No one expected Orson to
say anything. Some years ago a slab of rock
had fallen from the roof of a mine and
crushed his voice box. The two miners
grabbed their metal candleholders and
descended into the shaft.

Shortly a rhythmic pounding from the
depths told T. Greene and Warm Stove that
work on deepening the shaft was under way
once again. The familiar ringing of steel
striking steel was like fine music, a sym-
phony of progress along the road to riches.

"I sure hope we strike it soon," Lanny Payton said. "That little nest egg I had tucked away won't last long at the rate we're spending it."

Warm Stove Williams gave a hard shudder. "Don't go frettin' until we get some depth. Then it might take a little tunnelin' to find where the gold is."

Lanny focused fevered eyes on the shaft as if she could see into the earth. "There's a rich vein down there. I can feel it in my bones."

"Yep," T. Greene assured, "ain't no doubt about us hittin' it rich. The fact is certain as the Second Comin'."

Woody Ash clicked the brass telescope into focus and peered through an opening in the trees.

"Well, tell me, man, what's going on down there, have they hit anything yet?" Cushman Pierce grumbled.

"I can't see down the damn' shaft," Woody answered.

"Cursing is a sin, my friend," the preacher scolded. "We need the Lord's help, not his wrath."

"Sorry," Woody said. He handed the telescope to Cushman. "At least the vein they're digging on is the same as ours. If they strike ore, we should, too."

The preacher squinted through the telescope. "From here, they appear more worried than anything."

The undertaker sighed. "They're the ones spending money to see if there's anything down there. It don't cost us nothing to keep an eye on 'em."

"Amen, brother, patience is a virtue."

"When they go home tonight," Woody said in a whisper, "we should go down that shaft of theirs and take ourselves a peek."

"Trespassing on the property of another is a sin," Cushman Pierce said.

"Nope," Woody said firmly. "Until a claim's patented, it ain't private property. And the way I see it, that vein they're working is ours. It just so happens a little of it leaked over onto their side."

The preacher mulled that concept for a moment. "You may be correct, brother. After giving the matter some thought, I don't believe visiting their shaft after dark would be sinful at all."

"Thought you'd see it that way," Woody said.

"The pathway to heaven is a narrow one. I must set an example for all to follow."

The undertaker sighed and leaned against a tree. "We'd better get some rest and tonight I'll follow your example down their shaft. Then we'll see if this vein has any gold worth mining."

Jake Crabtree gave a smile and farewell wave to the twentieth visitor he'd entertained that afternoon. Being the center of attention was a wonderful feeling.

Isaac Beekman had written a fine and truthful article about him and his Merry Widow Mine. Every visitor had brought along a copy of the special edition of *The Baker City Bedrock,* folded in their pocket. The power of the press was an amazing thing. Once the callers gazed on his vein of ore, they had said they were going to stay and prospect the area. Jake Crabtree was the brilliant prospector who had started it all.

Building a town sounded like a better idea the more he thought on the matter. The way things were shaping up, Slab Creek would be bigger than Baker City. Perhaps he ought to think on making the town bigger than he'd planned.

In his mind's eye, Jake could envision towering smokestacks reaching to the heavens from a sprawling five-story building that covered the draw works. He could almost feel the earth tremble when the steam cylinders chugged to turn the hoist, bringing up another load of rich ore from far below the earth. Free enterprise at its finest and it all started because of Jacob Aloysius Crabtree and, of course, Dr. Gage MacNair.

I plumb forgot about old Doc, Jake thought, crashing back to reality from his lofty perch of dreams. *He's going to be in need of a resting place right soon.* It would be a pity to have that surveyor plot a cemetery only to find the place was as lousy with gold as Doc's last grave site had turned out to be.

Jake felt tired from all of the visiting that had gone on and the thinking he'd been required to do. He trudged up to his cabin, went inside, and poked a few small twigs of dry tamarack into the firebox of his stove. Soon he'd have a roaring fire and boil up a pot of coffee.

He grabbed a cigar from his rapidly dwindling supply and lit it. Having store-bought smokes certainly beat rolling his own, using pages out of Slappy's Bible. Now that he was a rich man, he would pass the Word onto someone less fortunate.

The food he'd stashed away from the planned funeral had nearly been consumed. Even Ulysses refused to eat the roast beef, which had taken on a decidedly green color. Jake sniffed it and agreed with his tomcat's judgment. There was a single pie left. Jake had a suspicion it might be mincemeat. That was why he'd waited until now to tackle the god-awful thing.

Ulysses began rubbing against his leg and purring loudly.

"Careful cat, or I might give you some," Jake said. "That'd break you from begging."

Through the open doorway Jake noticed the sun had dropped behind the mountains and the sky had become pewter gray. The clouds spoke of snow or rain, and cold. He wished he hadn't shot out his only window. Then he could keep an eye on the weather from the comforts of his cabin. He took a long puff on his cigar, blew a smoke ring, then got up to close the door for the night.

"Hello the house!" a friendly voice boomed, startling Jake considerably. He hadn't heard anyone approach.

"Hello, yourself," Jake said, poking his head outside. He noticed a roan horse tied to a tree and a skinny man with a pock-marked face standing alongside. "Come on inside. From the looks of things we might get us a storm. I've got a fire going. We'll have some coffee ready right soon."

"Sounds great," the visitor said. "I just wanted to ride up here and congratulate you on striking it rich." He reached into his saddlebags and extracted two bottles of whiskey. "Thought we might have a drink together."

Jake's eyes widened with delight at the sight of those amber bottles. "That's mighty thoughtful of you. I'd be obliged."

The man walked inside and set the bottles on the table. He flashed a black-toothed grin. "I reckon everyone knows your name, Mister Crabtree." Now that he was close, Jake noticed the lanky man's complexion was an unhealthy, pasty shade of yellow. "Allow me to introduce myself, my name is McCutchan . . . Rincón McCutchan."

CHAPTER TEN

It was difficult for Rincón McCutchan not to say anything about the huge black spider perched on top of the lawyer's head. He supposed it was a tarantula, even though he'd never heard of one growing to be so large. The spider had orange bands on its many leg joints and fiery red eyes that kept their malevolent gaze focused directly on him. The fact Henry Hayes Hedgepath didn't seem to notice the thing told Rincón the spider must be another spook. At least, he surely hoped so. Dealing with the hawk-nosed lawyer was uncomfortable enough without his wearing a tarantula on his head.

The lawyer spoke in his usual monotone: "So, Mister McCutchan, you mentioned you had a business proposal that might be of interest to me."

"Well, Henry it's about that. . . ."

"Stop right there!" the lawyer demanded, and slapped his hand on the desk for emphasis. "You will address me as *Mister* Hedgepath. All business dealings should remain formal. It removes any possibility of friendship entering into the relationship."

Rincón sputtered: "Sorry, sir . . . uh . . . Mister Hedgepath, I meant no disrespect." From where he sat the spider no longer looked as vicious. The arrogant lawyer had black piggish eyes that were undoubtedly windows into the netherworld. Underneath the spider, steel gray hair was combed straight back and hung a foot below the collar of his shirt. Rincón couldn't begin to guess the man's age. The bony lawyer might be anywhere from forty to seventy years old. Not that it mattered. After this outburst, the attorney would be playing poker with the devil — just as soon as he was no longer of any use.

"I merely wanted to set forth the ground rules for any business relationship between us," Hedgepath said coldly.

Rincón McCutchan decided to let the lawyer play his game and actually believe he might live to gain from this deal. Despite having been shot by four different people, he had yet to put a bullet into anyone. Plugging the man across the desk wearing a dreadful spider for a hat would be a wonderful place to start.

"Yes, *Mister* Hedgepath," Rincón said, "I see your point and agree fully. Any deal worth millions of dollars should be carefully entered into and recorded."

The first hint of a smile Rincón had ever seen the attorney exhibit crossed his normally lifeless face. "Ah, Mister McCutchan, such lofty figures could only come from a gold mine. By chance you wouldn't be referring to the recent strike made by one Jacob A. Crabtree?"

Rincón was taken aback. He knew the shyster kept up with what was going on, but his directness was shocking. "Yes, sir, Mister Hedgepath. I spent most of last night drinking whiskey with Crabtree up at that cabin of his. Before it got dark I also got a look at the vein." He reached into his pocket, extracted a chunk of shiny rock the size of his fist, and carefully laid it on the lawyer's massive oak desk. "The strike is for real."

The lawyer leaned back and laced his bony fingers behind his head. The tarantula didn't seem to mind. "And what, may I ask, are you suggesting?"

"What I'm proposing *Mister* Hedgepath is a partnership to make us both rich. Crabtree is a hayseed. I'm sayin', if I was to put up a location notice dating back before the strike, we'd win that mine in court."

"Interesting, Mister McCutchan, very interesting." The spider sprang from the lawyer's head to perch on a shelf. "The problem is, Crabtree's claims have been duly recorded in the county records for years. I have already checked. The paths of the law are diverse and sinuous, Mister Mc-Cutchan. I have many avenues to explore. It would be a perilous task to enter onto the Merry Widow Mine and lay claim to it."

Rincón's head began throbbing. The scarecrow-looking attorney had no real idea just how perilous claim jumping could be. That was why he was here: to avoid getting shot again. "Crabtree's also going to lay out a town up there. He's got a surveyor coming, probably today, to get started on it."

Hedgepath suddenly looked *very* interested. "Now, that is a piece of news. If I am unable to legally separate Mister Crabtree from his mine, the venture could still be quite profitable, my dear sir, quite profitable, indeed."

Rincón had no idea what the lawyer was ranting about. "I don't understand." Then he remembered quickly to add: "*Mister* Hedgepath."

"And now, Mister McCutchan, you may begin to understand why I do not carry bullets around inside my person as you do. Ah, yes, I know of your malady." The attorney hesitated for effect. "My goals are always directed to the long-term approach to winning. Rashness may, on occasion, be disastrous."

Or fatal, Rincón thought. "What are you suggesting, sir?"

"Profit, Mister McCutchan, possibly a great deal of profit. Do you know what generally makes more money in a boom town than the mines themselves?" Hedgepath did not wait for an answer. "It's mining the miners. A saloon with gambling and a few ladies of the night would be extremely profitable. Run the faro tables crooked, mark the cards, and water the whiskey . . . the latter I'm *certain* you're skilled at, are you not?"

Rincón coughed. "I may have slipped a nip or two."

"More like four cases. You may rest assured that I shall take my due out of your share of our future profits."

"Then, sir, I guess we're gonna partner on a saloon?"

"A partnership is a subjective term, Mister McCutchan. I trust you have matching funds available for our endeavor?"

"Uh . . . no, sir, but I'd sure pay you back right soon." Rincón couldn't keep up with

the twists and turns the lawyer was presenting.

Hedgepath grinned. His ivory teeth were
closely set and sharply pointed. The lawyer's
black eyes sparked like flint. "If I take most
of the risk, it is only fair that my share be
slightly more than yours. To be agreeable,
Mister McCutchan, I shall stipulate that,
should I be successful in legally gaining title
to this Merry Widow Mine, the profits of
that venture shall also be added to our
proposed partnership."

"How much more?" Rincón asked.

"How much more what?"

Rincón gritted his teeth; his head throbbed
with pain. He noticed the tarantula's red
eyes had grown to the size of dimes. "How
much more, *Mister* Hedgepath?"

"Excellent. I *do* wish to keep this strictly
a business proposition. Generosity will
certainly be my downfall, but if you agree
to operate the saloon, I shall continue your
salary of two dollars a day and dispense to
you twenty percent of the net profits from
the venture."

This was not turning out to be a good day
for Rincón. He'd had worse, however. At
least no one had shot him. The problem
was, the shyster made some sort of twisted
sense in his proposal. Rincón risked noth-

ing, yet kept his salary coming in and received twenty percent of what he knew would certainly be fat profits. Once everything had been figured out, it would be easy enough to arrange an accident. Pushing the bony lawyer down a mine shaft would be a delightful task and make up for having to call him "mister" or "sir." He wanted to conclude this meeting and get a drink. Also, that blasted spider had grown a foot in just the past minute and developed long white fangs that had droplets of venom clinging to them like morning dew.

"Well, Mister McCutchan," the lawyer's harsh voice grated, "please give me your decision as my terms are not only most generous, they're also not negotiable."

Rincón felt his head was going to explode. "I reckon that's fair. Let's get to it." A scowl from the shyster reminded him. "Mister Hedgepath."

"*Excellent.* I simply love it when a plan comes together. I shall prepare our agreement for signature. In the meanwhile, I do believe the saloon is due to open. Also, I must remind you that complete silence is necessary. I do plan to check into Mister Crabtree's claim holdings, but it must be done with due diligence."

The spider had grown to the size of a

whiskey barrel. Rincón didn't know which to fear more, the tarantula or the lawyer. Regardless, it was time to get out of there. "You can count on me, Mister Hedgepath."

The lawyer leaned forward and placed bony elbows on the desk, causing the spider's fangs to begin dripping poison. "My dear Mister McCutchan," he said with a hiss, "and that is the way it shall remain. Dissolving a partnership is always such a *painful* ordeal."

Rincón swallowed, stood up, and spun to leave, anxious for the fresh air and to be away from both the shyster and the spook.

"Mister McCutchan," the lawyer said as Rincón was headed out the door, "please feel free to imbibe to relieve those terrible headaches you must be suffering. I am quite aware of the effects lead bullets leaking into a person's system must cause. As our agreement is for net profits, this act of generosity on my part shall reap rewards for us both."

Rincón McCutchan didn't bother to answer. He simply nodded and shut the door behind him. For some odd reason he felt more afraid of that skinny, hawkish lawyer than anyone, even those who had shot him. When the time was ripe, killing Hedgepath would be the most gratifying accomplishment of his life.

■ ■ ■ ■

Horace Tabor stood in a spring snowstorm while feather-sized flakes built on his hat and tattered Albert overcoat. He was just outside the door of his store in Oro City, Colorado, but dreaded going inside worse than a visit to the dentist.

His shrill-voiced wife, Augusta, undoubtedly awaited his entrance with all the pleasantness of a bear trap. Freezing to death was supposed to be a pleasant way to go; a person simply drifted off into peaceful oblivion. He had only been gone a few hours longer than he said he would be. He'd run across a prospector friend, then had gone to the man's cabin and played cribbage for a while. Come to think on the matter, he had been gone all day. Still, freezing to death somehow seemed preferable to listening to Augusta's screeching. That woman's voice could stampede mules.

Tabor wiggled his soup-strainer mustache, shook the snow from his overcoat, and decided to face the music rather than freeze.

"Horace Tabor, you're tracking in mud," Augusta chided. "If I've told you once, I've told you a thousand times . . . clean your boots before you come inside."

109

"Yes, dear, I'm sorry," Tabor said, keeping his eyes to the plank floor. "I know I'm late, but I ran across some news that'll make us rich."

"Not another of your crack-brained schemes, Horace. I'll not listen to another. You've dragged me to the last forsaken mining camp you're going to."

"But, dear. . . ."

"Don't 'but dear' me. I know you were playing cards all day."

Tabor stroked his mustache and regarded his wife with misgivings. The stern-faced woman with wire-rimmed glasses perched high on her beak bore no resemblance to the beautiful and sweet girl he'd married years ago. It was as if she had been possessed by a demon. Horace had read about such things happening. For certain, something had changed Augusta for the worse. She lowered the temperature in a room twenty degrees by her very presence.

Tabor hung his coat and hat on the hall tree by the door. When he turned, he held a newspaper in his hand. It was a worn copy of *The Baker City Bedrock*. "Dear, they've struck gold in eastern Oregon."

"I don't care if they found Solomon's mines up there. I'm not budging an inch."

Horace was glad there were no customers

in the store to witness Augusta's tirade. Someday, when he got rich, he'd have to look around and see if he could find a better-looking wife that didn't have a demon inside her.

"Then, my dear, you should stay here where you're happy. I'm certain the trip will be fraught with untold peril. However, my sweet, it is my duty as a husband to venture forth into an unknown frontier with the fond hopes of easing your burdens."

"Horace, you and your silver tongue should never have left politics," Augusta said with resignation. "I know you're going, anyway. Just cut the balderdash about doing it for me." She walked behind the counter, bent over, and brought out a small metal box. "I've managed to keep back two hundred dollars from my hard work. Take it, Horace. Go chase your rainbows. I married you for better or worse. The Lord only knows how little of the better I've seen or how much of the worse I've suffered because of you."

Tabor reached out and grabbed the money before Augusta had second thoughts. She was more unpredictable than a grizzly bear with a sore tooth. "Someday, my dear, you'll have a mansion on a hill and servants to ease your toil."

Augusta snorted. "I'd settle for a husband who'll do a day's work."

"Patience, my sweet. I'll return a rich man. I can feel it in my bones."

"I hope those aren't the same bones that told you about Buckskin Joe and Central City. Horace Tabor, you're forty-two years old. You can't keep following every strike that happens."

"You used to have faith in me," Tabor said with a hint of sadness. "I wish you still did."

Augusta's expression remained stoic. "Let's get you packed up. One thing I've learned, if you're going to have any chance at all, you've gotta get there ahead of most."

Less than an hour later, Horace Tabor hefted his bulging portmanteaus onto the evening stage. The driver cracked his whip and the Concord stagecoach groaned as it made deep tracks in the mud. Horace Tabor quickly forgot about his stern wife and smiled as he thought of the riches that surely awaited him in the Blue Mountains of Oregon.

CHAPTER ELEVEN

Clarence Buhlman ever so carefully leveled the bubbles on his transit. In Jake Crabtree's opinion the picky surveyor was taking an insufferable amount of time just to lay out a town. Buhlman seemed to move at the speed of molasses poured in January. It had, for some unfathomable reason, taken the engineer and his helper an entire day just to get started. First he said he had to establish true north from magnetic north or find the declination, whatever that meant. After that had been accomplished, the surveyor had blazed a huge pine tree, then taped from it to a rock outcrop where he chiseled a huge cross.

"That's a tie point for our stadia," Buhlman had told Jake when asked.

"Don't want no stadium," Jake had replied. "Just lay out the town like I asked you to do."

The engineer had given him a strange look

and explained. "Mister Crabtree, I'm sure you are aware that the fundamental principle of the stadia is the geometric theorem that in similar triangles homologous sides are proportional."

"Now that you brought up the subject, I reckon you're right," Jake had answered after a long moment. "I see you know your stuff, so I'll leave you to your work."

Whatever it was the surveyor had said, Jake decided the words alone had probably cost him fifty dollars. Keeping watch on the proceedings from the shade while puffing on a cigar would be cheaper than asking questions. All that college-educated excuse for a surveyor needed to do was simply drive some pegs into the ground so people could get busy building. His new friend, Rincón McCutchan, had mentioned that he wanted to put up a saloon. A grand idea if he'd ever heard one. Last evening, when Packy Jackson came for another load of ore, he'd unloaded a case of whiskey Rincón had sent along. It was good Kentucky bourbon, the best Jake could remember. He decided a great friend like McCutchan should be given a prime lot for his saloon.

Jake could allow himself to feel magnanimous. If anything could be said about the gold vein, it was that it seemed to be getting wider and richer. There was no reason Jake Crabtree could fathom why that vein wouldn't be longer than a telegraph wire and extend deeper than the Grand Cañon. The Merry Widow was unquestionably the Mother Lode of the Blue Mountains. The town of Slab Creek was taking shape at a far slower pace than Jake wanted. He took a heavy puff on his cigar and left the comfortable shade of a towering pine where he'd been sitting and petting Ulysses.

Clarence Buhlman cast a jaundiced eye at Jake when he approached with his cat following at his heels. He stepped back from his transit to keep anything from bumping into it and destroying the delicate settings.

"How's it going?" Jake asked the surveyor. "Sure need to get some lots ready to deed over."

Buhlman sighed. He hated to be interrupted. "We have established twelve lots along the business section that you may sell. While you are here, I need to know the street names for the plat map."

Jake chewed on his cigar. He had been somewhat chagrined the reporter had talked him out of naming the town after himself. People needed a reminder of just who had first found gold in these parts.

"The main street will be called Crabtree

115

Boulevard," Jake announced. "Then the next one over should be named MacNair Avenue. While we're in the business of making up labels for signs, I want the park where the kids will go to play called Crabtree Square. That way the little tykes will have someone to look up to as an example."

Buhlman sucked in a deep breath to camouflage his moan. "Yes, sir." He made some notes on a scrap of paper. "That's what will go on the plat."

"Glad to have some lots ready to go," Jake said happily. "I've got a friend who wants to put up a saloon."

"That's generally the first business that goes up in any mining camp," Buhlman said. "Then a general store and a hotel."

Jake was irritated to hear his town referred to as a mining camp. Slab Creek was destined to be bigger than Baker City. He bent over, picked up his cat, and started to walk away. "Oh, if you need another name for a street, make it Ulysses Avenue."

"Sir," Buhlman said, his tone serious, "while we're working up here, would you like for us to survey out your claim boundaries and amend the location certificates for patent?"

Clarence Buhlman's request was not only as confusing as his "stadium" theory, it sounded downright expensive. "Nope, not right now, anyway. Just lay out the town so folks can start moving in."

The surveyor shook his head as Jake went off. To his way of thinking, applying for a government patent should be the foremost priority. Until that had been done the ground claimed as the Merry Widow Mine was still federal land and the title open to possible dispute. *Oh, well,* he thought, *at least I tried to help.*

The purple haze of a spring evening had settled across the rugged Blue Mountains when Packy Jackson and two of Jake Crabtree's hired hands finished loading the ore wagon. Packy knew Jake had three men working for him and wondered where the other miner was. A bearded young man came walking out of the trees, carrying an empty gunnysack over his shoulder.

"I . . . I'll head up to the cabin an' get us some dynamite," this miner said quickly, looking guilty as John Wilkes Booth running from Ford's Theater.

Packy knew the men were stealing ore. Anger boiled in his soul, then he had an attack of reality. The miners weren't doing anything he wasn't. That depression behind the rock pile would have a few hundred more pounds of high-grade stuffed into it before the night was done.

"You boys take care," Packy said. He climbed up to the driver's seat and unlocked the brake. The load of ore sparkled in the waning light like jewels in a king's crown. With the crack of a whip the wagon groaned forward. Another shipment of high-grade gold from Jake Crabtree's Merry Widow Mine was on its way to the mill. A fair amount of it would actually wind up there.

"Dag-nab it, Cushman, don't go and burn the bacon again!" Woody Ash scolded.

The preacher pulled back the long-handled skillet from the campfire and shook it. "Perhaps, brother Ash, you would care to do the cooking? The flapjacks you made yesterday are still laying behind the log where we tossed 'em. A porcupine would likely break a tooth trying to take a bite out of one."

Woody sighed. "It's durn' hard to make up a batch of griddle cakes without any baking powder. I'm comin' to the conclusion that it'd be an easier task to sink our ten-foot discovery shaft and spend the money to record our claim than keep camping out up here spyin' on our neighbors. When it rained the other night, I got as cold as a tax collector's heart. If I caught the ague and croaked, I'd be in a fix. There ain't another undertaker any closer than Cañon City. He'd likely charge a fortune to come all the way over here an' plant me."

Cushman Pierce grabbed a long stick and moved the sizzling bacon around. "Never fear, my Christian friend. I would excavate a hole and toss you in without charge."

"You don't have to be so dad-blamed nonchalant about it. Getting laid away proper is a mighty important thing."

The preacher was getting tired of listening to his partner's whining. "If we'd eaten those flapjacks you made, we'd both be standing at the pearly gates. Or, at least, I would . . . sometimes I fear for your immortal soul, brother Ash."

"Well, I'm beginnin' to fear about my business. Folks could be dropping like flies down in Baker City and here I am partnered up with a sky pilot that burns bacon. What do you say we do the work and hold onto the claim, then get back to living like sane people?"

"If that vein they're sinking richens up a little, I'd be all for it, brother Ash. It's a gratifying feeling to know a Baptist's money is going into that hole instead of some upstanding citizen's."

Woody said: "After dark we'll go check out their diggings again. It would be a blessing if they've hit gold."

"Blessings, brother Ash," said Cushman Pierce, "are bestowed by the good Lord upon the godly and the deserving."

"Then how do you explain Jake Crabtree striking it rich?"

The preacher frowned and shook the skillet from side to side. "The ways of the Lord can seem mysterious at times."

The undertaker lifted his head when he heard the distant creaking of Jackson's ore wagon taking another shipment to market. "Still can't figger Jake Crabtree findin' anything more than a whorehouse."

"Patience, brother Ash. In good time, the Lord's will shall be revealed."

"While we're waiting, don't burn the bacon." Woody snorted.

Warm Stove Williams shuddered and pulled his heavy coat tighter. "I can't figger out that undertaker an' preacher just campin' on their claim. Don't take that much work or money to dig a ten-foot-deep hole. Now, back in my day. . . ."

"I'm more concerned about *this* day," Lanny Payton interrupted. "We've got to get that shaft down."

Since going into the mining business, the nurse had started dressing like a man, right down to wearing pants, boots, and a slouch hat. T. Greene had made a quarter bet with Warm Stove that she'd be either smoking cigarettes or chewing tobacco before the shaft was thirty feet deep. Lanny had gotten the worse case of gold fever the old men had ever seen.

"They're waitin' tuh see if we strike anything before exertin' either themselves or their pocketbook," T. Greene declared. "Happens in ever' minin' camp. Don't let 'em worry you none, Lanny. We got the best part of the vein."

"I know that," Lanny said. "It just galls me that your pistol misfired. If it hadn't, we'd have us a whole claim, instead of just part of one."

T. Greene Moss batted a piece of quartz around with a cane. "Probably it was fer the best. Shootin' a preacher sometimes upsets folks tolerable much."

Lanny sneered. "Cushman Pierce is a Presbyterian. Most likely you'd have gotten a jury full of Baptists and gotten off scot-free. Then we would have another thousand feet of vein to mine."

The Dugan brothers climbed from the shaft and panted to catch their breath.

Lanny strode over. "How's the vein looking?"

Seth Dugan heard the same question every time he poked his head above ground. He always had the same answer. "Just the same, ma'am, not one bit smaller." It generally paid to be optimistic and not mention the fact it wasn't getting bigger, either. "We filled the bucket with some ore before we came up."

"Well, crank it up here where we can see it," Lanny demanded.

Seth and his brother obediently went to the wooden windlass and winched up the wooden bucket. Before it could be swung over and set on the ground, Lanny pounced on it like a cat on a mouse.

"Look at this, partner," she said after grabbing a chunk and sticking it into T. Greene's wrinkled hand. "I swear that's gold I'm looking at."

The sun had dropped below the horizon, but even in the poor light the old miner could see metal glisten. His heart began to race and his hands shook worse than Warm Stove's.

"You're right about the fact I should 'a' shot that preacher, Lanny. Fer sure as the Pope's Catholic, we've come inta gold!"

"Well, I'll be a suck-egg dog," Warm Stove

Williams said. "That vein made gold, after all."

His hand shivered so badly he dropped a piece of the quartz he had picked from the bucket. Even by the dreary light he'd seen enough to know his partner and Lanny Payton had struck rich ore. His name did not appear on any of the claim papers. Only the unspoken bond between him and T. Greene assured his share.

Lanny Payton bent over and retrieved the piece of high-grade. Tears of joy and relief streaked down her dusty and wrinkled cheeks. "I knew it was down there all the time. I could feel it in my soul."

T. Greene Moss sidled over to the shaft, his canes *clicking.* The old man peered into the depths. "Gonna be the richest gol-durn' mine in the whole blessed state of Oregon with Idyho tossed in fer good measure."

The Dugan brothers sat on a log and watched the proceedings with a dispassionate eye. They were happy the old folks had found ore, but it meant nothing to them. Somehow it didn't seem fair. They had done all the hard work. The only hope they held of making some real money was the possibility of making off with a few hundred pounds of high-grade.

Night began to claim the waning light. In

the west, the evening star twinkled against the gathering blackness like a fleck of yellow gold. Cold washed down from the snow-capped peaks, sending shudders through Warm Stove Williams's frail body.

T. Greene Moss worked himself around with his canes to face his partner. "Warm Stove, why don't you an' Lanny grab up some wood an' build me a fire. Then you two head back tuh town an' have a warm night. There's an extry blanket in the wagon. I'm gonna stay here an' guard the mine."

"Nobody knows we found ore," Lanny said. "Surely we can all go home and come back in the morning without somebody high-grading us."

T. Greene glowered at the Dugan brothers. "When a body's found gold, it's always temptation enough tuh turn even a priest into a thief. Been around too many strikes not tuh know that's God's own truth. Reckon Warm Stove an' me's helped ourselves tuh our share when opportunity knocked." The old miner tapped his coat with the handle of a cane. "Got my six-shooter fixed. Put in fresh powder an' primers. No way I'm leavin' this here mine. Just bring back plenty of grub an' supplies 'cause this mine's gonna be watched over like a sick baby, come hell or high water."

Jake Crabtree had just finished cinching his worn saddle onto Henrietta when Clarence Buhlman and his scruffy helper came walking up, wearing expressions like they both had been eating green persimmons. The morning had broken cloudless and the warming rays of the sun were shooting through openings among the towering pine and greening tamarack trees. Jake was headed for Baker City to visit the mill, pick up his gold from the first ore shipment, and go to the bank. He also had plans made for a suitable celebration later. He didn't want to be delayed by listening to some "stadium" theory.

"You fellows look like you've got a problem," Jake said somewhat curtly.

Buhlman stepped close and shook his head. "No, Mister Crabtree, the surveying is going fine. Slim and I were running a line down the creek. Well, sir, there's something that reeked awful, like something dead that's been there a long while. We investigated and found a coffin shoved back into a clump of spruce trees. That is where the smell is coming from."

Jake cocked his head. "Doc MacNair's in the box you're talking about. I reckon we oughta get around to buryin' him."

"Doctor Gage MacNair!" The surveyor was aghast. "He died weeks ago."

"Time does have a way of getting away from a person," Jake said. "I'll tend to the situation. In the meanwhile, it might be a good idea to plot out that cemetery we talked about."

Buhlman said: "I believe that is an *excellent* suggestion."

Jake said: "I'll tell the men at the mine to go dig a few test graves. I don't want to plant my good friend in some hole that has a gold vein in it. We'd just have to move him later on."

The surveyor shook his head sadly. "Doctor MacNair was a good man. I doubt if a dozen people will show up for the service, even if there is one. That's a terrible shame."

Jake pondered Buhlman's words for a long moment. "If you'll see to the grave digging, I'll make sure he's laid away proper."

The surveyor sighed. "We'll do that. Perhaps you might also send for a sack of quicklime."

Jake put a foot in the stirrup and swung onto the saddle. He sniffed the air and wrinkled his nose. "Reckon that's a good idea. The cemetery you'll be working on is mostly upwind, so get to crackin'."

■ ■ ■ ■

Booming, constant thunder on a clear day greeted Jake when he reined his brown mule to a stop in front of the Virtue Mill. The sprawling wooden building on the banks of the Powder River rumbled like an approaching storm. Henrietta's eyes were wide with trepidation from the ominous noises and the trembling of the earth beneath her hoofs. Black clouds billowed skyward from two of the four smokestacks. An occasional *hiss* of steam or menacing crunching sound from inside the rambling structure only served to spook the mule more.

Jake tied the reins securely to the wood railing, then spent a few minutes petting and talking soothingly to his frightened mule. From all of the rattling, rumbling, and banging going on inside that huge mill building, he wasn't surprised it took a while for Henrietta to settle down.

"You hang in there, old girl," Jake said, stroking the mule's neck. "We won't be here any longer than necessary. Then we'll go to a quiet saloon."

A small sign that said Office in small white letters over a door on the upper level of the huge mill building indicated where he needed to go. Jake thought about knocking first, then realized he could pound on the door for the rest of the day and likely no one would hear. Jake opened the entryway and was surprised to find an orderly office room with wainscot walls and two oak roll-top desks.

A slender, clean-shaven man with close-cropped, silver hair spun to meet him. Another man, a fleshy young fellow with black muttonchop whiskers, kept his attention focused on an open ledger book.

"I'm Ben Treadway, the manager here. May I help you, sir?" the silver-haired man asked without a hint of welcome. He was obviously a man who didn't like to be disturbed.

"My name is Crabtree, Jake Crabtree. I own the Merry Widow Mine."

Ben Treadway's stoic expression flowed into a warm smile. "Why, Mister Crabtree, how nice to make your acquaintance. The ore you have sent us is some of the richest I've ever seen."

Jake was surprised by the strength the mill operator displayed with his handshake. Undoubtedly this man and hard work were well acquainted, a strange occurrence to be found in anyone who called themselves a manager.

"Glad to meet you," Jake said. "I'm hoping I've got some gold to sell."

"Certainly, sir," Treadway said with a smile. "The sponge from your first load of ore is ready for you to take delivery."

"Reckon gold would do me more good than a sponge," Jake said.

The fat man, hunched over the ledger book, couldn't contain a gasp. Ben's expression turned stoic, then he chuckled. "I see you are a man of humor, Mister Crabtree."

Jake wondered why he'd been left out of the joke, but decided it would be wise to play along.

"Flannigan, go to the safe and bring out Mister Crabtree's sponges, while I go over the settlement sheet with him," Ben Treadway ordered.

The chubby bookkeeper appeared irritated by having to leave the comfort of his oak swivel chair. He stood up with a grunt, walked over to a tall floor safe, hunkered over the dial so Jake couldn't observe the numbers, and began the task of entering in the combination.

Treadway thumbed through some papers and momentarily extracted a yellow sheet of paper that he laid out for Jake's inspection. "And here, sir, is the settlement from your first load of ore."

Jake eyed the incomprehensible columns of figures. "You want to go over it with me?"

"Certainly," Treadway said without hesitation. "The gross weight of the ore was three thousand, one hundred, and seventy-eight pounds. After deducting five percent for moisture, we have three thousand, and nineteen pounds."

The fact that rock had any water in it was news to Jake, but he decided it might be wise to let the mill man continue.

"We recovered three hundred twenty-seven ounces of amalgam. This assayed out at six hundred fine which gave us a net of one hundred ninety-six ounces. Once you have deposited the sponge in the Virtue Bank, a draft will be deducted automatically for our charges of ten percent. That will give you a respectable one hundred seventy-six point four ounces of gold."

"That's pretty good, ain't it?" Jake's head was spinning worse than if he'd drunk a quart of bad whiskey.

"Good! My dear sir," Treadway exclaimed, "that ore assayed at over one hundred thirty ounces per ton! A very remarkable showing, indeed."

The fat man with muttonchop whiskers set down three brassy-looking, porous, round cylinders on the desk. Without a word he trudged back, plopped down in the swivel chair, and continued his scrutiny of the clothbound ledger book.

Treadway beamed. "Gold sponge is beautiful, is it not, Mister Crabtree? If you'll sign the receipt, the doré is yours."

Jake nodded in agreement. His education in gold mining now included what the word sponge meant. He signed where Treadway pointed, then reached over and hefted one of the yellow plugs. "Sure does have the weight to it."

"Yes, indeed," Treadway replied. "Gold is one of the heaviest of the elements. A cubic inch weighs about ten ounces."

"Well, I'd better haul this over to the bank," Jake said as he cradled the cylinders into the crook of his arm. "I've got a passel of bills to pay."

"Keep the ore coming, Mister Crabtree," the manager said. "I assure you we will do our best to keep your trust."

"I see you know your stuff. That's good enough for me."

The manager opened the door for him. The fresh air felt wonderful. Jake walked over and stuffed the gold sponges into the saddlebags. He was as anxious as Henrietta to be away from the thundering mill that shook the ground beneath their very feet.

131

■ ■ ■ ■

Otis A. McElroy, cashier was etched in a brass plate that set alongside the black wrought-iron teller's cage. Jake placed the heavy gold sponges in front of the stern-faced older man. "I want to deposit this and set up an account."

The cashier regarded him through small, wire-rimmed glasses that perched on the very tip of his nose. "You must be Jacob Crabtree. May I see the settlement sheet, please?"

"Who said I was coming over?" Jake questioned.

"Why, Mister Treadway, of course. The Virtue Mill is owned by Colonel Ruckle, as is this bank. I believe you have a considerable amount of money coming to you."

The teller's statement caused Jake to grin. "And this is just the first of it."

"How fortunate for you," the hawkish McElroy said curtly. He carefully weighed each of the sponges. "I find our weights agree with Treadway's."

"Well, tell me, how much do I have coming to me?"

The teller added up some figures with a stub of pencil. "After deductions, we arrive at one hundred seventy-six ounces. At seventeen dollars per that is the delightful sum of two thousand, nine hundred, and ninety-eight dollars."

Jake knew he'd been swindled, but for the life of him couldn't figure out how it had been accomplished.

The cashier said: "Would you care to have all of this credited to your account, Mister Crabtree? A draft on this bank is good as cash."

"That's a good idea. Give me a bunch of those drafts, but I need some cash. How many half eagles do you have?"

Otis McElroy looked puzzled. "Five-dollar gold pieces? That is a strange request. Give me a moment to add them up."

Finally the clerk returned. "We can part with three hundred of them, sir. That is fifteen hundred dollars' worth."

"Reckon your cipher is correct," Jake said. "Bag 'em up and keep them here until in the morning. Right now give me a couple of hundred bucks anyway you've got handy."

The startled teller began counting out Jake's two hundred dollars. "The three hundred gold coins are a very strange request, Mister Crabtree. May I inquire as to what need you have for so many half eagles?"

Jake said loudly: "We're going to have a funeral for Doctor MacNair up at the Merry Widow Mine tomorrow afternoon at three o'clock. Whoever shows up and pays their respects gets five dollars for their troubles."

McElroy quickly slid ten double eagles through the cage window and watched as the crazy miner grabbed them up and stuck them into his pocket. It would be a relief to have a man who paid people to go to a funeral out of the Virtue Bank.

CHAPTER TWELVE

"Your wife is a very sick little lady, Mister Antrim," Dr. Franklin Kincaid said solemnly. "Galloping consumption is a malady not to be taken lightly"

The young mining man was plainly worried. "Doctor, we've only been married a short while. Catherine has two sons to raise by her previous husband. I was hoping the dry climate here in Silver City, New Mexico Territory would be helpful."

"Helpful, yes," the doctor said, "but to be perfectly honest with you, I cannot hold much hope for the future."

Antrim asked: "How about the sanatorium back East in Boston? I've been reading that it has a good record of cure."

"Ah, yes," Dr. Kincaid said. "The Heidelman Institute does have an envious reputation. However, the cost of a stay there would be quite expensive."

"But might not the Heidelman Institute

be our best hope?" Antrim asked with concern.

Dr. Kincaid pursed his lips. "Please forgive my brusqueness, but if you can afford such treatments, it very well may be your wife's *only* hope."

William Antrim walked from the doctor's office in a daze. The clear azure sky and warm spring day went unnoticed. Catherine had fallen ill days after they had married in March. Not only did he love and need her, so did Catherine's two boys, Joe and Henry. Especially Henry. That stepson's temper was something that had already caused problems. The lad was only seventeen, but he often flew into a rage. Antrim believed Henry wasn't a bad sort, just needed some guidance. Right now, coming up with enough money to save his wife's life was paramount. Antrim was a mine boss and successful as anyone who toiled for wages. The only way he knew to acquire a great deal of money was to go prospecting and make a quick gold strike.

Antrim knew just where to go and find out the latest scuttlebutt. With determination in his step, the miner headed for the Santa Rita Saloon. Preachers claimed alcohol greased the pathway to hell. Just as surely, whiskey could be relied on to loosen tight lips. If anyone had word of a new gold strike here, he could find out about it. Arriving at the adobe Santa Rita, he swung open the batwing doors and entered the smoky and dusky saloon. When he made out Bugsy Miller and Chicken Bill bellied up to the bar, he forced a smile and headed over for a visit.

"Howdy, boys," Antrim said as he plunked down a dollar on the bar. "Thought you two would be down pounding on rocks in the desert."

Chicken Bill smiled through his bushy white beard. Some years ago the lanky prospector's front teeth had been kicked out by a burro. When he talked, his words came with a whistle. "We done spent 'way too much time side-steppin' cactus. Bugsy an' me's headin' north fer the Mogollon country. Reckon gold can be found in purty country same as the desert."

Bugsy's eyes followed a green fly until it lit on the bar. He pulled a swatter out of his back pocket and smashed the insect into the woodwork. "Might be less bitin' bugs up there, too. Can't abide the things." Bugsy had gotten his nickname because of his intense hatred of any creature with more than four legs.

"They ain't no place that's not got creepy

crawleys runnin' around," Chicken Bill asserted. " 'Cept maybe Canada. Might be too cold fer 'em to git around up there."

A bartender came up, looking friendly. He smiled at Antrim. "What'll it be, my friend?"

"A mug of draft beer." Antrim glanced at the empty glasses in front of the prospectors. "Give my friends more of the whiskey they're drinking."

"Thankee, Antrim," Chicken Bill said. "Why ain't you at the mine workin'. Did the manager get smart an' fire you?"

Antrim's throat burned like he'd drunk bad whiskey when he thought as to why he had taken the day off. "Nope, just had some business that needed tending to."

Bugsy Miller's eyes kept searching for another fly to smash. "I reckon that's 'most always the case. This ol' world keeps right on spinnin' no matter who's wanderin' around on it."

"See what I gotta put up with," Chicken Bill retorted. "Not only is my pardner a fly-chasin', bug-squashin' annoyance, he's also tryin' to become a phillyosofarter to boot."

"The word is philosopher," Bugsy corrected curtly. "It mean's a man's got some thinkin' goin' on."

Chicken Bill squinted at his partner. "Seems to me the words wise-ass would cover the situation an' save a lot of breath in the process."

The bartender brought the round of drinks, taking the two veteran prospectors away from their usual bickering. Then the saloonkeeper focused his happy eyes on Bugsy. "I couldn't help but overhear your conversation. Reckon an educated person like you has read about the big gold strike up in Oregon?"

Chicken Bill and Bugsy Miller looked dumbstruck. Neither had ever learned how to read or write.

Antrim's face lit with excitement. "What's this about a strike?"

The bartender grinned and fished through a stack of newspapers on a shelf below the painting of a chubby nude blonde. "Here it is," he announced, and spread a copy of *The Baker City Bedrock* on the bar in front of them.

"My eye's are gettin' mighty poorly," Chicken Bill said. "Gonna have to get me some spec's before too much longer."

"I know the feelin'," Bugsy Miller said. "Since I busted mine, I ain't been able to read a durn' thing."

Antrim flashed the saloonkeeper a knowing smile and grabbed up the newspaper. When he finished reading, he laid the paper on the bar. Oregon was a long way to travel, but if he could come up with enough money to save Catherine, it would be worth the effort. Antrim had a faraway look in his eyes. "Boys, it sounds like there's a whole new rich gold mining district in Oregon to be opened up. It might be a wise move to head up there and get a claim before the place gets too crowded."

"Mighty cold in the wintertime," Chicken Bill said after chugging his shot of whiskey. "Snow gets ass-deep to a tall Indian. I don't hanker that."

"An' 'skeeters," Bugsy said with concern. "I can't abide them things."

Antrim made up his mind. "Well, boys, if you want to stand around in a saloon and fuss, go right ahead. I think I might not hesitate. If a man got to moving, he'd be there fairly soon. A person could travel most the way by train."

"We'll study on the matter," Chicken Bill said.

"An' the 'skeeters need to be considered," Bugsy said.

William Antrim motioned the bartender over. "Could I buy this paper?"

"Oh, go ahead and take it," the saloon-keeper said.

Antrim folded the copy of *The Baker City*

Bedrock. "Thanks," he said to the bartender.

The two prospectors didn't notice him leave. They were too busy arguing over what bugs could be found in the state of Oregon.

It was a source of distress to William Antrim just how swiftly consumption had devastated his wife. With a blood-flecked handkerchief grasped in her right hand, she sat on the divan wrapped in a quilt and regarded her husband.

"Dear," Catherine said with a raspy voice, "does Doctor Kincaid really believe this hospital in Boston may be able to cure me?"

"He's certain of it," William assured her. "All I have to do is come up with enough money."

"I know," she said. "But to run all the way to Oregon is such a risk."

"There's no talking me out of it," he said firmly. "You're what matters."

Antrim nodded toward the two gangly boys who stood by his side with worried looks on their young faces. "Joe will take good care of you until I can come back."

"Yes, sir," Joe McCarty said firmly. "Henry an' me will take good care of our mother, you can count on that."

Antrim shifted his gaze back to Catherine. "Dear, I'm of the mind that Henry should go with me. He's old enough to be a lot of help."

Catherine Antrim knew what her husband meant. Without William's stern guidance, her contentious seventeen-year-old son might get into trouble.

Henry wiped a lock of hair from his forehead. "Ma, if there's a chance we can come up with enough money to make you well again, I'd be obliged to go."

"Oh, Henry," Catherine sobbed.

Henry said: "Mister Antrim knows how to look for gold. If there's any way we can come back with a lot of money, we will. You just don't worry about nothin' while we're gone, 'cause I'll look after our safety."

Antrim smiled. "Now you listen to your son's good advice about not worrying. Before you know it, Henry and I'll be back."

Catherine sighed and motioned her family close. "Whatever happens is providence of the Lord. Just remember that I love you all."

Henry's lower lip quivered. "Ma, that would be like forgettin' how to breathe."

CHAPTER THIRTEEN

In the harsh reality of morning sunlight the soiled dove lying on Jake Crabtree's arm looked a lot less appealing than when he'd gone to bed with her.

"Whiskey can sure mess with a man's eyesight," Jake mumbled, hoping not to wake her. She was snoring loudly and the once cute, pouty smile of hers had disappeared into drawn, hollow cheeks. Then Jake saw the set of false teeth in a water glass on the nightstand beside the brass bed.

Jake drew his arm a few inches from under her stringy hair. She snorted and mascara-coated eyelashes fluttered open.

" 'Mornin', hon," she rasped, "you want a little more of Delma's sugar? You were a real tiger last night. A genuine roaring hunk of a tiger."

Jake used the opportunity to retrieve his arm. A quick escape seemed his best hope. "Love to, darling," he replied, "but I'm in mourning. My best friend up and died. I've got to see to his funeral."

The girl seemed genuinely sorry. "You poor man. When you're feelin' better, you come back and see little Delma."

Jake jumped into his clothes like the building was on fire. "You bet, but it might be a spell. I've got to see to his widow and the ten little ones he left behind."

Jake felt in his pocket and came out with a ten-dollar gold piece. A silver dollar would have done fine, but the closer Jake looked at Delma, the less money mattered and speed counted. "Here you go," he said, tossing her the eagle.

Her eyes opened wide. "Lover," she cooed, "you sure you ain't got time for little Delma to give you somethin' to remember me by?"

Jake wondered with a start if possibly she already had. "Can't take the time. I'll see you again soon."

To Jake's relief, the soiled dove got up and wrapped her naked frame in a bulky robe. "I ain't heard of anyone dyin' lately. Who was the unfortunate?"

Jake bolted for the door. "Darlin', he's not from these parts."

After three stacks of flapjacks buried under mounds of chili and a dozen cups of steaming black coffee, Jake began to overlook last night's lapse of good sense. If he was going to drum up a decent crowd for Doc's funeral and get them to the mine by three this afternoon, he needed to get hopping.

"More coffee, Mister Crabtree?" the young waitress asked.

"Reckon not," Jake said. "Gotta get to moving." Then he took a moment to survey the waitress. A gold wedding band glistened on her ring finger.

"Ma'am," he asked, "would you and your husband like to make some extra money this afternoon?"

The girl seemed puzzled. "What do you mean?"

"Well, I'm sure you remember Doctor MacNair."

"Yes, sir."

"He's gonna get buried up at the Merry Widow Mine at three this afternoon. I know folks are busy and all, so I'm paying five dollars in gold to everyone that shows up. Well, up to three hundred folks that is, cause that's all the half eagles I was able to scrounge up."

The young lady was taken aback. "Why, Mister Crabtree, how generous of you. That's as much money as I make working here for days. If you don't mind, I can bring along my folks. Lord only knows how much they could use ten dollars."

"Head 'em up there. Now, I've got to rustle up a preacher that hasn't caught gold colic."

The waitress looked perplexed. "If you don't mind me saying so, you might try Preacher Pruett. He's a Baptist minister."

Jake cocked his head. "Preacher Pruett, ain't he the one that keeps trying to shut down Molly Spade's joint?"

"Yes, sir. The good reverend has made closing that den of iniquity one of his goals in life."

"Reckon he'll do just fine," Jake said firmly. "I've admiration for that man."

The moose head that hung high on the wall over the entrance to the Belle of Baker Saloon had come to life. It bothered Rincón McCutchan immensely to have not only its red eyes but the entire head turn to follow his every movement. Having to deal with a spook early in the day was a terrible agony. Rincón ignored the glaring moose head and poured a tumbler full of Kentucky bourbon. He motioned with the bottle and nodded at Jake Crabtree with a broad smile. "Care for a taste?"

After the way his normal good sense had

failed him last night, Jake didn't feel up to another wrestling match with John Barleycorn. "Thanks, friend, but I've got to see to Doc's funeral. We're gonna lay him to his eternal rest this afternoon. The poor man's getting in tolerable need of it."

Rincón McCutchan furrowed his brow. "I'd suppose that is something that requires tending. It's been a warm spring."

"Yep," Jake said. "I hired Preacher Pruett to come up and say the words over him."

"Preacher Pruett's long-winded enough. God will go ahead an' let Doc into heaven just to get him to shut up. I don't mind preachers until they shut down a good saloon or whorehouse."

Jake squinted his eyes. "Wish there was a *good* whorehouse in these parts for a preacher to close."

Rincón noticed the moose had opened its mouth to display twin rows of pointed teeth. "I've been thinking that I might run a covey in Slab Creek. If I did, they'd be prime material."

The bartender now had Jake's full attention. "About that building lot, Rincón. I'm plain gonna give it to you."

Rincón forced his eyes from the moose head and grinned. "You don't know how much I appreciate that, Jake. Just as soon as

I get the deed, I'll hire a crew and start building."

"I'll run by the lawyer and have a deed drawn up for you before I head up to the funeral."

Rincón said: "Henry Hayes Hedgepath, that owns this joint, would handle the paperwork and likely not charge you a dime for his troubles."

Jake wiggled his mustache and frowned. "After the way that skunk shystered poor widow Nolan out of this place, I wouldn't trust him to baby-sit a brick."

Rincón was jolted by Jake's warning, but he had signed an agreement with Hedgepath that any property received by him from Crabtree was to be included in their partnership. He couldn't fathom how he could do anything but make money on their ventures.

"All lawyers bear tolerable watching," Rincón said.

"Just can't wait to see your saloon in operation," Jake said. "Have you thought of a name for it yet?"

"Yep. How does the Red Lion strike you?"

Jake grinned. "Couldn't have done better myself. I'll be your first customer."

Rincón chugged the last of his whiskey. "Don't bring along any money. My friends drink for free on opening day."

"Look forward to it," Jake said. "Now, I've got to point Henrietta back home. Doc always was a patient sort, but some things can't be put off any longer."

The moose ignored Jake Crabtree when he walked underneath it and out the door. Then the blasted thing started snorting fire out of its black nose. Rincón McCutchan refilled his glass with whiskey. His head hurt and the moose was acting up. If only Hedgepath could be successful in jumping Jake's mine, he would be rolling in money. Then a doctor could remove those lead slugs and he wouldn't have to keep putting up with spooks.

"You heard me right, Packy," Jake said to the freighter. "I want you to run a stagecoach up to Slab Creek. I want as many folks hauled up to Doc's funeral as you can pile on."

"Yes, sir, Mister Crabtree," Packy Jackson said. "Lew Thorson's got a decent Concord stage for sale. If I had two hundred dollars, I'd buy the thing."

"Go and get it," Jake said as he scribbled out a bank draft. "I made this for two hundred and fifty dollars. I want a load of grieving mourners up at the mine by three o'clock."

Packy nodded. "They'll be there, Mister Crabtree. And thanks a lot for helpin' me out. I won't forget it." Packy thought of the growing pile of high-grade he had stashed. "Your generosity is appreciated more than you know."

The afternoon sky was a deep blue with a few fluffy white clouds high in the west. A slight breeze rustled the long needles of the towering fir and lodgepole pine trees. Standing high on the pile of dark dirt, the white-bearded preacher looked like Moses getting ready to part the Red Sea. In one hand he grasped a Bible while holding a walking stick in the other. He regarded Jake's approach with deep-set hazel eyes that seemed to peer inside a man's soul.

"Brother Crabtree," the preacher boomed. "I trust all is in order?"

Jake grinned and held out a twenty-dollar gold piece. The preacher tucked the walking stick under his arm and grabbed it.

"That's what I'm here to find out," Jake said as he eyeballed the surveyor and his helper. "I take it there ain't no vein of gold in the way this time?"

"No, sir," Clarence Buhlman replied. "There's no doubt in my mind about plotting a cemetery here."

Jake checked the hole. "Well, it does appear there ain't no gold." He sniffed the air and looked around. "Where is Doc, by the way?"

Buhlman pointed to the coffin. "We sprinkled in a sack of quicklime last evening."

"I'll pay a bonus for that," Jake said.

"Brothers, bring forth the deceased and place him alongside his resting place," the preacher commanded.

"Come on and line up," Jake said, reaching into his pockets and coming out with a handful of gold coins. "I'd take it right favorably if you fellows would carry Doc up here."

By the time the appointed hour of three o'clock came, Jake was out of half eagles. Packy Jackson's new stagecoach had been so loaded the horses were lathered and exhausted. Fifteen people had somehow found a way to fit either inside or on top of the conveyance.

Jake felt so bad about running out of money that he started writing out vouchers on the Virtue Bank. When the preacher stood high on the mound above the grave and began his ringing oratory, Jake's fingers hurt from doing so much writing.

An hour later, Jake wondered about his wisdom in paying Preacher Pruett twenty dollars for the service. Ten dollars' worth of praying and preaching should have been enough to get any sinner through the pearly gates.

Finally, to the relief of Jake and everyone on the mountain, Pruett wound down. While the preacher recited the Lord's Prayer, six men lowered the coffin into the open grave, then began shoveling in dirt. After a short while only a mound of fresh-turned earth marked the doctor's resting place.

Jake Crabtree walked quickly to his cabin and returned, packing a heavy black object. He had mounted two wooden posts onto the sign he'd taken from the doctor's stairway. Once the marker had been erected, women sobbed and even the preacher's lower lip trembled. Every eye that beheld the grave marker grew moist when they read the words etched into the heavy metal:

GAGE MACNAIR, M.D.
OFFICE UPSTAIRS

"I can't for the life of me figure out why Crabtree went and paid that zephyr of a Baptist to preach over Doc MacNair,"

Reverend Pierce grumbled. "I said enough good words for free to get the job done."

Woody Ash snorted. "Well, I wish Presbyterians could dig holes as good as they complain. I kept saying we oughta go ahead an' put it down, but, oh, no, we couldn't do that. We had to sneak, an' spy, an' generally act like loons until they hit ore. Now we gotta go ahead and do the dad-blasted work anyway."

"Brother Ash" — Cushman Pierce glared at the undertaker — "my God-given patience with your constant whining is coming to an end. Maybe we should dissolve our relationship."

"Don't want you for any of *my* relation," Woody said, tossing his pick from their shallow hole.

Cushman stepped close to Woody and glared up at him. The top of the preacher's head came even with the undertaker's Adam's apple. "I've got fifty dollars of my wife's sewing money stuck away. It's yours, if you'll go back to burying dead people and sign your interest over to me."

"Well, now, ain't you the generous one with your poor, hard-working wife's money. With T. Greene Moss and Lanny in pay dirt, fifty dollars sounds like a lame pay day."

"What have you got to offer? All you've

done lately is whine about being broke. If I get a tad more upset with you, brother Ash, you may have need of a grave right shortly."

"I keep a-tellin' you, I'm not your dad-blasted brother!" Woody yelled. "That pious Pete talk of yours is gonna get your nose popped."

The minister shot a glance at the undertaker's huge knotted fist and decided to let diplomacy settle the matter. "Perhaps we have been together under adverse conditions too long bro . . . Woody."

Woody relaxed his fist and pondered the preacher's words. Cushman was talking hard cash to get him out of this claim. The undertaking business was a lot less fuss than owning a mine. At least, his usual clientele didn't go running off at the mouth.

"Cushman," Woody Ash said, "I may have come up with an idea that'll not only keep us from trying to kill each other, but would pay us for our trouble. I reckon it'll take a good hundred bucks to get my hearse fixed up, once I get the thing unstuck from those trees."

"You mentioned the word *us,*" Cushman said.

"Why, we're partners in this here claim. Have been since the day we went crazy together."

Cushman Pierce was suddenly very interested in hearing the undertaker's plan. Being able to preach the good word to his flock on Sunday mornings and sleep in a decent bed at night seemed a lot more desirable than owning half interest in a claim. "Tell me your plan, bro . . . partner."

Seth and Orson Dugan shoveled freshly blasted rock while T. Greene Moss, Lanny Payton, and Warm Stove Williams watched expectantly. The new location notice contained the names of them all.

"Dag-gone it, Lanny, that sure was decent of you tuh include Warm Stove in fer an interest," T. Greene said. "I never reckoned on Woody Ash an' the Bible whacker sellin' out like they done. Less messy than shootin' 'em, though."

Warm Stove shivered heavily. "They sure don't know what we've struck or they wouldn't've sold fer a million much less for a measly five hundred dollars."

"Boys," Lanny said, "I'm just thankful to have the money. All of those years of working as a nurse, scrimping and saving, are going to pay off big."

The grizzled old miner studied the situation for a while before he spoke. "Buyin' this claim was a powerful good move,

155

Lanny. The Golden Ruckus Mine now has a solid two thousand feet along the vein. That's enough ground to attract a big outfit if we ever decided to sell out."

Lanny Payton looked dumbstruck. "I don't know why we'd want to go and do something like that. It appears to me, if the mine's worth a million dollars to some big company, it oughta be worth more to us."

Warm Stove pulled his heavy peajacket tightly with a shudder and started to say something when T. Greene spoke.

"Yer right, Lanny. We'll do right well a-minin' it ourselves."

Lanny Payton pulled a chunk of gold-laced quartz from the pocket of her shirt. "A few tons of this and we'll all be on easy street. How much longer before we can ship a load of ore?"

T. Greene shuffled around to face her. "We oughta have at least one wagonload fer Packy to haul to the mill by tomorrow."

Lanny smiled, her eyes staring into the dark trees. "I hope the crew gets that cabin done. Sure be nice to stay out here."

"They're framin' it now," T. Greene said. "Not much longer an' it'll be ready."

"I hope they put a bodacious heater in the place," Warm Stove said. "I surely hanker that. Be a pleasure to sit in a chair nice an' close to a roarin' fire an' not be freezin'.'"

Lanny Payton turned her gaze to the shaft on their new claim. "That rich gold will run forever. I can feel it in my soul."

T. Green Moss and Warm Stove Williams hoped desperately in *their* souls that Lanny Payton was correct in her assessment.

Horace Tabor took off his black felt bowler and mopped a trickle of sweat from his forehead. Back in Oro City seldom did a single summer day nudge the mercury in a thermometer past seventy degrees. His reception in Oregon had been strange. First, he'd been offered a free stagecoach ride from Baker City. Then, upon his arrival, a gangly man had poked a five-dollar gold piece into his hand to attend a funeral.

Horace had pitched his tent on a newly pegged lot after the surveyor told him Jake Crabtree, who owned the town, wouldn't mind.

Tabor wanted to stake a claim of his own. That was where the real money lay. After traversing the heavily timbered country for a mile in every direction, he guessed there were possibly five hundred people camped in these rugged mountains. Blazed trees, newly erected wood posts, and rock cairns were in abundance everywhere he'd been.

The entire area had already been claimed. Due to the dense tree cover many boundaries overlapped and people were arguing over who had been first with their location notices. The place was a fertile breeding ground for lawyers if he'd ever seen one. At least, he hadn't heard of anyone being shot yet. He knew all too well that it would only be a matter of time until someone used a more direct approach than hiring a lawyer. Bullets were more dependable and didn't charge by the hour.

As he resumed his expedition, Tabor decided to spend some more time in the outlying areas. It was always a possibility he could stake a claim or two, quickly sell out, and at least gain back his expenses. Back in Oro City, all that awaited him was Beelzebub's minion, his wife Augusta.

CHAPTER FOURTEEN

Jake Crabtree was sitting under a tall tamarack and petting Ulysses. The slow-paced surveyor and his unwashed helper now had sixty lots plotted out. Best of all, his new friend, Rincón McCutchan, had begun construction on the saloon. A crew of twenty men working twelve-hour shifts had made an impressive start. The board-and-batten two-story structure was taking form with delightful speed. In a matter of days the Red Lion would be operating around the clock.

Jake wondered briefly as to how the bartender had been able to afford the venture. He dismissed his question as immaterial. Results were what mattered, and Rincón's saloon was certainly going up with splendid rapidity.

Jake Crabtree stood, lit a cigar, and admired what he had wrought here in the wilderness. All of this wonderful progression of civilization was due to his diligence and long suffering of purpose. Not that Doc's money hadn't come in handy. Jake felt certain his old friend and benefactor now had a golden harp to play for eternity. Yet, as he thought on the matter, something struck him. Whort Pigg! He hadn't bothered to tell Whort or Jenny about the funeral. They would have wanted to be there. Jake decided to hire Packy Jackson to make a special trip to Whort's ranch with his new stagecoach and haul them up to see where Doc had been buried.

"You must be Jake Crabtree?" a pleasant voice asked, jerking him from his thoughts.

"That I am, sir," Jake answered, shaking the proffered hand.

The stranger was a balding chap who sported a bushy, black soup-strainer mustache and had sparkling gray, mischievous eyes.

"My name is Tabor, Horace Tabor from Oro City down in Colorado Territory. I have been prospecting and mining for several years now. My congratulations on striking rich ore."

Jake beamed. "Thank you, my good man. After many years of adversity, dame fortune has finally seen fit to smile upon me. Would you care to visit the mine and see the vein for yourself? I'd be happy to give you a tour."

Tabor's bushy brown eyebrows raised in surprise. Seldom did anyone owning a mine rich in free gold allow a stranger to visit.

"If it wouldn't be too much trouble, Mister Crabtree, I'd certainly appreciate that a great deal. I always like to study an ore body when I have the opportunity."

"Reckon this vein'll knock your eyes out," Jake said proudly, turning to lead the way. "Did you ever hit it?"

Tabor thought for a moment and measured his reply. "I've had some success. One summer I took out over fifteen thousand dollars." He was careful to leave out the part about losing it all the following year. Horace Tabor had been reminded of that fact by Augusta so many times he didn't want ever to hear it mentioned again.

"That's a tolerable amount," Jake said over his shoulder as they headed for the mine. A moment later the men reached the wooden windlass that had been built over the shaft.

"Frank," Jake said to a bearded man who stood with his hands in his pockets. "Rustle us up some candles and a rock pick. My friend, Tabor, here wants to see the vein. I'd reckon he oughta pry out a chuck of rich gold for himself so he can remember the visit."

"You're a very generous man, Mister Crabtree," Tabor said, trying to hide his dismay over Crabtree's utter disregard for protecting the treasure house he had opened.

When they emerged from the depths of the mine, Horace Tabor's pockets were stuffed with gold. He happily estimated that he could sell it for a hundred dollars allowing him to stay away from Augusta longer.

Tabor was duly impressed by the foot to eighteen-inch wide vein. What he noted, and decided to keep silent about, was the fact that the rich gold only appeared on the north side of the shaft. At the bottom of the workings the rich ore vein seemed to be narrowing considerably. All of the earmarks of a pocket mine were present. Horace Tabor had studied enough geology to realize nearly all mines that produced millions of dollars were not rich. The ores were consistent in value, the veins wide and able to sustain a large daily tonnage at low cost. Small high-grade pockets always created great excitement due to their extreme value. It was a certainty, to Tabor's thinking, the mine would be exhausted in short order. He felt sorry for Jake Crabtree, but doubted the man would listen to his advice.

"She's a real beauty, ain't she, Tabor?" Jake said happily.

Tabor honestly answered. "Yes, sir. Have you thought of bringing in a mining engineer to do a report? A professional opinion is often a wise move."

Jake shook his head in dismay. "Can't figger out why I'd want to go and do that. I plan to mine it myself."

"A laudable ambition," Horace said. "Very soon you should be able to run some levels and put up some raises for stoping."

"Yep, plan on doing just that," Jake said quickly. He had absolutely no idea what Tabor had said. Right now watching his town being built was far more important than some "stope" thing could be. "While I'm showing you around, why don't we go take a gander at the new town of Slab Creek?"

"I'd like that," Tabor said agreeably.

"We're gonna have a nice park here by the creek," Jake said with a wave of his arm. "Crabtree Square, it's called. A hundred years from now little tykes will still be playin' here."

"That sounds wonderful," Tabor said.

"This is the main street of Slab Creek. It's called Crabtree Boulevard. We're gonna have a saloon open shortly."

"Lovely place," Tabor said truthfully. He pointed through a thicket of lodgepole pines to his tent. "I'm afraid I have been camping on one of your lots since my arrival. The surveyor said you wouldn't mind."

"Mind!" Jake boomed. "Not only am I glad you're here, I'll have a deed drawn up and give the lot to you. Experienced mining folks like you are a welcome addition to Slab Creek."

"Why, thank you, Mister Crabtree," Tabor said, dumbstruck. "I don't know how to thank you."

"You can start by calling me Jake."

Tabor smiled. "I'll be proud to."

Jake laughed. "Let's drop by the saloon. There's someone I want you to meet."

Jake hesitated outside the newly framed door to the Red Lion. Horace Tabor stepped to his side.

"Can't wait for the place to open," Jake said. "But we don't have to wait until then for me to buy you a drink."

A rough-looking man with black, greasy hair spilling out from underneath a rumpled hat stepped through the entrance way to greet them. A pale, pockmarked face with rheumy eyes fixed a cold glare on the man by Jake Crabtree's side.

Horace Tabor's eyes narrowed to slits. He jerked open his jacket. A split second later he had his pocket pistol out and cocked. With less hesitation than a striking rattlesnake, Tabor fired both barrels into the middle of Rincón McCutchan's chest.

CHAPTER FIFTEEN

The thunderous blast from the small pistol knocked Rincón back a step. He swatted at some smoking embers alongside the twin black holes in his shirt.

"Dag-nab it, Tabor," Rincón fumed. "This was a good shirt. I just boiled it last month. Ain't you ever heard of lettin' bygones be bygones?"

Jake, Horace Tabor, and the few workmen who had witnessed the incident could only stare in awe while waiting for Rincón McCutchan to fall over dead. Not only did the saloonkeeper appear uninjured, his only concern seemed to be putting out the fire that had started in his shirt.

"You OK, Rincón?" Jake managed to ask.

McCutchan grinned and thumped his chest with his knuckles, giving off a metallic sound. "Sure, I'm fine. I plain can't afford to get shot any more so I had a blacksmith make me some body armor. I even wear it when I go to bed. This is the first time I've had a chance to try it out. I'd venture it worked right fine."

Tabor's face flushed red and he tried to fish some cartridges out of his pocket but the chunks of gold slowed his progress.

Jake reached over and grabbed the pistol. "Why in tarnation did you go and shoot Rincón for? The man's just buildin' a saloon."

Tabor's gray eyes shot daggers at Rincón McCutchan. "Jake, that scalawag's a claim jumper of the worst sort. I already put two slugs into him down in Central City. I guess he's so mean the devil won't have him."

Rincón gave a sickly grin. "Now, Horace, that matter was a simple misunderstanding."

"I caught you red-handed changing my location papers," Tabor insisted. "What I'd like to know is why you ain't got the decency to die like a reasonable man should."

Rincón McCutchan's watery eyes surveyed Jake Crabtree and the gathering workmen. He knew he needed to put on a good show to avoid having folks not trust him until he had skinned them out of their money.

"Now, boys," Rincón said soothingly, "Horace Tabor is just upset over a little misunderstanding that happened a long time ago. Just to show how nice a person I really am, I'm gonna open the saloon an' the drinks are on me."

"That seems like a peaceable offer," Jake said.

Tabor's eyes returned to narrow slits as he glared at Rincón. "A head shot ought to do the trick." He spun to face Jake. "Give me back my gun. That sidewinder will croak if I shoot him in his head."

Jake frowned. "Nope, I ain't gonna allow anyone to get shot when he's buying drinks. That'd set a terrible precedent."

Tabor sighed. "Rincón McCutchan's a venom that'll poison this town, Jake."

"Let's have that drink now," Rincón said cheerfully, sweeping his hand at the gathering crowd. He stared at Tabor and motioned toward the door. "That drink is for you, too, Tabor. There's been no harm done, except to my shirt. I'm plumb ready to bury the hatchet."

Jake Crabtree spoke up. "Sounds like a reasonable man talkin', Horace. Let's go have us a snort and forget about shooting anyone."

Tabor's voice was sharp with anger: "Jake, you're rubbin' elbows with a rattlesnake. I'm heading back to my tent. This town's going into the crapper on greased skids."

Rincón had a broad smile on his pale face. He realized the six-foot-tall chipmunk that ran out of his saloon and accompanied Tabor on his departure was another spook. It felt agreeable to have both of them gone. "Come on in, boys."

Jake hesitated. There was something about Tabor's words that bothered him. Right now, Rincón had opened the bar. Whiskey drinking always took priority over spending time with a pickle puss.

Henry McCarty was in a sullen mood. He was put out by the fact that his stepfather wouldn't let him wear a revolver. The gray mule he sat astride did little to elevate his spirits. By any reckoning, the cantankerous animal should have passed away from old age long ago. Every few miles the mule would stop dead in its tracks and blow and puff like a steam engine. If that wasn't enough embarrassment for the young man to endure, he was forced to ride lightly in the saddle from a melon-sized bruise from where the beast had bitten him on the butt.

"Mister Antrim," Henry said, painfully crawling from the saddle, "I think that Charlie Farmer feller at the livery stable pulled a shecoonery on us with these mules.

Mine's so old it ain't likely to see another sunrise."

"Best we could do under the circumstances," Antrim said. "The mule I'm riding ain't up to winning any races, either."

"Fifty dollars apiece for a worn-out mule is just like robbin' folks," Henry grumbled.

"Now, kid," Antrim said, "we can cover a lot more ground from a mule than on foot."

Henry McCarty glared at his puffing mule and rubbed his posterior. "I surely hope that mule don't up and die natural. I'm looking powerful forward to shootin' him later on."

Antrim had heard nothing but complaints from the kid ever since he'd been bitten by the mule. It was time to change the subject. "I've a good feeling about this place, Henry. It might be a good idea to move upslope and head to the town that way. Gold can sometimes be found not far from a road where hundreds of people have traveled."

Henry stepped far enough away from his mule to be safe and looked around quizzically. "Mister Antrim, are you a-sayin' there's gold right here?"

William Antrim smiled. He knew how anxious Henry was to strike gold and the terrible price they would pay for failure. "Maybe not under your feet, but in mineral country it pays to keep a sharp eye peeled.

Red, burnt-looking rocks with dull quartz in it is a good indicator. There's a saying that's well to remember . . . gold wears an iron hat."

"You know a bunch about the business, sir," Henry said. He looked down and kicked the ground with the toe of his boot. "There's somethin' I've been a wantin' to tell you, but it ain't an easy task."

William Antrim's expression turned serious. "What might that be?"

Henry kept his gaze to the earth. "I'm glad you married my ma."

Silence lay heavily for a long moment. Antrim worked the lump from his throat. "Son, I appreciate that. Now let's set out to do what we come for."

Packy Jackson couldn't have been a happier man. In a year, two at the most, he would be able to tap his stash of high-grade. Out of the loads of sparkling gold-laden quartz he'd freighted to the Virtue Mill so far, a solid ton lay hidden out in that depression alongside the road. Packy figured the check from his future gold "strike" would net him around eighteen hundred dollars, a literal fortune. Best of all, he wouldn't face the Almighty's wrath come Judgment Day. After tithing ten percent of the proceeds, just like the Good Book commanded, his soul would be safe from perdition.

Packy Jackson was more than happy to do Jake a favor when the man had asked him to make a special trip with the stage to take Whort Pigg and his good-looking wife to Slab Creek. Wearing a smile of satisfaction, Packy climbed aboard the driver's seat of the empty stagecoach, took hold of the jerk line, and started the horses into motion for the short trip to the Silver Spur Ranch. In spite of some ominous dark clouds in the western sky this morning, the day had turned clear and warm. Perhaps Jenny would wear a nice tight-fitting dress that would show off her trim figure. He could always hope.

"Well, I'll be switched!" Whort Pigg exclaimed when the stage groaned to a halt in front of Jake Crabtree's cabin. "Look at this place, Jenny. There's a town getting built up here."

Jenny was amazed as she surveyed the booming new town of Slab Creek with amazement. Wide streets had been cleared through the thick trees. Cabins with fresh chinking between hewn logs were on the closest street. Below them was a huge two-story structure. Workmen were just now erecting a large white sign over the doorway that proclaimed the Red Lion Saloon in bright scarlet letters.

Whort nodded toward the sprawling building. "Well, hon, leastwise we know where to find Jake."

Packy Jackson swung the door wide and placed a short, heavy, wooden footstool for Jenny to step down on when she departed the high coach.

"Glad you folks made it up here," Jake's familiar voice boomed from the open door of his cabin. Even Jenny showed surprise that the mine owner wasn't inside the saloon.

Jake sauntered outside, blowing on a steaming cup of coffee. A balding middle-aged man with a soup-strainer mustache followed behind.

"Whort, Jenny," Jake said, moving aside, "I want you to meet a friend of mine from Colorado. This here's Horace Tabor."

Tabor beamed at the lovely auburn-haired young lady. If Augusta looked half as attractive, he would still be in Oro City. He stepped close, bowed, then pecked a kiss on the back of her proffered hand. "Your servant, madam."

Jenny was taken aback by Horace Tabor's refreshing manners. She curtsied graciously.

"I am pleased to make your acquaintance, my good sir."

Whort Pigg's face pinched into a frown. He quickly strode over and said gruffly: "I'm her husband an' Jake's friend, Whort. Glad to meet you, Tabor."

Horace kept his smile. Being around a beautiful woman always put him in a good mood. "Likewise, sir," he said. "Jake has told me about how you two were in the war along with the poor deceased Doctor Mac-Nair."

Jake swept an arm toward the budding town. "Slab Creek is gonna make a nice city."

Whort shot a glance at the Red Lion. "Don't imagine how a body could ask for more. Reckon being within walking distance of a saloon is sort of like goin' to heaven."

Jake Crabtree shook his head worriedly. "I've come to have doubts about the fellow that's runnin' the joint. Tabor's been telling me why he shot him down in Colorado, then again yesterday. Rincón McCutchan just might not be an upstanding citizen."

Jenny's eyes widened. "Mister Tabor actually shot a man yesterday?"

Tabor shrugged. "It was a waste of ammo. Rincón wears body armor nowadays. When I plugged him in Central City, I caused

174

some serious hurt, but the bullets didn't take."

Whort sighed. "Now I reckon you'll understand why Jenny and I are happy ranching. The next buildings to go up here will likely be an undertaker's parlor and a lawyer's office." He eyed Jake. "This Rincón character hasn't tried to jump your mine, has he?"

"Nope," Jake said. "He can't do it. I've had 'em staked for years. Maybe Horace bouncing those bullets off him made an impression."

"I surly hope so," Jenny said. "Shooting people is serious business. Isn't the sheriff around to protect folks?"

"Alton Kingman!" Jake exclaimed. "The only time he leaves his office in Baker City is to go to the courthouse and pick up his pay check. He wouldn't come to Slab Creek if a dozen folks got shot."

Whort decided to change the subject. "I'm sorry we missed Doc's burial service. We sure heard a lot about it later. If you'll show us to his grave, we'll let you keep your ten dollars."

Jake swallowed. "I just wanted a good turn out."

Jenny said: "That's OK, Jake, we're here now."

She walked over and stepped up to the open stage door. Jenny reached inside and grabbed up a large bouquet of pink peonies. "I brought these for Doc's grave."

"You know," Jake said, "all those folks at Doc's funeral and not a one of 'em brought a single flower."

Whort stuck his hands into his pockets and surveyed the workmen, scurrying around the new boom town. "Gold does that to folks."

CHAPTER SIXTEEN

Rincón McCutchan thought the vulture perched on top of Henry Hayes Hedgepath's gray head was an appropriate addition to the seedy lawyer's vestments. He knew the blasted red-headed buzzard was just another spook, but when the bird spread its wings wide and carrion drooled from its hooked beak, the specter appeared almost likeable compared to the lawyer.

"So your sordid past has begun to cause us problems," Hedgepath said with a sneer from behind the expanse of his huge desk. "I cannot say this comes as any great surprise."

Rincón countered: "Well, it sure as hell surprised *me* when Horace Tabor yanked out a pistol and started shooting."

The vulture folded its wings and the lawyer took on a pained expression. "Mister McCutchan, please refrain from the use of fulminates in my office. I find them debasing to its sanctity."

A blank look washed Rincón's pockmarked face. "Huh?"

Hedgepath shook his head sadly. "Don't use any curse words in my presence."

"Oh, yes, sir, I'm sorry."

"Now tell me, Mister McCutchan, how did you avoid being injured or worse in this fracas?"

Rincón grinned and pounded his knuckles on his chest. The heavy sound was akin to thumping on a cast iron stove. "Body armor. Those bullets didn't even make a dent."

The lawyer nodded his approval. Given his own occupation, it might be judicious to invest in some bulletproof undergarments himself. "A wise move. It was unfortunate you did not have the same protection in Central City. I believe this Horace Tabor was one of the men who nearly caused your demise there."

Rincón shrugged. "He's just a sorehead. I thought his claim had lapsed an' was putting up my own location papers when he showed up."

Hedgepath gave a knowing look. "I'm *certain* that was the case. What we must concern ourselves with is damage control. My understanding is Jake Crabtree was present at the incident?"

Rincón nodded and wondered just how the bony lawyer managed to know everything that happened. "Yep, he was there all right. I ain't seen hide nor hair of Crabtree in my place since."

"*Our* place," the lawyer corrected. "It is possible Crabtree is simply busy with his mining operations."

"Could be that's the case. But Tabor's been spendin' a lot of time with him, an' the surveyor's about got the town plotted up."

The lawyer's gray eyes sparked. "Just the town? Are you saying Crabtree did not have his mining claims surveyed while he had a surveyor hired?"

"Nope," Rincón replied with a shrug. "Jake's just layin' out the town."

"And you felt this gem of information wasn't worth passing along?"

The buzzard arched its neck and stared at Rincón. "I thought you was plannin' to do some legal shenanigans to jump the mine?"

"A fact such as this is precisely what I need to perform what you so crudely term 'legal shenanigans', Mister McCutchan. In the future I wish to be kept abreast of *all* details of what you see or hear in *our* saloon."

"Yes, sir, sorry Mister Hedgepath. It won't

happen again."

The lawyer sighed and pored over some notes on his desk. "I see you have two faro tables and one roulette wheel. I trust the operators will be adept in their profitable manipulation?"

Rincón cocked his head and thought for a moment. "Are you askin' if they can cheat good?"

"Coarsely worded, but accurate."

"Why, Henry, we'll clean out everybody an' do it so slick they won't know how it happened."

"*Mister* McCutchan," the lawyer snarled and the turkey buzzard spread its black wings. "I have asked you before to refrain from a show of familiarity."

"Sorry, Mister Hedgepath, sir, it won't happen again."

Henry Hayes Hedgepath squinted his flinty eyes and grinned, showing his perfect, small, pointed teeth. "A partnership is very much like a marriage vow. They are binding until death do us part."

For the first time, pure fear trickled down Rincón's spine like icy footsteps from a venomous scorpion. He fought down the urge to bolt from his chair and not stop until he ran out of land. "Uh . . . sir, we're going to need some girls to work the cribs upstairs. I'd be right pleased to go an' recruit us some."

The lawyer continued his malevolent grin. "That will not be necessary. I have made arrangements with Madam Molly Spade to handle the matter."

Rincón masked his disappointment. He had been looking forward to checking out whores for weeks. The ominous lawyer was terribly correct about not spending the money, however. That would leave more for him later on, after Hedgepath's demise.

"That'll be good, sir," Rincón agreed with a forced smile. "The way Slab Creek's booming, those girls will get a workout for sure."

"I trust you are correct in that assessment."

The lawyer leaned back in his swivel chair and laced his fingers behind his head. The vulture ignored him and kept its beady eyes fixed on Rincón. "Regardless, when we wind up owning the Merry Widow Mine, there will be no cause for regret."

Rincón's smile turned genuine. "No, sir, there sure won't."

Hedgepath clucked his tongue. "I believe your presence is necessary at the Red Lion."

"Yes, sir." Rincón stood and spun to leave. *Until death do us part,* a vile-sounding, liquid voice intoned as he turned the brass doorknob. Rincón knew it wasn't the lawyer and decided the blasted buzzard had learned how to talk. Having an occasional spook to contend with was bad enough. When they began to speak, it was an added agony.

Until death do us part, the vulture rasped again.

The moment Rincón was outside the lawyer's office, he jerked a sliver flask of whiskey from his jacket pocket and drank it dry in one long, satisfying gulp.

Isaac Beekman poked a hunk of black tobacco into his mouth. The corpulent newspaperman sighed as he read the rejection letter for his latest novel. He had a difficult time understanding just how bloody blind Eastern editors were. Here he had written a masterpiece of action, adventure, and purpose blended with a lesson in morality, and the manuscript had been rejected and returned in less time than the postal service was known for being capable of moving mail.

"That man simply doesn't know good literature when he sees it," Beekman grumbled aloud. "I cannot, for the life of me, understand how he retains his employment."

He slid open a drawer on his massive desk and added Milo Nettleman's rejection to the growing stack. He spit a wad of tobacco juice in the general direction of the brass spittoon and began to devote his talents to another future bestseller.

So far Beekman had nearly thirty pages completed and now he had a title: CRIMSON SKIES; OR, MILO'S CHECKMATE AT INDIAN CREEK. Diligent research on his part had disclosed that Randolph Press in New York was a bitter rival of Slayton Publishing. By renaming his not so bright hero after Slayton's moronic editor, the novel would certainly be snapped up with a huge advance.

"What d'ya you mean I'm overdrawn?" Jake Crabtree grumbled. "I've still got plenty of those drafts that you gave me."

Otis McElroy clenched his teeth and took a moment to reply. His employer had made it abundantly clear that Jake Crabtree was to be treated with respect. It rankled the cashier to be nice to an idiot. "Sir," McElroy said, "you have written vouchers for more money than you had in your account. The bank realizes you are a valued client. Therefore, we have honored the overdrafts for only a nominal service charge of one dollar for each draft."

"How many was that, anyway?" Jake asked, remembering how badly his fingers hurt after writing all of those vouchers at the funeral.

The hawkish clerk peered through his wire-rimmed glasses at a ledger book. "One hundred and seventy-eight to be precise. All of them were for the grand sum of five dollars each."

"You mean to say, it cost me a dollar to give away five?"

The cashier was scarcely able to conceal his elation. "Sir, that is bank policy when a customer writes drafts and there are insufficient funds in the account."

"But I had ore at the mill," Jake retorted.

"Oh, we here at the Virtue Bank realize that, sir. Unfortunately the mill is a separate entity altogether. Until the check for the new ore shipment was physically in our possession, the matter was totally out of our hands."

Jake frowned. "We're talking about the same hands that got one hundred and seventy-eight of my dollars?"

Otis A. McElroy's eyes flashed with gratification. "That is a fact of business."

"Well, how much do I have since I got robbed?"

The cashier felt it would be prudent to limit his reply to what was written in the ledger book. "Three-thousand, two-hundred dollars even."

Jake fingered the bank drafts in his shirt pocket. "Now you're a telling me I can write these darn' things for up to that amount without paying a dollar for the privilege?"

"That is a fact, Mister Crabtree."

"Can I get two hundred in cash?" Jake asked.

"Certainly, sir. Would you like that in gold?"

"I brought in gold to the mill and I'd like to leave here with the same stuff. Is there a blasted charge for getting my money out, too?"

McElroy gave a vulpine grin. "No, Mister Crabtree, no charge for cash withdrawals."

Jake grabbed up the gold eagles after they were counted out. "Tell me, do you know what town in Missouri Frank and Jesse James hail from?"

McElroy shook his head in surprise. "No, sir, I don't. What a strange question to ask."

"No, it ain't strange at all," Jake said. "I'm planning on writing them a letter and tell 'em to come over here and learn how to rob folks proper. I'll even give 'em your name. Now, *you* have a nice day, Mister McElroy."

■ ■ ■ ■

A mile past the turn-off to the gold camp of
Sumpter, Henry McCarty's mule broke
wind and stopped in the middle of the road.
It began wheezing and Henry and Antrim
realized the animal wasn't going another
foot until it had rested.

"Never gave mules much thought before,"
Henry said as he painfully climbed from the
saddle and backed away. While the old beast
seemed on the verge of death, it still might
bite. "But I'd reckon they're about the or-
neriest critters on earth. For the life of me I
can't figger them tellin' us his name was
Swifty."

William Antrim surveyed his stepson's
panting mule with a jaundiced eye. "From
the looks of things, he got that name a
bunch of years ago."

"Yes, sir," Henry agreed. "It's too bad ol'
Swifty was too stove up to head cross-
country like you wanted to do."

Antrim said: "Well, the road here is wide
enough a wagon could get around your
mule, so we might as well look this area
over."

Henry gave a buck-toothed grin of satisfaction. "Which way do we go?"

Antrim nodded toward the tree-covered slope. "Let's head up there. A man never knows where he'll find gold. Sometimes it turns up in the darnedest places."

Henry rubbed his sore rear end, shot a scathing glare at the mule, and climbed to the top of a low bank. His curious eyes noticed where a pile of brush heaped up over a depression had obviously been recently shuffled about. He stepped down and pulled the scrub from the hole.

"Mister Antrim," he said, his voice tight with consternation. "I think you oughta come see this."

Antrim smiled. To the desperate boy, anything that had a shine to it would appear to be the Mother Lode. Teaching young Henry what a gold outcrop looked like would take a lot of patience. Then he saw the object of the boy's attentions and his eyes widened.

"Henry," Antrim said, nervously scouring the surrounding countryside, "you know that pistol in the saddlebag?"

"Yes, sir."

"Go get it and strap it on. I said, once we found something rich to protect, you could wear it. The time's come. There's a lot of high-grade cached here. Whoever stole this gold in the first place won't take kindly to us relieving them of it."

With incredulity Henry McCarty stared at the hoard of glistening yellow metal that he had uncovered. It was only their second day in the Oregon mountains, and now, thanks to a nearly dead mule, they were rich. Finding gold had turned out to be a lot easier than he'd been led to believe. "Mister Antrim," Henry asked, "are you saying some thieves have already stole this gold and buried it here?"

"That's most certainly the case," Antrim answered. "No one would stash rich ore if they had come by it legal."

Henry shrugged. "I can't abide thieves, but I reckon there's no harm in *us* takin' it since we didn't steal it in the first place."

"Yeah," Antrim agreed. "I've even got an idea how to do it legal."

Henry jumped down from the bank. He approached the wheezing mule carefully to avoid getting bitten again. A moment later he had his stepfather's Navy revolver strapped around his narrow waist. The young man slid the heavy pistol in and out of its well-oiled holster a few times before the creaking of an approaching wagon added a fresh urgency to his skill at handling a firearm.

A wagon pulled by four draft horses slowly

came into view. The pudgy driver reined the heavy, loaded wagon around the mule that showed no signs of moving. The moment the wagon groaned out of sight, Henry began looking around for his stepfather when Antrim rose from the depression that held their golden cache and brushed dirt from his clothes.

"Reckon I'm just jumpy," Henry said as he joined his stepfather. "He hardly paid us any mind."

"Being jumpy can save your life, boy. Lots of folks have been killed for a lot less than what's in this hole."

Henry surveyed the cache. "How much do you figger is down there?"

"That's hard to say, but I'm betting on well over a thousand dollars."

Henry looked concerned. "I hoped it would be more than that."

"It's a good start. We won't really know how much gold is here until we dig it out."

The boy brightened. "That's great, sir. You mentioned we could do this legal?"

Antrim grinned. "Well, sort of anyway. There's two kinds of claims a person can stake. The first is a lode. The other is a placer claim. It gives ownership to gold that's just layin' loose. We're gonna stake a placer claim on this. While not everybody might agree with my thinking, it'll keep us on the right side of the law."

"I cotton to the idea of not crossin' the law, Mister Antrim."

"Still, you should practice a lot with that gun. We may need to defend our claim." Antrim was growing increasingly attached to his stepson.

CHAPTER SEVENTEEN

Lanny Payton bent and watched by flickering yellow candlelight as Orson Dugan tamped a cartridge of dynamite into a lifter hole. The nurse stood and moved over to give Orson more room. She slid a leather pouch from her wool shirt, took out a two-fingered pinch of snuff, and added the tobacco to the wad behind her lower lip. Using snuff had become commonplace with Lanny.

"Sure is a mighty pretty sight," she said wistfully as she surveyed the gold-laden vein.

Orson glanced up, nodded in agreement, then returned to loading the holes with sticks of dynamite. The miner wished the old busybody would climb out of the shaft and leave him alone. Being unable to speak, he rushed the job. Once the first fuse had been lit, Lanny Payton would be out of his way in a hurry.

The gold imbedded in a six-inch-wide seam of white quartz glistened in the candle-light like jewels in the crown of Solomon. To Lanny Payton's gold-fevered eyes, the pay streak looked like a crack in the pearly gates. A few more feet into the mountain and they would open gold as plentiful as that which paved God's own streets.

Orson Dugan shook Lanny from her delightful reverie by grabbing the candle-holder from its niche and motioning with his head toward the ladder. The miner was ready to light the fuses. Lanny took one last, longing glance at the vein of gold and started for the surface.

Orson took a moment to roll a cigarette. The nurse wasn't on the skinny side. It would be a disaster to light the fuses only to find Lanny had run out of steam halfway to the surface. The miner also took this opportunity to pry loose a few high-grade pieces of gold and add them to what he'd already stashed away deep in the pockets of his mud-plastered Levi's. Orson took the lack of any noise to indicate that Lanny Payton had reached the surface. Normally a miner would yell "fire in the hole" before lighting any fuse, but in his case no one could expect that.

Satisfied that each of the fourteen fuses

was burning its way to the dynamite, Dugan climbed the ladder and scrambled to the fresh, clean air of a warm Oregon afternoon.

Two deep-booming thuds put a smile on T. Greene's bearded face. A heavy woofing sound signified the cut holes had moved a lot of rock. They waited for the lifters to fire, but heard only a low, continuous thundering from the depths of the shaft.

"What is it, what's wrong?" Lanny shouted when she read the worried looks on the miner's faces.

"We got trouble," T. Greene said simply.

Seth Dugan stepped to the collar of the mine and peered downward. "It's comin' up, T. Greene. The darn stuff's only a dozen feet down already."

"What's wrong?" Lanny demanded again. "Why won't somebody tell me?"

T. Greene clicked around on his canes so he could look in the shaft. An expression of dismay shone in his rheumy eyes. "You'd better come see fer yourself, Lanny."

One glance into the depths answered all questions. Water filled the shaft to within a few feet of the surface. Lanny felt faint with the same pain in her chest that used to rise from her stomach when a patient died. Only this wasn't the death of a beloved patient she was witnessing, it was the demise of her dreams.

"Oh, my God!" Lanny exclaimed.

"We blasted into a dad-burn' underground river," T. Greene said.

Lanny wailed. "But the mine was dry. I was just down there."

Seth Dugan shook his head sadly. "It's a tolerable shame you had to hit water so soon. A few more shipments of ore, then you might have had the money for a steam pump that'd handle a flow of water this big."

"We can pump it out," Lanny said firmly. "I know we can."

T. Greene Moss and the Dugan brothers exchanged knowing glances. Even a distant hope should be allowed a chance to flourish.

Jake Crabtree was in a quandary. He couldn't shake the disturbing feeling that Horace Tabor might be correct in his assessment of Rincón McCutchan's character. In spite of a tendency to be trigger-happy, Horace seemed to be a level-headed man with nearly as much knowledge of the prospecting business as Jake himself possessed. Rincón was still friendly enough, but Jake had begun to notice some disturbing goings on inside the Red Lion Saloon. He paid two bits for a shot of whiskey just like everyone else, only his came from a special bottle. The other patrons received a vile-looking glass of popskull that seemed to assure their loss at any of the gaming tables.

Tonight, Jake decided, would tell the tale on Rincón's saloon. Not a person in Slab Creek had failed to hear that the first load of whores had set up shop in the Red Lion.

"It's a terrible shame you're a married man," Jake said to Tabor as he dumped a steaming bucket of hot water into a copper washbasin. "That condition limits a man's recreational activities something awful."

Horace Tabor grimaced when Augusta's stern, demon-infested image flashed through his mind. "It can be a vexation, but if that claim jumper had a bevy of beauties giving it away, I'd pass. A corkscrew's straighter than that McCutchan's black soul."

Jake wore an amused expression when he began lathering his face before shaving. "After you went and shot Rincón, I figured you didn't care much for the man."

"It causes stomach problems if you hold your feelings in."

"Reckon your gut's in great shape," Jake quipped.

Horace nodded in agreement. "Shooting

scalawags always helps. I hope you're careful around him. You can bet on Rincón McCutchan doing the same thing to you that you're planning on doing to one of those whores."

Jake chuckled, then turned serious. "Horace, I'm beginning to concern myself a tad with the goin's on at the Red Lion. I'm keeping my eyes open."

Tabor sighed. "I hope you are, Jake. I really do."

Wearing a fresh-boiled shirt and cleanly shaven with a splash of toilet water on his cheeks, Jake entered the saloon. He had five shots of whiskey to get in the proper mood while watching the comings and goings up and down the stairs. Strangely enough, the traffic seemed pretty light for the first time soiled doves had been available in Slab Creek.

"I'd have thought you'd have a line waitin'," Jake mentioned to Rincón.

"Prime merchandise is expensive. I'm havin' to charge five bucks a toss. Not too many folks seem to want to pay for quality."

Jake choked on his bourbon. *"Five dollars!* Why, Mollie Spade only charges a buck in her joint."

Rincón grinned. "The shipment came straight out of Portland. I've been savin' room Number Four just for you. The little gal in there'll spin your lariat."

A man Jake recognized as a teamster for Packy Jackson objected loudly to losing twenty dollars on the roulette wheel. Two toughs who worked for Rincón calmed him down with a blackjack.

"I run an orderly place," Rincón said.

"That's obvious," Jake said as the bloody, unconscious man was tossed out the door.

Rincón gave a sickly grin and plunked a round brass slug onto the plank bar. "This is how we're handlin' the gals up here. Keeps 'em from cheatin'."

Jake picked up the brass token and studied it. One side held the engraving of a lion's head. On the reverse was written: **Good for one screw.**

"Hand it to the lady an' that takes care of the matter," Rincón declared.

Jake nodded and cocked his head to eyeball the upstairs door with a crude 4 painted on it.

"Ahem," Rincón sputtered. "I'll be needin' the five."

Jake fished out an eagle. "This'll cover my drinks, too," he said. "I hope that gal's worth a whole five dollars. I never thought I'd ever pay that much for a poke."

Rincón grabbed up the gold coin. "Everyone gets their money's worth at the Red Lion."

"Come on in lover," a honey sweet voice cooed in answer to Jake's knock.

Wearing a smirk of anticipation Jake entered and closed the door behind him. The girl stood with her back to him brushing her auburn hair. She wore a tight-fitting chemise that accented her bony frame like a wet sheet draped over a range cow that had suffered through a dry summer.

Jake's worst nightmare came true when she turned and grinned at him with a toothless smile.

"Well, hello again, hon," she purred. "I see you have come lookin' for some more of little Delma's sugar."

CHAPTER EIGHTEEN

"I'm tellin' you, Tabor," Jake Crabtree fumed, "you've been right all along about McCutchan being a low-down skunk. That miserable excuse for a human being saddled me with a whore so blame ugly a train would jump its tracks rather than run over her."

Horace Tabor held the brass token between his thumb and forefinger and studied it in the flickering light of the kerosene lamp.

"Can't accuse Rincón of lying none," Horace said with a smirk. "It says right here in big letters that you're gonna get screwed."

"I got me an idea," Jake said. "Rincón charges two bits for a shot of rotgut and his tables are crooked as a dog's hind leg. Add in some whores so ugly they'd stampede cattle and you know what I have to do?"

Horace Tabor took a sip of whiskey and surveyed Jake through the wavering yellow light. "You're fixing to open your own joint."

"Yep," Jake agreed. "Slab Creek's *my* town. I can't see no other choice but to run him plumb out of business."

"What are you planning to call the place?" Tabor asked.

Jake lowered his eyebrows. "The Merry Widow's like owning a mint. How about if I name my saloon The Mint?"

"I like it," Tabor said. "And if you run it square, you'll take Rincón's business away for sure."

"That's what I'm plannin' on."

"One thing you gotta remember." Tabor patted the pistol in his pocket. "Rincón's not going to take favorable to your doing that. He doesn't wear bulletproof underwear because folks like him."

Jake spun his nearly empty glass worriedly. "I reckon it would be a wise move to hire a guard or two."

"I doubt if you'd get the place built without it catching fire if you don't."

Jake nodded. "I always thought I was a pretty good judge of character."

"That's an easier task when you don't have much money. A rich man has a mighty hard time telling who his real friends are."

"I'm learning."

Tabor grabbed the bottle and refilled their glasses. "You know anything about running a saloon? If you're going to stock the joint with some soiled doves, you'll need to find someone who knows the ropes. One woman is trouble enough. I can only imagine the trouble a half-dozen or so of the species might cause."

Jake chuckled. "You have a point, but I'm hiring the carpenters tomorrow. While the building's goin' up, I want my manager to go to Portland and come back with a whole covey of cute little ladies. If my timing is right, the brass beds will be ready and waitin' for 'em when they get here."

Tabor looked puzzled. "You know someone who'll run the place and not rob you blind?"

"Yep," Jake said firmly. "And that man, Horace Tabor, is you."

Tabor chugged a mouthful of whiskey and closed his eyes. The vision of his stern-faced, demon-infested wife was all too vivid. His bushy mustache tweaked up at the edges. "Reckon I could do that for you Jake, me being a friend and all."

"Then let's drink to it," Jake said, holding up his glass.

Tabor clinked his glass to Jake's and beamed. While he hadn't found a gold mine, the summer was definitely shaping up to be a good one.

■ ■ ■ ■

"That freight wagon owner's a real unfriendly sort," Henry McCarty remarked to his stepfather.

William Antrim watched as Packy Jackson grimaced and tossed another shovel full of the high-grade gold into the back of his ore wagon.

Antrim said: "I agree, Henry. That man does have an ornery attitude. He even made me show him our claim papers before he'd haul the load to the mill. I thought that was a bit strange, like we might have been the ones who stole it in the first place."

"I just can't abide a thief," Henry said loudly enough to draw a scathing glare from the freighter. "How much do you reckon this'll bring us?" Henry asked again.

Antrim surveyed the growing wagonload of ore and what was left in the cache. "This is very high-grade ore, some of the richest you'll likely ever see. I'd be real surprised if this load don't fetch us a couple of thousand dollars."

Packy Jackson swallowed hard before he remembered he had a wad of tobacco in his mouth and began to choke.

"You gonna be OK, sir?" Henry asked

with concern.

"I'm just fine," the freighter wheezed. "I'd get the job done faster iffen you would leave me be."

Henry said: "We're keepin' an eye on our gold an' I'm gonna ride along with you when you take it to the mill."

"I ain't no thief," Packy Jackson growled.

"No one here ever said you was," Antrim answered calmly.

The freighter tossed another shovel full of ore onto the wagon, spat what remained of his chew at Henry's feet, and said: "You two think you're really somethin'. Come out here an' find a load of gold that somebody sweat blood to mine out and claim it for yourselves. I can't figger how that's right."

Henry patted of his revolver. "Judge Colt says it's ours."

"I ain't accusin'," Packy said quickly. "I just don't think it's fair."

Antrim stepped closer. "Are you sayin' you know who put this stolen ore here?"

Packy shook his head. "Nope, I sure don't."

"Then, perhaps," Antrim said, "it might be a good idea to do the job we hired you for and leave the moralizing to preachers. For all we know, whoever stole it in the first place has already been hung."

"They don't hang high-graders," Packy said firmly.

Antrim gave him a cold grin. "That depends on the situation. A lot of ore thieves have gotten suspended sentences from a tree for their efforts."

The color fled Packy Jackson's face. "I'm just here to load my wagon."

Antrim placed a hand on Henry's shoulder. "Come on, son, let's take a walk and let the man get his work done."

"This here Cope and Maxwell pump might dry up the shaft," T. Greene Moss said, pointing to an ad in *The Mining and Scientific Press*. "Trouble with any steam pump is they'll eat a forest tuh keep up the pressure. We'd likely need fifty cords of wood laid back before we fire the boiler. Once we get tuh pumpin', we can't stop fer nothin', otherwise the water'll just come right back up an' we'd loose what we gained."

Lanny Payton's face took on a faraway expression. She knew in every fiber of her heart the blast that had opened the watercourse also had laid bare the treasure of kings. There was still twelve hundred dollars in her bank account. T. Greene thought the single ore shipment they had made would bring them around eight hundred dollars. *That will give us two thousand dollars,* she thought. *With that much money and God on our side we could pump out the Pacific Ocean. Moses parted the Red Sea with nothing but a stick.*

"How much will everything cost us?" Lanny asked.

T. Green leaned over and took a pencil to a piece of foolscap. After a few moments of figuring he said: "It ain't only the pump an' boiler we gotta buy, there's also casing an' pump rod. Then the freight's gotta be added in. Then we have tuh hire the thing set an' the wood cut."

Lanny's expression grew worried. "How much have you come up to?"

T. Greene's silver eyebrows narrowed as he went over his arithmetic. "I can't say fer certain on the freight. The pump itself weighs right at two tons. Iffen I allow fer the fact that they'll rob us blind, the whole shebang adds up to about eighteen hundred dollars."

Lanny stuffed more snuff under her lip, sneezed, then grabbed the piece of paper from T. Green's hand and studied it. "Boys, it's going to be really close."

T. Greene used his arms to shift his crippled body to where he could face Lanny. "Pardner, you've been bank rollin' this mine

205

ever since we staked the thing. We might could sell out an' get yer money back."

Lanny looked dumbstruck. "We can't sell the richest mine in the whole state of Oregon just because we have a little problem with water. I don't want to hear any more talk of selling out."

T. Greene nodded his white-cropped head. "That's fine, pard. I just wanted tuh let ya know it'd be all right with us iffen you wanted to."

"We're buying a pump," Lanny proclaimed.

T. Greene Moss had seen too many cases of gold fever to think Lanny would ever let go of the mine, but it seemed only right to bring up the possibility. To save money, Lanny had given up her home in Baker City and had begun bunking with Warm Stove and him at the cabin by the mine shaft. T. Green chuckled inwardly at what rumors would have been flying about had this situation happened a few years ago, he and his partner living with a woman, a sin-filled situation if there ever was one.

As he knew she would, Lanny kept rambling on about the mine. T. Greene wished they could converse about something else. Perhaps they could simply plan what they would have for dinner. That would be pleasurable. He felt a strange tugging sensation in his heart when he was around Lanny. There had been a time when he would have called it love. Nowadays, even speaking of such a thing, would be foolish. Lanny Payton loved only gold.

CHAPTER NINETEEN

The moment William Antrim set eyes on the gold vein in the Merry Widow Mine he knew exactly where the cache of ore he and Henry sent to the mill had come from. The rock was identical. Antrim knew it wouldn't be prudent to divulge that fact to the friendly mine owner standing by their side. He fervently hoped his young stepson wouldn't have a slip of the tongue.

Jake Crabtree beamed and motioned to the glistening vein. "Sure is a beaut, ain't it."

"Yes, sir," William and Henry answered.

"Help yourselves to a chunk or two," Jake said with a smile. "I'd like for you two folks to have something to remember your visit."

I'm fairly sure we've already helped ourselves to plenty, William thought. "Thank you, Mister Crabtree, I'm certain the boy will appreciate that. He's never seen a rich vein of ore in place before. The education will be a big help to him learning how to prospect."

Jake surveyed the gangly youth. "Being a prospector is a wonderful calling, son. I'd be obliged to help you learn the business. There's a lot of things I can teach you that you likely wouldn't learn nowhere else."

Henry flashed a buck-toothed grin. "Sir, I'd appreciate that a whole lot. The only problem is . . . I ain't got a whole lot of time with my ma bein' sick with the gallopin' consumption. We gotta strike it right soon an' get her to a clinic back East."

Jake's expression turned sad. "Sorry to hear that. Where is she?"

Antrim spoke up: "At our home down in New Mexico. The doc said there was a clinic on the East Coast that could cure her, so I quit my job as a mine boss and Henry an' me came up here, hoping to make a strike so we'd have money enough to pay for the treatments."

"You're an experienced miner?" Jake questioned.

"Yes, sir," Antrim replied. "That's all I've ever done."

Jake mulled the situation for a moment. "Mister Antrim, while I'm an expert at prospecting, I ain't got time to run a mine the size of this one. If you'd take the job of managing it, I'd be proud to offer you six hundred dollars a month."

Antrim swallowed. The salary was unbelievable. As mine foreman in Silver City he'd been paid four dollars for a ten-hour day. "Sir," he said, "I'd be proud to take you up on that offer. The wage is very generous and I'll watch after your property like it's my own."

"But Mister Antrim," Henry said, "we can't give up on findin' our own mine."

Antrim put his hand on Henry's narrow shoulder. "Jake Crabtree's wonderful wage will likely see to your mother's care. What you need to do is learn from Mister Crabtree and go prospecting."

"I'll teach him everything I know," Jake said. "With my guidance he'll have to work hard at *not* finding gold. I've got a real nose for the stuff."

Henry lowered his head. "I'll do my best . . . for my mom I'd do 'most anything."

Jake worked a lump from his throat. "Well, let's go topside and let everyone know who their new boss is."

A lone white cloud hung in a still, azure sky when they emerged from the mine shaft. Jake motioned with a nod of his head to a man shoveling ore onto a freight wagon. "This here's Packy Jackson. He hauls the

210

ore to the mill."

The freighter shot a startled glance and returned to his task.

"Packy," Jake said, "William Antrim's just taken over as my mine boss. You'll be working for him from now on."

Packy Jackson bolted like he'd been shot. He dropped his shovel and spun around, a look of disbelief on his face. He tried to think of something to say that wouldn't get him hung, but all he was able to muster was an open-mouthed gawk.

"You OK, Packy?" Jake asked.

"Uh . . . yeah," the freighter mumbled. "I was just surprised to hear the news. I'd figured on you keepin' runnin' the place yourself."

"Got too much to do these days," Jake replied.

"Henry," Antrim said, "tomorrow's soon enough to start on your prospecting lessons. That ore's plenty rich. I want you to strap on your gun and ride along with Mister Jackson and protect him from robbers and such."

"Yes, sir," Henry replied. "I'd be proud to look after Mister Crabtree's interests."

Henry McCarty made up his mind never to become a freighter. From the grimace of pure pain on Packy Jackson's visage, his

211

back had to be hurting him something fierce.

Horace Tabor found it difficult to keep from staring at Madam Doily Lace's well-exposed and ample cleavage. He realized the lady hadn't bought such an expensive low-cut dress to have her obvious charms ignored, yet manners must be observed.

"Another glass of sherry, Mister Tabor?" Madam Lace asked, her deep voice purring like a contented cat.

"That would be delightful," he answered, and leaned back in the luxurious chair to enjoy the view while she poured from the bottle of delectable wine.

The madam slinked back into her chair across a low ornate walnut table from Tabor and regarded him with eyes that twinkled like blue ice. She took a demure sip of her sherry, then her expression changed from seductive to that of a businesswoman. Being a chameleon was a necessity in her profession.

"If I understand you correctly, sir," she said firmly, "you wish me to send a few of my young ladies to the boom town of Slab Creek where they will work in a saloon managed by you?"

Tabor nodded and took a puff on his

cigar. "The girls will work strictly for you, ma'am. All we're going to do is furnish the rooms for them and let the boys know they're there."

Doily Lace cut to the deal. "How much will your establishment take from what my girls earn?"

Tabor looked appalled. "Why, ma'am, Crabtree and me don't want anything. We're simply trying to put up a quality saloon. There's simply not a good-looking dove in the whole town. I'm here to rectify that problem."

The madam cocked her head. This wasn't what she had expected to hear. "What about rent? You're going to charge a lot to use your rooms?"

"No, not at all," Horace said, confounding her further. "The rooms are free and the ladies can cook their meals in the kitchen. Any and all money they make is theirs . . . yours . . . to keep."

A smile washed across the madam's painted face. "I dare say, Mister Tabor, your town sounds like it is in desperate need of some feminine companionship. I feel it's my civic duty to help out." She hesitated a moment. "I like my girls' safety taken care of. Will you assure me they'll be watched after?"

Tabor patted his pocket pistol. "Ma'am, if anyone tries to take more advantage of one of your gals than they've paid for, I'll shoot them myself."

"You're an astute man, Mister Tabor. I like that quality in a person."

"Thank you, Madam Lace. Might I inquire as to what your little ladies will charge for a po . . . their time?"

Doily laughed. "Why, dearie, under the terms you've laid out we can afford to be generous. Two bucks for the basics will be fair to everyone concerned. If someone wants more . . . well . . . that's always negotiable."

Horace felt his cheeks flush. He wasn't used to such straight talk from a lovely lady.

Doily Lace giggled. "Have another glass of sherry and please stay the night. I've already heard of Slab Creek, and, I must confess, I've thought of checking into opening a place there. It was most opportune for you to show up when you did."

"Yes, ma'am," was all Horace could muster.

"Please join me and the girls for breakfast. This will give you time to get better acquainted. We'll be having clam cakes and eggs."

Tabor eyed the elaborate grandfather

clock. It was two in the afternoon.

The madam grinned like a fox. "I'll be sending along four girls for now. You really should take the time to get to know each of them before taking off on such an arduous trip. Generosity such as yours should be rewarded, Mister Tabor."

Horace Tabor's luminous eyes widened with surprise. His mind worked overtime to assess the situation, then he remembered he *was* working for Jake Crabtree. Augusta was always scolding him to get a job. Perhaps he should follow his wife's good advice for once.

"Madam Lace," Horace said, his eyes mischievous, "it's going to be a real business doing pleasure with you."

Henry Hayes Hedgepath drummed his dainty fingers on the massive oak desk and glared at Rincón who tried to ignore the rattlesnake writhing around the lawyer's scrawny neck. "I am most dissatisfied with your performance, Mister McCutchan." The lawyer's voice came as a hiss. "*Most* dissatisfied."

Rincón tried not to wince when the snake coiled around, poked its triangular head into the lawyer's mouth, and wiggled down his gullet. "Mister Hedgepath," he said, taking a moment to recover from the spook, "if Molly Spade had sent up a good-lookin' gal or two, Crabtree wouldn't be building his own saloon."

"The man does seem to have rather discerning taste for a man of limited intellectual capacities. And Miss Spade's ladies do have a certain lack of pulchritude. But the failure of the Red Lion to show a decent return bodes ill for our net profit venture."

Rincón ran a thumb along his pockmarked cheek. "It's plenty hard to make money in a saloon if there's not a lot of folks strikin' it rich. I'd reckon the only valuable property up there is Crabtree's."

"Mister McCutchan, I congratulate you on your cognition."

Rincón chewed on his lower lip. He couldn't decide if he'd been paid a compliment or not. If he could have afforded one, he would hire a lawyer of his own to tell him what this one was talking about. "Uh . . . Henry . . . I mean, Mister Hedgepath," Rincón said, "I was surely hoping you might be able to pull off some of that legal claim jumpin' we discussed."

The lawyer grinned and displayed his pearly white, sharp-pointed teeth. "Ah, Mister McCutchan, your perspicacity never fails to impress me. My diligence has literally been directed toward us reaching that end." Rincón's blank stare caused Hedgepath to elaborate on the matter. "Jake Crabtree's dipsomania and indolence have left us with an auspicious situation."

"Huh?"

Henry Hayes Hedgepath sighed and leaned back in his chair. "We *are* going to jump the Merry Widow Mine."

A vulpine grin washed over Rincón's face. "Well, that's some rip-snortin' good news. When's this gonna come about?"

The lawyer proclaimed with obvious satisfaction: "The laws are quite specific when it comes to staking and filing a mining claim. First, a person must erect a location monument. Then he must place a copy of the location notice there, and then file a duplicate with the county recorder."

"How does the jumpin' part fit in?" Rincón interrupted.

"Ah, yes, you are one for the direct approach. I like that in a person. The flaw in Crabtree's claim staking was failure to mark all of his claim corners. Myself, along with surveyor Buhlman, and Father Ledbetter of our local Catholic church were unable to locate but three monuments. Since Mister Crabtree has two claims, we should have found six." McCutchan's blank glare caused

Henry Hayes Hedgepath to continue. "An improperly staked claim is held by the courts to be open ground. I have filed claims, under our partnership name, over the Merry Widow Mine."

"So the mine's ours?" Rincón was incredulous that it could be done so easily. If he had partnered with a lawyer years ago, he wouldn't be suffering from spooks.

Hedgepath leaned his elbows on the desk and tented his fingers. "It is only a beginning. There is the matter of possession and the very real possibility some soft-hearted judge may rule against us."

The word "possession" stuck in Rincón's craw and brought back painful memories. "You mean to tell me I gotta go ahead an' use a gun to jump the place? Folks know all about my body armor, thanks to Tabor."

The attorney sighed. "It grieves me deeply to think you believe I would ever place my valued business partner in harm's way. While it is true we must physically occupy the mine itself, there is no hurry to accomplish that."

No matter how much the lawyer rattled on, Rincón could still envision getting shot. His look of concern caused the attorney to lean back and chuckle. His dull laughter caused icy pin pricks to work their way down Rincón's back.

Hedgepath intoned: " 'The lion and the belly-pinched wolf keep their fur dry, un-bonneted he runs, and bids what will take all.' "

"Huh?"

Hedgepath frowned. "It is a quote from Shakespeare . . . *King Lear* to be precise. I thought it appropriate to the moment." He focused on a side door to his office and boomed. "Please come in, Mister Galt."

The door swung wide and Rincón nearly bolted. What had to be the most frightening spook to date sauntered into the lawyer's office. At least Rincón *hoped* it was a spook. The visage was that of a tall, lanky man with a pearl-handled pistol hung low on his hip, gunfighter style. The stranger wore a large black hat with a wide brim that had long silver hair spilling from under its rim. Pink eyes glared lifelessly from a ghostly white face. The fact that the lawyer grinned and followed the man's progress gave Rincón the uneasy feeling he wasn't dealing with a spook.

"Mister McCutchan," Hedgepath said proudly, nodding to the striking figure, "meet Great Man Galt, the fastest gun-fighter in the West."

"He ain't *the* gunslinger, Great Man Galt,

is he?" Rincón asked with awe.

Everyone in the West had heard tales of the famous albino's exploits and of how many men he had killed. Estimates ranged all the way up to one hundred. However, the gunman looking like a ghost had yet to receive so much as a scratch. This prowess at avoiding bullets impressed Rincón greatly.

"You may address me directly," Galt said to Rincón with a semblance of a smile on his chalky, whiskerless face. "I have not been paid to kill you, so you have nothing to fear from me. To answer your question, my god-given name is 'Great Man.' My parents held great hopes for my success."

The icy pin pricks were working their way down Rincón's backbone again. Dealing with a cold-hearted lawyer, spooks, and jumping claims were enough to handle. Now he had an added worry in the form of a pasty-faced killer to put up with. Galt's voice came as a shock. It was soft and melodious, like the peal of fine silver bells. The way the gunfighter looked, he should have hissed like a snake.

"You see, Mister McCutchan," Hedgepath said, "I *do* care for your safety. Considering Mister Galt's expediency with a firearm, I fail to see how there will be much difficulty taking possession of the Merry Widow."

Rincón nodded in silence. *Having this guy come after you with a gun would cause anyone with half a brain to pee down their leg. I've seen lots of spooks lately, but Galt's scarier than any of them.*

Galt focused his ghostly smile on the lawyer. "One point of business has not been made clear to me, sir. That this Crabtree person and his friend, Horace Tabor, are to be evicted from your property I understand. What I need to know is, what if they resist?"

Hedgepath leaned forward, placed his elbows on the desk, and said through pointed teeth: "Why, Mister Galt, you are to kill them where they stand."

CHAPTER TWENTY

Jake Crabtree couldn't have been a happier man. He sat in the shade of a tall, spreading tamarack tree, smoking a cigar as he watched the finishing touches being performed on his new saloon. He scratched Ulysses behind the ears and the sleek black tomcat immediately hopped in his lap and began purring loudly.

"Your puttin' on some tolerable weight there, cat," Jake said. "Reckon that's fairly safe. Me being rich and all, I ain't likely to have to stew you up."

Jake chuckled and smiled proudly at his wonderful town of Slab Creek. He was responsible for its very existence and he looked upon its growth and nurture as a doting and loving father would an only child. Jake mused that he had no idea how much money he'd spent lately. It really didn't matter. To expedite his desires, Otis A. McElroy, the crusty clerk at the bank, had set up a loan. Jake only had to sign a few papers of some sort to be assured none of those bank drafts he wrote would bounce.

"Yes, sir, Ulysses," he said happily, "it sure is a right smart feeling to be a wealthy man."

Jake shifted his gaze to his latest endeavor. The Mint Saloon was a fashionable false fronted, two-story building constructed of the finest Oregon fir available. Upstairs, Jake had six rooms ready to go. Lace curtains adorned the windows and each held a sturdy brass bed. All that was required was the stocking of a few soiled doves and his saloon would be ready for its grand opening. Just as soon as that slowpoke Horace Tabor returned from Portland with a coach load of strumpets, that is.

Jake watched as one of Packy Jackson's wagons creaked in, loaded with a huge Majestic range destined for the kitchen. Women liked to cook and wash clothes and things, so it was just as well Tabor was taking his sweet time about returning. Jake felt badly that he hadn't had the time to show Henry McCarty how to find a rich mine. Since Antrim insisted, for some odd reason, that Henry ride along with each of the ore shipments, Jake decided to pay the boy. Then he'd remembered Tabor's warning about Rincón's possibly burning down the saloon. To guard his property and keep Henry occupied until he could show him how to get rich, Jake had bought the kid a new pistol and a Winchester rifle as a gift and had started paying him ten dollars a day to watch after his interests.

The sidearm was one of those new Colt "Peacemakers." Jake figured the boy must have burned up ten boxes of cartridges getting the feel of it. One thing was certain: the kid knew how to draw and shoot with lightning speed, far faster than anyone he'd ever even heard of, except, perhaps, the legendary Great Man Galt. Jake grabbed up Ulysses and tossed him aside. He stood and watched as a dozen or so workmen started to unload the huge cook stove. Those lunkheads needed someone of his expertise to tell them how to go about the task or they would likely make a botch of the affair.

Lanny Payton nervously added to the lump of snuff wadded behind her lower lip. The Dugan brothers along with four freighters were unloading the huge steam pump from an enormous wagon. It had required a team of ten horses to move the heavy piece of machinery from the railroad station in Baker City.

"Don't you fret none, Lanny," T. Greene

Moss said, leaning on his canes by her side. "These here fellers knows what they're a-doin'."

"I surely hope so," she answered without taking her gaze from the proceedings. "Every dime we've got is bet on this piece of machinery."

"The freight sure was more than I figgered," T. Greene said. "I hated tuh borry five hundred bucks from the bank, but there just warn't no other choice."

"When's the boiler coming?" Warm Stove Williams asked as he walked up, holding his heavy coat wrapped tightly around his frail body. "I've sure got a hankerin' to have the thing fired up."

"It'll be a few days yet, pard," T. Greene said. "You'll get plenty heated up once it gets tuh goin'. You can crawl inside an' get a feel fer what ol' Scratch has in store for you once Gabriel toots his little horn."

Warm Stove scoffed: "You might oughta check the lay-out inside yourself, 'cause I'm bettin' you ain't gettin' no harp!"

Lanny Payton stared at the gaping dark maw of the flooded mine shaft. The gold was down there. She could see the glistening riches in her mind's eye. "We'll make it. Before long we'll all be rich as Croesus."

Neither Warm Stove Williams nor T.

225

Greene Moss had a clue as to who Croesus was, but both mouthed a silent prayer that their strike would turn out as well as his must have been. They both respected a successful miner, no matter what side he had fought on during the war.

Great Man Galt had grown a third eye smack in the middle of his forehead. Rincón McCutchan found it very annoying. Those blasted spooks were an awful aggravation to endure. Possibly not as much of an irritation as a hidebound lawyer, however. Henry Hayes Hedgepath had ordered the Red Lion closed. To make matters even worse, Rincón's salary had been stopped and he was forced to bunk in the back room of the Belle of Baker Saloon and spend his time with Galt.

"I understand Jake Crabtree is planning on a big celebration to open his saloon," Great Man Galt said in that melodious, chafing voice of his.

"Yep," Rincón answered after taking a long drink of whiskey. It was nine in the morning and they were the only people in the saloon so they could talk freely. "The fool's giving out free drinks the whole darn' day. That man's spendin' money like there's no tomorrow."

Galt chimed in: "For Crabtree, there may not *be* many tomorrows."

Rincón shrugged. His head hurt too badly to worry about upsetting a three-eyed gunslinger. "Well, I wish you'd get to it."

"I have found it prudent to act within what passes for the law. It would be a disappointment to my mother if I was to get hung."

"You *are* gonna kill Crabtree an' Tabor, ain't you?"

"You have no patience, Rincón. Rash behavior reaps the whirlwind."

"We ain't talkin' about no blasted wind. Are you plannin' on pluggin' them or not?"

Great Man Galt sipped on a cup of coffee, then grinned. "My, my, but we are in a foul mood this morning, aren't we?"

A sharp pain ripped through Rincón's skull. "I sure hanker to see that Horace Tabor feller shot. Just how good are you with that gun, anyway?"

The grin remained on Galt's ghostly face. "Would you care to find out?"

Rincón chugged his glass of whiskey. "I'd reckon that'd be a good idea. Let's grab some bottles and go down to the river an' get in some target practice."

Great Man Galt's laugh pealed. "My dear friend, you misunderstand. When I draw my gun, people die."

Rincón's hand trembled when he refilled his glass. "I didn't mean nothin'. Reckon I'll take a bottle an' go back to my room an' read a book."

"I would suggest you crack a Bible," Galt said coldly. "With your attitude, I'm rather certain Judgment Day will be coming quite soon."

Rincón McCutchan didn't know now who to fear most, the seedy lawyer or the pasty-faced gunman with three pink eyes. When this deal was over, he'd hire a gunslinger of his own to do both of them in.

CHAPTER TWENTY-ONE

William Antrim watched with a critical eye as the horse whim hoist, only recently installed, slowly cranked a steel bucket loaded with rock from the depths of the mine. It was gratifying to have such a piece of efficient machinery in operation.

Henry McCarty watched the operation for a few moments with obvious satisfaction. "Mister Antrim," he said with pride, "you really know your stuff when it comes to minin'."

Antrim said: "Modern methods are the way to go."

"Jake Crabtree thinks he's got a Mother Lode."

Antrim looked around to assure himself they were alone. "Now, Henry, this is just between us, but I'm afraid the Merry Widow is playing out. Most of the rich high-grade like you found in the cache is gone."

"Does Mister Crabtree know about this?"

Henry wondered.

"He's too busy building his saloon to worry about the mine. I doubt he'd believe the facts if I told him. I've got a crew taking out what ore we have in sight. That'll keep money rolling in . . . for a spell anyway."

"Sir, I sure am in a stew about what to do."

"How's that, Henry?"

"Well, Mister Crabtree's payin' me ten whole dollars a day to keep an eye on his saloon. I might do a whole bunch better if I went prospecting, instead."

William Antrim placed a muscular arm around the boy's lanky shoulders. "Henry, you're becoming a man and there's some decisions you've got to make for yourself. It wouldn't be fair of me if I told you what to do."

Henry McCarty shuffled his boots in the dusty ground. "Maybe with Mister Crabtree payin' me so well I oughta stick with him."

Antrim nodded. "You've got a good head on your shoulders. We need every dollar we can scrape together."

"Yes, sir," Henry said, hoisting the rifle Jake had bought him. "I'd best go do what Mister Crabtree's hired me to do."

"You be careful, son. Rincón McCutchan's hanging out with that gunfighter, Great Man Galt. Don't go and try to be a hero. If they show up here, you come and get some of the boys from the mine to back you up."

"Shucks, Mister Antrim," Henry said with a shrug, "there's only two of 'em. It'd seem a shame to bother other folks."

"Galt is supposed to be the fastest gunman in these parts."

Henry patted the handle of his Colt revolver. "That may be true, but I'm not from these parts."

Packy Jackson downed his fifteenth shot of whiskey and pounded his empty glass on the plank bar of Bill Webster's Blue Mountain Saloon.

"I'm coming, for Pete's sake!" Webster boomed. "What are you trying to do, embalm your liver in one afternoon?"

Packy slurred: "I got things on muh mind. Poor ol' preacher Pruett ain't gonna get that pianner he's been pinin' for all these years."

The bartender squinted his thin eyebrows. "You're drinking yourself stupid just because the Baptists can't caterwaul to piano music? Seems to me a git-fiddle or maybe a mouth organ would give 'em a tune to shoot for."

Fresh tears welled in Packy's rheumy eyes.

"It was to be muh tithe to keep from burnin' in hell. Now it's all gone an' I don't wanna get hung."

Bill Webster shook his head sadly. It was always a shame when anyone lost their mind, let alone a good customer. "Packy, I know the Baptists are plenty strict, but I'd think hanging someone for not buying a piano would be a stretch."

Packy glared at the bartender. "Ain't nuthin' anyone can do now 'cept leave the bottle and let me be."

"It's your funeral," Bill Webster said with a shrug.

"Ulysses," Jake Crabtree said to his tomcat, "I surely wish Horace Tabor would get off his duff and get back here to Slab Creek. The Fourth of July's only two days away. It'd be a tolerable shame to miss being able to mix the two celebrations into one whale of a shindig."

The cat nuzzled Jake's neck, then curled up in his lap for a relaxing nap. When his master sat in the shade of a tree, there was always plenty of time before anything was liable to happen.

"I sure hope Tabor has an eye for pretty doves. That one whore that followed me up here from Baker City would've scared all the hair plumb off your body. You oughta thank your lucky stars you was off chasing a rat. . . ."

The *creaking* of the stagecoach approaching took Jake from his visit with Ulysses. He gently picked the purring tomcat from his lap, laid him on a soft bed of pine needles, and went to meet the stage.

A few out-of-work miners were lollygagging around the saloon. From the lecherous stares some of those hangers-on were giving Packy's coach, Jake assumed Horace Tabor was returning with a delectable selection of sporting girls. The stagecoach driver hopped down, packing a stool for the fair-but-frail to step on to ease their departure from the high coach. The broad grin underneath the man's tobacco-stained beard told Jake that Tabor must have been able to round up some really good merchandise. Molly Spade's girls would likely spook the horses, let alone cause a stage driver to display manners.

The luscious sight of a trim ankle beneath a frilly yellow dress caused Jake Crabtree's heart to skip a beat. "Dad-gum it, Tabor," Jake muttered under his breath. "You plumb went and outdone yourself. This girl's looks would clean out a bank."

The comely lass with emerald eyes and

shoulder-length, flame-red hair looked quizzically at the burgeoning town. The young beauty was obviously in need of someone to show her where to set up shop.

"Welcome to Slab Creek, ma'am," Jake said, stepping close and offering his hand. "I'd be obliged to show you to your room, and, if you're not too tuckered, I've got a hankering to be your first customer."

The redhead fixed her icy green eyes on Jake. "My good sir, I am afraid you may have me mistaken for another."

"Ain't no mistake on my part, ma'am," Jake said. He fished an eagle from his pocket and handed it to her. "Let's head upstairs."

"Sir!" she exclaimed haughtily. "I am not some lady of easy virtue."

Jake reached into his pocket again. "At your prices I'm afraid pickings might be a little slim in these parts. Most men hereabouts can only afford a couple of bucks to get a poke."

The young lady's cheeks turned as crimson as her hair. "I am looking for a Jacob Crabtree."

Jake beamed. "That's me, ma'am, at your service."

"I have heard enough about you that somehow I shouldn't be shocked at your rudeness," the lady said coldly. "My name is Cecilia MacNair. Doctor Gage MacNair was my brother. According to my attorney I have inherited half interest in this gold mine from my late brother's estate."

The color drained from Jake's face. "Oh, fudge," he sputtered. It suddenly dawned on him what Doc had tried to tell him just before he passed away. He'd not only had a sister, but a mighty pretty one at that. The flame-red hair was a dead giveaway. Briefly Jake wondered why Doc hadn't mentioned her before. Then he realized it had been to keep her safe from the likes of him. Doc always had been a decent judge of character.

Cecilia MacNair reached into her reticule and extracted a stack of papers. "This is my brother's will, and I'm certain you will recognize his signature. It was on all of those checks he gave you."

Jake lowered his eyes and his mind raced for some way to ease his embarrassment. "I'm tolerable sorry for the mistake, Miss MacNair. I was plumb expecting someone else to be on that stage."

A taunting grin crossed her ruby lips. "I'd say that was obvious. Would you please examine the documents?"

Jake thumbed quickly through the papers. "There ain't no doubt about you being my partner in all of this." He swept a hand along Crabtree Boulevard. "Miss MacNair, your brother's shrewd investments are gonna make you a very wealthy lady."

"From what I have been told, the Merry Widow Mine *is* quite rich. Since fate has brought us together, I feel you should call me Cecilia. The trip has been a tiring one. Could you please show me where I may freshen up?"

Jake cast a jaundiced eye at the completed saloon. "Reckon if I put you up there, it might cause considerable confusion. I'll tell you what, Miss . . . Cecilia . . . why don't I let you have my cabin and I'll start bunking at the saloon."

Cecilia gave Jake a cute smile that caused his knees to feel rubbery. "I appreciate your hospitality, Mister Crabtree, and I'm glad there will be no problems with my receiving my inheritance."

Jake said: "I'm only sorry that Doc ain't here to see what his grubstake has accomplished. This is gonna be the biggest town in Oregon. And once the saloon gets to running, we'll have another money-maker on our hands."

Cecilia sighed and fluffed her fiery hair, sending out a sweet aroma of lilacs. "I visited with my attorney, Cyrus T. Pettibone, in Baker City before I came up. He informed me *exactly* what type of business the Mint Saloon will be conducting. My education and skills as a schoolteacher don't lend themselves to operating a house of ill repute."

Jake snorted. "The place ain't gonna have a bad reputation. The girls won't roll nobody."

Cecilia sighed. "Perhaps we should discuss these matters privately, once I have rested."

Jake motioned to the stage driver. "Tote the lady's grip over to my cabin." He tossed the scruffy Jehu a silver dollar which brought a scowl to Cecilia's face. By every account Jake had blown a small fortune and would undoubtedly continue doing so unless checked. A quick division of property would likely be the only way she could ever receive anything from her inheritance.

"Howdy, ma'am," Henry McCarty said, stepping forward with his hat held to his chest. "I'd be right pleased to show you to Mister Crabtree's place."

Jake frowned at the way the boy's eyes flitted over Cecilia's trim form. "This here's our mine boss, William Antrim's stepson, Henry. He's seventeen."

Henry winced when Jake mentioned his age, but kept his innocent, buck-toothed grin. "Proud to make your acquaintance ma'am. If there's anything you need, I'll be happy to fetch it for you."

"Thank you," Cecilia said. "It will be a comfort to have a gentleman such as you to call on."

Henry's cheeks flushed to mimic Cecilia's hair. "Yesum," he stuttered.

"Lookee yonder, boys," some fellow hollered excitedly. "Here comes the *real* whores!"

Jake felt his heart stop in the middle of a beat. He spun to behold Horace Tabor approaching, driving a surrey. There was the stub of a cigar clenched in his teeth and close by his side sat a black-haired vixen wearing a red, tight-fitting dress. Three more doves were riding in the back seat. From the way Tabor was listing to one side, Jake knew instantly that he was pickled.

Both Cecilia and Henry watched aghast as Horace pulled the wagon close and reined to a stop.

"Howdy, Jake," Tabor slurred. "God, I love Oregon." He slid over to leave the wagon and tumbled from the seat to wind up in a heap at Cecilia's feet.

"Reckon we oughta get you to bed," Jake said to Horace who was struggling to sit upright.

"He needs to stay *out* of bed and get some

rest," the black-haired girl said as she swung down from the wagon. She helped Tabor to his feet. "This man's a real tiger."

"Wonderful trip," Tabor said, then his crimson eyes fixed on Cecilia with obvious puzzlement. "Can't say as I recollect you, or was you the one that's got the rose tattooed on her butt? God, I love Oregon."

Jake swallowed and stepped forward. "Horace, this is Cecilia MacNair. She's my partner."

"Dang!" Tabor exclaimed. "You done got hitched."

Jake said quickly: "We're not married. She just inherited half of the mine."

Horace blinked his bloodshot eyes. "How did you half die?"

"I'm French Rita," the raven-haired girl said and extended her hand to Jake. She nodded to the three blonde ladies who were now standing alongside the surrey. "First there's Ida Belle, then Velvet, and Mabel. We're all mighty glad to be here."

"God, I love Oregon," Horace spluttered once again. Then to Jake's relief he crumpled to the ground and began snoring.

French Rita looked down at Tabor. "That poor man's been at it for five straight days. I've known lots of men that's been away from women for a long while, but this man

239

was in worse need than any of them."

Jake clucked his tongue. "I do reckon he'll have his memories."

French Rita smiled at the Mint Saloon. "Is this where we set up shop?"

"Yep," Jake answered, then noticed the glowering look he was receiving from Cecilia. "We was gonna wait and hold the grand opening on the Fourth of July."

"But, honey," French Rita pouted, "we're ready for business right now with anyone that's got two dollars."

"I got two bucks!" the grubby stage driver yelled out.

Henry McCarty said to Cecilia: "Ma'am, I was wonderin' if you'd like to see your place 'bout now."

Relief washed across the redhead's face and she beamed at Henry. "Yes, I would. It's nice to know there is at least *one* gentleman in this town."

Jake watched as Henry escorted Cecilia to his cabin. "I don't know what she's so blamed upset about," he said to French Rita. "That girl has got half of the profits coming. Guess I've got some learning to do when it comes to women."

The raven-haired dove ran a silky hand along Jake's cheek. "For a few dollars, I'd be happy to give you some lessons."

Jake Crabtree fished out the eagle he'd offered Cecilia. "Let's go to school," he said with a vulpine grin.

Three full days had passed since Rincón had been plagued by any spooks. Now with Hedgepath's appearance in the Belle of Baker, they were out with a vengeance. The moose head over the door was back to life and snorting flames out of its black nose. Great Man Galt's third eye had returned, and worst of all there were rattlesnakes everywhere. They slithered in profusion along the bar and floor. Some coiled around spittoons and the whiskey bottles along the back bar.

The lawyer took a dainty sip of coffee from a china cup while extending his pinky finger. " 'For law is strict and war is nothing more.' "

"Huh?" Rincón said.

Hedgepath grinned. "A little quote from the bard. Really, Mister McCutchan, you should read more classic literature."

Great Man Galt said dryly: "I convinced him to read the Bible some."

"Ah, yes, the Good Book," the lawyer said. "A tome so delightfully loaded with contradictions and petty rules. It is a wonderful vessel that has given much sustenance to

241

the livelihood of barristers."

"Are we ready to jump Crabtree's mine yet?" Rincón asked. He hated big words he didn't understand.

Hedgepath said with disdain: "May I remind you both that huge rewards are at stake here, rewards that will be reaped by all of us."

"How much longer before we can start harvestin'?" Rincón asked.

Galt added: "I find myself asking the same question."

The lawyer sighed and said through clenched, pointed teeth: "When all is in readiness, I shall loose the dogs of war."

Rincón winced when a sharp pain sliced through his head. "Can I shoot Tabor then? You know how much I've been hankerin' to."

Hedgepath's thin grin remained. "When the law is on our side, you may kill anyone who stands in your way. The courts are quite lenient to persons defending their property."

Galt said: "Not getting hung would be worth the wait."

Rincón McCutchan nodded in agreement. Being able to shoot someone like Horace Tabor and not have to suffer a penalty would be a fair exchange for putting up with a skinflint lawyer, even one who caused the spooks to come out.

The noted mining attorney and Congressional hopeful, Cyrus Tiberius Pettibone, ran a pudgy hand through a silver beard that was neatly trimmed and regarded the beautiful young lady sitting across his cluttered desk. "Unfortunately, my dear, the only records available of the production from the Merry Widow Mine are the mill receipts and deposits made into Jake Crabtree's bank account. I must say that, considering the large amounts of money involved, it is most unusual no books have been kept."

Cecilia sighed knowingly. "We *are* talking about Jake Crabtree."

Pettibone cut a slice from a plug of tobacco. "He *is* a rather carefree soul. I believe him to be innocent of any attempt to defraud you. At the time he received these payments . . . which add up to the grand sum of thirty-nine thousand dollars . . . Crabtree was acting under the impression Doctor MacNair had no relatives. You did say he voiced no opposition to your claim?"

"No, sir, none at all. At first he appeared shocked, but once he read my brother's will, he simply grinned and said there was plenty of gold in the mine to go around."

Pettibone said: "By all accounts he's been spending money quite freely."

Cecilia pinched her lips. "My biggest concern at the moment is that Mint Saloon he's opened. I find owning an interest in such an indecent establishment to be distasteful in the extreme."

The lawyer poked the chew of tobacco into his mouth. "I can understand how that could be a cause of embarrassment to you."

The redhead's vexation was evident. "Can't Jake simply buy out my interest?"

Cyrus Pettibone grabbed a paper from the jumble on his desk and pored over it a moment. "I don't know how that would be possible," he said sadly shaking his head. "It appears the saloon is financed by money borrowed from the Virtue Bank with the mine pledged as collateral."

"Jake Crabtree has blown all the money and mortgaged the mine?"

"That is the state of affairs, but on the brighter side I hear the saloon is doing a booming business and the mine *is* still shipping ore."

Cecilia was dumbstruck. "Are you suggesting I take part in the operation of a sinful business?"

The attorney dismissed her concerns with

a wave of his hand. "Miss MacNair, I can sympathize with your feelings, but the mine may again ship rich ore."

"What do you mean . . . rich ore *again*?"

Pettibone spit a wad of tobacco into a brass cuspidor. "The grade of ore has fallen off drastically. It might be wise to hire a mining engineer to do a report on the property."

"That sounds expensive."

Pettibone shrugged. "The mining business is not for the faint of heart."

Anger rose in the young lady like bile. "Give me the name of this mining engineer. Jake Crabtree has just inherited a *working* partner."

Pettibone smiled in satisfaction. He felt gratified Cecilia MacNair was showing the backbone to take charge. "My dear lady, welcome to the mining business and . . . ah . . . the operation of *other* enterprises."

Cecilia said: "When I get back to Slab Creek, Jake Crabtree's going to think the wrath of God striking would be preferable to having me as his partner."

"Ma'am," Pettibone chuckled, "I think your train's on the right track."

Chapter Twenty-Two

"Tarnation, but you're a stubborn woman!" Jake roared at Cecilia. "I plumb went and told everybody in the country that we was holding a shindig for the Fourth of July. The steers are standin' in the pen just waiting to get barbecued."

Cecilia placed her hands on her hips and glared up into Jake's steel gray eyes. Everyone in the Mint Saloon was obviously enjoying the show except Tabor. Since he'd sobered up, any noise was an agony to his system.

"Uh . . . miss," Tabor said politely, "perhaps this matter should be discussed in a discreet manner, somewhere nice and quiet."

"Right here is fine!" Cecilia yelled, bringing furrows to Tabor's brow. "The fact that I own half of this place gives me the prerogative to shout if I feel like it."

"What in the heck is a prerogative?" Jake

questioned. "If you're gonna use big words, we ain't never gonna work nothing out."

Horace Tabor extended a trembling hand, palm down, and motioned for quiet. "Jake, Cecilia's just saying she has the right to her own opinion. There's no reason we can't settle things without being so blasted loud about the affair." He tweaked his bushy soup-strainer mustache and forced a smile. "Jake, possibly Cecilia would consent to cooking up the livestock and letting everyone buy their own drinks?"

A chorus of agonized moans escaped the lips of the saloon full of miners to echo off the plank walls.

Cecilia's scowl softened as she turned to face Horace. "I would find that most acceptable. Mister Tabor, you have a natural talent for negotiation. You should become a politician."

"He ain't enough of a crook to make a success of it." Jake cocked an eyebrow. "But he did do a right smart job of getting drunk and sorting whores. On second thought, he might make a go of it in politics."

"The ladies upstairs are leaving," Cecilia said flatly. "I refuse to be a party to debauchery."

Jake Crabtree shook his head at Tabor. "There she goes again, using big words nobody but a Philadelphia lawyer would understand. Horace, please explain to her that she don't have to come to no party if she's not of a mind to."

Tabor spoke up quickly to forestall another outburst. When Cecilia yelled, she reminded him of Augusta. Thinking about his demon-infested wife was an affliction to the delightful memories of Portland. "Please, miss," he said, wearing a pained expression, "don't yell any more. I've been around gunfights that were quieter than this discussion has been. As to those little ladies upstairs, well, they are necessary to the survival of this saloon."

"Dag-nab it, Tabor!" Jake protested. "If women had a head for business, they'd be allowed to vote. But they ain't."

Jake Crabtree noticed Cecilia's face flush with anger, but he failed to see the empty whiskey bottle she'd snatched from a nearby table until it crashed into the side of his head.

"Dang!" a miner exclaimed. "She's done gone an' killed 'im."

Cecilia's icy green eyes focused on the prostrate form of her partner. "He's not dead. He just got whacked on the head that he wasn't using. Any man who thinks a woman can't run a business has got another think coming." A smile of satisfaction settled over Cecilia's countenance. "Mister Tabor, will you please tell him, once he finishes his nap, that the ladies of ill-repute may stay. As for tomorrow's celebration, we will go ahead with the cook out, but everyone . . . even he . . . will pay for their drinks."

Horace Tabor had witnessed demons infest women before and knew there was no option but to agree with anything they wanted. "Yes, miss."

Cecilia spun and stalked from the saloon. Not a man in attendance uttered a word of disapproval over her decision to cancel the free drinks.

Tabor rolled sympathetic eyes to his unconscious friend. "Jake, you sure have a way with women. Most guys have to marry them before they rate this kind of attention."

A soft rapping on the cabin door took Cecilia from her book. She sat upright and grasped the heavy iron skillet. If the visitor turned out to be Jake Crabtree, he would have another lump on his head if he weren't in an apologetic mood.

She swallowed to clear her throat and not betray her distress. "Come in. It's not locked."

The heavy, crude door squeaked open to

expose Henry McCarty with a rifle cradled in the crook of his arm and concern on his beardless face. "I'm sure sorry to bother you, ma'am, but I thought I'd best come an' see if there's anything you need."

Cecilia smiled with relief and gratitude. Aside from Horace Tabor, the lanky young man appeared to be the only other male in Slab Creek with any manners. "Why, how kind of you, Henry. I am afraid I lost my temper with Mister Crabtree. I hope he is all right."

A sly grin washed across Henry's face. "He was standin' at the bar drinkin' when I left, so I reckon he'll live. He seems mighty upset about women sufferin'. I don't know what he's talkin' about."

Cecilia laughed. "He's upset about the suffrage movement."

Henry cocked his head in puzzlement. "I don't cotton to the idea of any lady sufferin'."

"The word suffrage means the right to vote. In this country a woman is not allowed to vote and some of us feel that is not fair."

"Can't reckon as how I can see where it is, either, ma'am. Every person that lives in this country has to live by rules. It would only seem fair that ladies have a say as to who makes up those rules. I'd guess that makes me a suffragette, too."

Cecilia chuckled. "Just tell people you're for equal rights, Henry. The term suffragette is reserved for us womenfolk. I must tell you, I certainly wish a lot more men had your courage and understanding."

Henry shuffled his boots. "Aw, shucks, ma'am."

Cecilia asked: "Henry, do you plan on going to town anytime soon? There are a few things I would like."

"Yes, ma'am." Henry nodded. "Mister Antrim, wants me to ride in on the ore wagon this afternoon to guard it. I'd be right proud to fetch whatever you want."

Cecilia stepped over to the table, picked up a pencil, and began writing on a scrap of paper. "I really appreciate your doing this for me."

Henry McCarty hung his head. "If it's all the same, ma'am, why don't you just tell me what you need. I won't forget nothin'."

Cecilia ignored the boy's pleading and kept working on her list. "Just hand this list to the clerk," she said, fishing money from her reticule. "There are a few things ladies need that men might find embarrassing to shop for."

Henry's cheeks reddened. "Yes, ma'am."

Cecilia handed over the list along with a

five-dollar gold piece. "If you would like to learn how to read," she said, "I'd be delighted to tutor you."

"I'm able to read a newspaper and such, but I couldn't bother you to learn me more."

"The correct word is 'teach,' Henry. Not learn. As far as me not having time to tutor you, I probably have more time on my hands now than ever."

Henry pursed his lips. "I'd like to learn more, ma'am, but I still gotta guard Mister Crabtree's saloon and mine."

Cecilia made a moue. "Remember, I am his partner. We can find time to work together that will not interfere with your job."

Henry McCarty's cheeks flushed anew at the thought of spending time with the most beautiful lady he had ever set eyes on. His heart thumped heavily in his chest as he struggled for words. Finally he simply nodded, spun, and headed off into the trees.

"It's magnificent," Lanny Payton said with awe as she inspected the new boiler. "I never thought it would be so big. The thing must weigh several tons."

"Yep," T. Greene Moss said as he whacked it with one of his canes. "Six tons of lap-riveted iron. That's why it cost so much, gettin' the thing hauled in."

Warm Stove Williams ran a trembling hand along the fire door of the monstrous boiler. "Sure oughta put out a bunch of heat once it gets goin'."

T. Greene snorted. "Ain't no fire this side of Lucifer's joint that'd heat you up enough to stop your constant whinin' about bein' cold."

"When can we start pumping water?" Lanny asked with concern. The vast treasure chest of gold below their feet beckoned with a siren's song. She had no time to waste on needless bickering.

T. Greene Moss sidled around on his pair of canes to face the nurse. "Tomorrow's the Fourth of July an' Jake's throwin' a big shindig at that new saloon of his, but we'll get to crackin' afterwards an' oughta start the pump in a week or so."

Worry etched itself deep in Lanny's brow. "This is no time to celebrate. We should stay here and work."

"I wish we could," T. Greene said, shuffling his canes. "But we need the Dugans. They're gonna be at the party in Slab Creek. I'd surely say that if ol' Warm Stove an' me was back contractin', we wouldn't pass up no celebration, either."

"We did have our times," Warm Stove said with a far-off, placid look on his wrinkled face. He was thinking back to when he and his friend had believed youth was something that lasted forever. "Jake Crabtree's barbecuin' up half the livestock in Oregon an' the dinner's free."

"Isn't there *something* we can do here at the mine?" Lanny pleaded.

Warm Stove ignored the nurse's entreaties. "I've got two quarters saved up. At a nickel fer a glass of beer, I oughta be able to inflict some decent damage on the next day."

T. Greene Moss clucked his tongue at Lanny's scowling stare. "Come on, partner, lets go have a little relaxation. That gold's been down there since creation."

"You boys go and have your fun," Lanny said while staring at the mine. "I'll stay here and guard the place. Keep anyone from stealing tools we'll be needing."

"We'll bring you back some roast beef," T. Greene Moss finally said.

"I'd like that," Lanny answered absently. She was thinking of gold.

A hush born of fear and awe washed through the gathering at the Mint Saloon when the famous gunfighter, Great Man

Galt, accompanied by Rincón McCutchan strode in and made their way to the bar. Burley miners moved quickly aside to give them room. No one who wished to continue their hold on this mortal coil would dare anger the pasty-faced killer who regarded them with cold, pink eyes.

It rankled McCutchan that no one paid him any mind. "Whiskey!" he boomed, sending a quarter ringing onto the plank bar.

Woody Ash, who had been plagued by a town full of healthy people for a month and was reduced from undertaking to tending bar, ignored Rincón to wait hurriedly on Galt. "What'll it be, sir?"

"Just a mug of beer," Galt answered with his chime-like voice.

There was little doubt in the undertaker's mind that he would receive a customer or two due to this man with the ghostly face. Carefully Woody filled the mug to overflowing and scraped away the foam with his finger before presenting it to the gunslinger.

"Thank you, my friend," Galt said. He laid a quarter on the counter. "Keep the change for your excellent service."

Woody nodded his gratitude. If more folks tipped him, bartending would pay better than burying people. It was indoor work, too.

"Where's my dratted whiskey?" Rincón roared.

Great Man Galt frowned at his companion. "Patience, my friend. The man is busy."

Woody poured Rincón a shot of the worst whiskey he had. The man had never been known to leave a tip.

Jake Crabtree was sitting at a table with T. Greene Moss, Warm Stove Williams, and Isaac Beekman. The newspaper editor had come up to cover the celebration. Two tons of succulent meat roasting on spits outside the bar was an added inducement for him to make the trek to Slab Creek. At the moment, Jake focused his eyes toward the row of rooms upstairs. "Sure hope Horace Tabor's got a few more dollars on him."

Isaac Beekman ignored Jake and looked at the pink-eyed gunman. "My gracious, I believe that man is the legendary Great Man Galt. He's a renowned hired gun."

"Likely he just came up to join the party," Jake said without concern. He couldn't fathom why he should worry about some gunfighter, even one who looked like he stepped out of a nightmare. "I am considerable ill at ease about Tabor's showin' up and Rincón plugging him. Warm Stove, why don't you go up and let Horace in on the fact that he's liable to get shot if he don't keep dallyin' with French Rita for a spell."

Warm Stove gave a shiver and scooted back his chair. "I'll go inform the poor soul he'd best spend some more time with the whore."

T. Greene chuckled. "Wish somebody'd cause me that amount of sufferin'."

Shortly after Warm Stove returned to the table, Great Man Galt and Rincón Mc-Cutchan finished their drinks and sauntered out through the batwing doors. Jake Crabtree joined the crowd in the saloon by breathing a sigh of relief.

Woody Ash carried a tray of full beer mugs to Jake's table and began setting them out. "Well, they sure didn't stick around long. Rincón only had a taste of rotgut. That normally just primes his pump."

"Leastwise, no one got shot," T. Greene said. "Reckon they just wanted tuh be sociable. Think we oughta tell Tabor it's safe to come out?"

Jake took a swig of beer. "Nah, it'd be a shame if he left while he still had money."

Woody Ash looked at Jake and asked: "Is it true that your new fireball partner, Cecilia, said that you were supposed to pay for your own drinks?"

257

Jake reached into his shirt pocket and brought out a draft on the Virtue Bank. "I'll write this out for twenty bucks. It's the same as cash."

Woody grabbed the check. "Works for me," the undertaker said happily.

Another shiver wracked Warm Stove's frail body. The old miner sipped his beer and said to Jake: "Wimmin are strange critters. I'd speculate that redhead'll be tolerable upset 'bout that draft. Now back in my day. . . ."

"Things weren't no diff'rent then, ya ol' coot," T. Greene growled. "I'd reckon the lady'll figger ten bucks of that money's hers, or is my cipherin' off?"

Jake fidgeted with his handlebar mustache. "You know, now that you mention the fact, I'd reckon you've got a point." He grabbed another draft from his pocket and began writing on it. "I'll make her out a check for ten dollars. That oughta square the matter."

T. Greene motioned toward the door. "Do you reckon I could get some of the roast beef whacked off an' put in a gunnysack with a rope hooked to it so's I can drape the thing over my neck. There ain't no other way I can pack nothin'."

"Tell Henry to give you whatever you need," Jake said, surprised by the old man's request. "Ain't you gonna stick around for a while? Nobody's passed out so far. The party's just getting started."

T. Greene Moss took a long moment working his canes before he could stand. "Lanny's down there all by herself. I tol' her I'd fetch her back somethin' tuh eat."

Jake watched as T. Greene sidled his way through the batwing doors.

After a moment Warm Stove said: "You know, we've been partnered up for over thirty years. I know that old codger better than God. If T. Greene weren't so old an' crippled up, I'd say he was in love with Lanny Payton."

Jake Crabtree felt a burning in his throat. "Reckon that's better than never loving anyone at all."

Warm Stove stared at his beer with watery gray eyes. "I'd reckon."

Chapter Twenty-Three

Rincón McCutchan reined his horse to a stop at the Merry Widow Mine. He dismounted and tied the traces to a scrawny tamarack. With a satisfied look on his pockmarked face he waved his hand across the silent mining operation. "Part of this is gonna be owned by me right soon."

Great Man Galt stepped to Rincón's side and adjusted his wide-brim black hat to shelter his eyes from the sun. "I'd have to wonder just what a lawyer's idea of net profits would boil down to?"

Rincón dismissed the question with a shrug. "It's all on paper. We got ourselves a legal contract."

Galt asked: "And who, may I ask, drew up this contract?"

"Hedgepath's a good lawyer."

"Then you have nothing to worry about," Galt said with a ghostly smile.

Rincón grumbled: "We might as well poke

around while we're here."

Galt headed for a glistening heap of rock that had been carefully placed on a sheet of rusty metal. "This looks like a pile of ore."

"Yeah, but the *real* ore's down the shaft," Rincón said.

Great Man Galt smiled and bent over to paw through the rocks. He had a terrible, unreasoning fear of close spaces. There was no way Rincón would ever get him to enter the mine.

Rincón McCutchan gasped when he saw the coiled timber rattler next to where the gunslinger was poking around. Then he relaxed. It had to be another of those blasted spooks. If the rattlesnake was real, a gunfighter of Galt's reputation would have seen it by now. A scream of agony and fright echoed from the tall trees. Galt bolted upright and threw the snake that had attached its fangs to his hand to the ground.

"Oh, my God!" the gunfighter yelled. "I've been snake bit!"

Rincón shook his head in puzzlement. He really needed to get those lead bullets removed. It would be a blessing to know what was real and what wasn't.

"Quit your blasted hollerin' and jumpin' around, Galt. We'll get you back to Baker City and rustle up a doc."

"I'm going to die, I know it!" The gunman held his hand close to his chest and began to sob. "I'm dying. I just know it."

"Well, get on your horse first," Rincón spat.

It felt good to Rincón to be able to boss Galt around for a change. If the hired gunslinger croaked, it would save him money. A man should always look on the bright side.

"I must say, gentlemen, that I am very disappointed in the both of you," Henry Hayes Hedgepath said, barely masking his cold fury. "The affidavit that I needed from Buhlman is now in hand. Then you two go to Slab Creek . . . against my implicit orders not to . . . and now Galt has been incapacitated."

"Doc, tell me the truth, am I going to die?" Galt pleaded.

Clayton Chalmers was a dentist; he was also quite drunk. Considering his patient's reputation, he didn't feel it prudent to reveal these facts. "You'll be fine, if the wounds don't get infected, or if you don't take a turn for the worse."

Galt glanced at his gun hand, which was swollen to the size of a small watermelon. He gave out a pitiful groan and rolled over to stare at the wall.

"We just went to check out the situation," Rincón said apologetically. "Rattlesnakes ain't a common occurrence hereabouts."

The lawyer sniffed. "It appears that's not *always* the case. Does it not? Now we must delay our plans. What I would like to know is how *both* of you failed to notice that snake until after it had struck."

Great Man Galt gave out another groan.

"I'll leave him some laudanum for the pain," the dentist said quickly. It was a holiday and he still had celebrating to do. "It'll cause him to sleep."

"How long will it be before he regains the use of his hand?" Hedgepath questioned.

Chalmers shrugged his shoulders. "A week, maybe two. These things are hard to predict." He held out his palm. "Five dollars."

Henry Hayes Hedgepath fished a five-dollar gold piece from his money purse and handed it over with a scowl.

Dr. Chalmers grabbed the coin and headed back to his revelry, listing slightly to starboard. "I'll drop by tomorrow," he added over his shoulder.

"I'm going to die. I can feel it!" Great Man Galt sobbed.

Rincón grabbed the blue bottle the dentist

had left. "Take this, it'll make you feel better."

Galt did as Rincón ordered, then the gunfighter laid back down and started crying softly. In a moment he began to snore.

Rincón commented: "Wish I'd had some laudanum earlier, then I wouldn't have had to listen to his caterwaulin' all the way back to town."

Hedgepath said firmly: "I expect you to see to Galt's well being."

"Henry . . . uh . . . Mister Hedgepath, sir. We was doin' what we thought best."

"Thinking, Mister McCutchan, is what *I* am trained to do. In the future I expect you to rely solely on my judgment in *all* matters."

Rincón's head was splitting. He wanted the sharp-tongued shyster to leave him be so he could drink some whiskey. "Yes, sir, it won't happen again."

Hedgepath took one last look at the snoring gunman before turning to leave. "I would certainly like to know how he failed to see that snake."

Rincón shrugged. "Accidents happen."

The lawyer hesitated in front of the door. He rolled his head to face Rincón and showed off his finely pointed teeth. "But for my fealty toward you as a partner, I would dissolve our relationship." Without waiting for an answer he strode off, slamming the door behind him.

Rincón had noticed a couple of coiled rattlesnakes in the lawyer's path. They might or might not be spooks. It was becoming so difficult to tell. He waited in silence for a moment. When he heard no screams of pain, he decided sadly those snakes had been spooks, after all. That was too bad. There never was a *real* rattlesnake around when you needed one.

"Blast it all," William Antrim said with a grimace.

He was inspecting the mine workings directly underneath where the richest of the gold ores had been extracted. No matter how carefully he examined the vein, there was no gold to be seen. He decided to hold off telling Jake Crabtree or Cecilia until he was certain the mine was exhausted. Likely enough the miners had already said plenty, but he doubted Jake would pay them any mind.

Antrim flung a piece of worthless quartz onto the muck pile. The rock thudded with an echo that reverberated from the stone walls like an empty promise. He walked to the shaft and climbed toward the fresh air and green trees. The closeness of the mine workings had become oppressive.

The captivating beauty of a cool summer evening in the Blue Mountains greeted him like a welcome friend. He stood to catch his breath from the long climb and listened to a calm breeze rustling through the spreading trees. Then he saw the shadowy form of man with a gun. Antrim breathed a sigh of relief when he realized it was Henry McCarty. The lanky boy stood stone still with slouched shoulders and bowed head. Instantly Antrim knew something was wrong and strode to his stepson's side.

When Henry turned to face him, a tear trickled down the boy's cheek and glistened in the setting sun like a thin icicle.

"What is it, son, what's wrong?" William asked.

"It's about Ma," Henry's voice was surprisingly strong.

"Has something happened to her? Tell me, son."

"Doctor Kincaid sent a telegraph. I managed to read most of it, but Lord how I wish I hadn't been able to."

Antrim carefully took the telegraph and moved it to face the dying sunlight.

To William Antrim, et al.

The Heidelman Institute has closed. I suggest your early return. Her remaining time could be brief.

Kincaid

The burley mine superintendent choked back a sob. His beautiful wife was still so young. That Eastern clinic had been a Holy Grail, a cure, life itself. Emptiness flooded into his heart to fill the void that is left when hope has fled.

"What are we going to do, Father?" Henry had never called William Antrim that before.

"We're going home to Silver City." William studied a distant snow-capped peak. "But not for a little while. We owe Jake Crabtree and Cecilia MacNair. A decent man never deserts his friends."

Henry took the telegraph from his stepfather's hands, refolded it, and stuck it back into his shirt pocket. "I'd reckon we oughta go back to our place. I'll fix us some venison directly."

William Antrim draped an arm around the boy's narrow shoulders. Silently they walked together through the gathering darkness to the little log cabin they shared on the banks of the small burbling stream known as Slab Creek.

■ ■ ■ ■

"Maybe now you'll get yer bones warmed while yer still on this side of perdition's gates," T. Greene Moss said to Warm Stove.

They watched as the Dugan brothers slid more logs into the blazing firebox of the huge boiler.

Warm Stove pulled his heavy coat tight around his frail body and backed closer to the fire. "Ain't workin' yet. I've been freezin' for years, you know."

T. Green clucked his tongue. "Reckon ol' Lucifer will have tuh pay extry fer coal once he gets hold of yer chilly soul. That's why you've lived so durn' long. God don't want you an' Satan can't afford you."

"It's a magnificent piece of machinery," Lanny Payton said dreamily.

Orson Dugan tapped the round brass steam pressure gauge that indicated eighty pounds of pressure and grinned his agreement to Lanny.

"We'd best wait until we have a head of at least a hundred pounds of steam built up before we turn on the pump," Seth Dugan commented.

"Toss in some more wood," Lanny ordered without taking her eyes from the gauge. "We need to get with it!"

"Won't be long now," T. Greene said with a nod to Lanny.

"Sure ain't puttin' out heat like it oughta," Warm Stove griped.

"Ninety-five pounds," Lanny said. Her voice was heavy with tension.

Minutes passed like poured molasses before the needle behind the glass face of the pressure gauge pointed to the magic figure of one hundred.

T. Greene Moss grinned. The grizzled old man balanced himself on one cane. With his free hand he reached out and gave the whistle cord a firm yank. A screech accompanied by a cloud of steam shook the countryside. "Let 'er rip!"

All eyes went to the black Cope & Maxwell engine. When the pressure hit the steam cylinder, the huge machine quaked ominously, then gave out a hiss and began chugging like a train. The six-foot high cast iron flywheel started to turn slowly. The walking beam, attached eccentrically to the flywheel, began its up-and-down movements, operating exactly like a small hand-operated well pump. Water began to flow from the drain pipe that had been run to a nearby gulch.

"It's working!" Lanny yelled.

"Never was no doubt about it," T. Greene

Moss said. "The only question waitin' to be answered is just how much water that mine's makin'. Right now, it's all up to God an' Cope an' Maxwell."

"We're pumping a river!" Lanny exclaimed.

After some adjusting of the valve by Orson, the huge engine began to smooth out, its jerky strokes and chugging becoming even as a heartbeat.

Several tense moments passed before the water level, which was only a few feet from the surface, could be seen lowering by inches. Progress was obviously going to be slow, but the huge pump was going to dry out the mine.

A smile of relief and satisfaction crossed Lanny's face. She extracted her snuff bag and poked a wad behind her lower lip. "Boys," she said, "we're all going to be rich."

"Thank you for coming to see me," Cecilia said to Jake Crabtree as he cautiously entered his old cabin.

Jake's head was fairly well healed and he didn't want to do anything to cause it to get whacked again. Worst of all was the rotund mining attorney, Cyrus T. Pettibone, who sat slouched in a chair sipping coffee and smiling contentedly as a cat that had just

270

eaten a nest full of baby birds.

"Mister Crabtree," Pettibone said with a nod, "how good to see you again."

"Reckon that might be your side of it," Jake said.

Cecilia said: "Mister Pettibone is here at my invitation. There is something we need to discuss."

Jake ran a finger gingerly across the purple bruise alongside his left eye. "I can't see where it'd be any more painful than the last time we talked business."

Pettibone ignored him. "There have been some rather . . . ah . . . *interesting* developments regarding the Merry Widow Mine that you need to be aware of."

"Well," Jake said testily, "get on with the awareness part or are you so blamed used to chargin' by the hour that I need to take a seat and rest a spell?"

The lawyer couldn't contain a chuckle; in spite of Jake's verbal jabs he was a likeable man. "Tell me, have you ever heard of Winthrop Sinrod or The Venture Corporation of San Francisco?"

Jake cocked his head. "Can't say that I have."

Pettibone said: "Winthrop is a very successful broker of mining stocks. His acquisition vehicle is The Venture Corporation, which owns mines in every Western state. Mister Sinrod has retained my services to make you an offer to buy your share of the Merry Widow Mine."

A rubbery feeling came to Jake's legs. He slid out a chair and plopped down into it. "We'd never want to sell out. That mine'll make us millions."

"Any gold mine is an unknown," the lawyer replied. "Cash in the bank is often preferable to the . . . ah . . . *problems* of ownership."

Cecilia poured a cup of coffee and set it down in front of Jake. "I have already sold," she said bluntly. "Thirty thousand dollars will give me a comfortable retirement."

"Thirty thousand dollars!" Jake exclaimed, aghast. "That's chicken feed compared to how much gold's in the Merry Widow."

The lawyer shrugged. "Miss MacNair has the legal authority to dispose of her property. I highly advise you to take the same generous offer."

"Why would I go and do a fool thing like that?" Jake questioned.

The lawyer folded his hands behind his head and regarded the prospector gravely. "I have reliable information that your claims have already been jumped. A court battle will be quite expensive. The Venture Corporation has inexhaustible funds. Do you have the ability to match them dollar for dollar to defend your property? If not, the court will diminish your interest accordingly. There is also a bank loan against the property. Once a suit is filed, that note will come due and the bank will freeze any assets to protect its interest. This will include ore at the mill, along with the Mint Saloon. Whoever buys this lien, which *will* be The Venture Corporation, acquires paramount title to the properties. Please believe me, Mister Crabtree, this offer being made to you will not be held open for a long period of time."

Jake was dumbfounded. "I reckon I oughta get a lawyer."

Pettibone nodded. "An excellent decision."

Jake Crabtree stood on shaky legs, turned, and strode away without a word. Something told him that he was feeling very much like a woman who had just been raped.

CHAPTER TWENTY-FOUR

"A body sure never has much warning before things start rolling downhill in the general direction of hell," Jake Crabtree said to Horace Tabor across their usual table at the Mint Saloon.

Tabor nodded in agreement and thought back on how easily Augusta had became infested by demons. "Some things are mighty hard to predict."

Jake sighed and took a sip of whiskey. "Ain't it the truth. Here I go and find the richest gold mine in Oregon and now I'm up to my butt in lawyers."

"Buzzards have more class than a Shylock," Tabor remarked after taking a puff on his cigar. "At least buzzards have the decency to wait until you're dead. Lawyers will pick your flesh off while you still have use for it."

"Cecilia's already left town," Jake said with a hint of sadness in his voice. "She took off on the afternoon stage. That was a pittance she sold out for."

Horace rolled his eyes to the upstairs rooms. "The company of a lovely woman is a real comfort to the soul. The thought that I might have to go back to Oro City gives me a cold chill and it has nothing to do with the weather there."

"French Rita does seem to enjoy it better than a man," Jake said.

"It's good to have a job you delight in."

"Horace," Jake said with a furrowed brow, "what would you do if you were in my shoes?"

Tabor rolled his cigar in his mouth. "Jake, do you have any money on you?"

"Nope, but I sure got lots of vouchers from the Virtue Bank."

"Write one out for about twenty dollars, cash it, and have another drink."

Jake shrugged his shoulders, then dutifully went to the register and did as his friend had asked. He returned and tossed two gold eagles onto the table. "Here you are. Might as well help yourself while you still can."

Horace Tabor grinned wickedly. "Heck, that money's not for me. It's for French Rita. Take a bottle upstairs with you and lay those coins on her nightstand. Don't show your face back down here until morning. By then I might have come up with a plan and you'll have a smile on your face again."

Jake leaned forward on the table. "You're asking a tolerable lot from me, Tabor. But I reckon I can force myself to do as you ask."

"I know it's bitter medicine," Horace Tabor said seriously. "But you will definitely feel better in the morning. Trust me on that."

"After today," Jake said, eyeing the upstairs rooms, "your advice about how to spend the night is about the *only* thing that I'd trust."

Great Man Galt stood before the full-length mirror beside the washstand. He glared coldly at his reflection with pink eyes. In less time than it took to blink, the pistol flew from its holster to level at his image. Galt grinned with satisfaction and twirled the gun back onto the well-oiled leather holster.

"Very good, Mister Galt," Hedgepath said. "I'm gratified to see that you have recovered. For the time has come 'to let slip the dogs of war.' "

"Are you sayin' we can jump the mine now?" Rincón McCutchan asked.

The lawyer forced a thin grin. "I believe

that was my point. You really should read some of Shakespeare. His works are most stimulating."

Rincón shot a glance at the huge spider with fiery red eyes perched on Hedgepath's silvery head. "When I get rich, I'll buy every one of his books."

Great Man Galt chuckled. "I'm sure Shakespeare will appreciate that."

"Gentlemen," Hedgepath said in a commanding tone, "you are to shoot someone only if they are armed and show enough hostility to cause a reasonable man to act in self-defense."

"How about Tabor?" Rincón pleaded. "You know how much I hanker to put some lead into his worthless carcass."

When the lawyer faced him, Rincón noticed the spider had grown two long white fangs that dripped with venom. The tarantula actually appeared to be grinning sardonically.

"Mister McCutchan," Hedgepath said with a sneer, "we have been over this ground before, have we not? If Crabtree's men, including Horace Tabor, agree to leave he property peaceably, they are to be left to do so unharmed. Do I make myself completely clear?"

"Yes, sir, we'll do as you say," Galt agreed.

McCutchan kept his gaze on the spider. The thing had hunkered down with its yellow-banded legs drawn in and for all of the world looked like it was preparing to spring from Hedgepath's head and attack. "Uh . . . yeah . . . I got you understood just fine."

Galt said: "Well, Mister Hedgepath, when do you wish us to do this little task for you?"

"Tomorrow morning," the lawyer replied. "I believe you should leave here quite early and be there before the crew shows up for work."

Galt shook his head sadly. "First, there is the matter of my fee, which remains unpaid. Perhaps there has been some *misunderstanding?*"

Rincón shivered when he heard the spider hiss the words — *all dead, all done* — twice in a row. That blasted tarantula was the worst spook yet. Except for the vulture the rest had had the decency to keep quiet.

The attorney's scrawny neck flushed and he snapped: "Payment shall be forthcoming *after* you have earned it, sir."

Henry Hayes Hedgepath's gaze had never left the gunfighter's ghostly face. Neither had he broken eye contact, yet when he looked down, Galt had a cocked pistol aimed at him.

The lawyer swallowed hard. "Would a check be acceptable, Mister Galt?"

"Provided it is made out for the full amount and I am able to cash it yet today," the gunman answered coldly.

Rincón McCutchan had never seen any man, let alone a lawyer, write out a check so fast.

Galt plucked the voucher from the lawyer's trembling hand. "I am very glad there was no misunderstanding, aren't you?"

Rincón's stock in the albino went up several points. He decided that it would be a ad day when he ordered Galt to be shot. There was always a thin chance the gunfighter might plug the lawyer first. Saving money was always a lofty goal.

"Tomorrow morning, Mister Galt," the lawyer said. His commanding tone of voice had vanished. "I am counting on you."

Great Man Galt glanced at the check. "Now," he chimed, "you may do so."

Hedgepath beat a hasty retreat through the doorway.

All dead, all done the spider hissed again and again from the hall.

"Well, friend McCutchan," Galt said as he twirled the revolver back into its holster, "I can see that our esteemed attorney understands a ruling from Judge Colt's

279

court without having to spend a lot of time researching the matter."

"Yes, sir," Rincón said with obvious respect. "I'm sure lookin' forward to workin' with you. There's no doubt at all now that gold mine'll be ours."

Galt feigned a look of hurt. "I am distressed that you had any question as to my ability. In the morning, should anyone show disbelief, they will die."

Rincón felt his spine turn icy. *All dead, all done* rang in his ears like an echo that refused to go away. For the first time in his life, Rincón McCutchan was afraid to face the coming dawn.

The lovely young woman with silky, waist-length, raven hair rolled over and took a *cigarillo* from a box on the nightstand. French Rita lit it and blew a smoke ring toward the unpainted ceiling. "It seems nothing in this world works out the way we want it to, does it?"

Jake Crabtree lay beside her on the feather-bed. "I trusted folks to do right by me. I'd reckon that makes me out to be three kinds of a fool."

French Rita ran her soft fingers down Jake's bare chest. "When a person loses their ability to trust, they also lose their soul and any reason to go on living."

Jake rolled his head toward her and questioned her with his eyes. He hadn't expected such a statement from a soiled dove.

"What I said surprised you," French Rita said. "It shouldn't. Whores learn a lot about life. More so than most, I suppose." She placed the small cigar between her ruby lips and stared upward, seeing far beyond the clapboard. "I didn't start out wanting to sell myself for a few dollars to any man with the money to pay me. Like I said, things often don't work out like we wish."

"You don't have to talk about this if you don't want to."

"It's all right," she said. "I've learned to bury the hurt, but not the hope."

Jake thought for a moment. "I've always wanted to accomplish something in this world. I reckon I *did* build a town, even if no one will remember who done it."

French Rita batted her painted eyelids. "*You'll* remember, that's what matters. The most important thing is to not grow bitter." Her gaze returned to Jake. "That's the hardest part of all."

Jake placed his own cigar in an ashtray. He reached over and stroked her rouged cheek. "You're a right fine lady and I'm glad to be here with you."

"Please blow out the lamp and hold me tight for a while?" she said softly.

Jake gathered her into his arms and embraced her with a sheltering hug. "Is there anything else I can do?"

"No." Her small voice cracked in the dark. "This is what I need these days."

"You just say the word, Mister Crabtree," Henry McCarty said with a pat to his rifle. "I'd be obliged to blow those claim jumpers clean off your mine."

Horace Tabor held out his palm in a plea for calm. "Now, hold on, boys, let's not go running off half cocked and get somebody shot." He focused on William Antrim, who stood at the head of the crew of obviously irate miners grouped together in the Mint Saloon. "Go over what happened one more time."

Antrim's features were tight with anger. "When the men and I went to start the day's work, two armed toughs were already at the mine and ran us off. It was that pink-eyed gunfighter, Great Man Galt, and Rincón McCutchan. . . ."

"What, exactly, did they tell you?" Tabor interrupted.

Antrim took a deep breath and measured his words. "That they were the representatives of the legal owner of the mine, Henry Hayes Hedgepath. Galt did most of the talking. Come to think on it, the only words Rincón spoke was to ask where you were, Mister Tabor."

Horace grinned. "I'm gratified to have been a disappointment to that sidewinder. Did the pasty-faced gunfighter make any threats?"

Antrim cleared his throat. "It came across more like a promise. Galt said that anyone who stuck around after he counted to three would be shot. Before he spoke the number two, we were on our way back here."

"That was the right thing to do," Jake said without hesitation. "I don't want anybody getting killed. What I've gotta do is come up with a plan."

"You wouldn't be in this fix if I'd done the job you paid me to do, Mister Crabtree," Henry McCarty said, his voice crisp with determination.

Jake shook his head. "Hold on there, Henry, you're just a kid. I can't have you going up against a hired gun like Great Man Galt."

Henry McCarty pondered Jake's words. "You know something, sir, as for Galt an' that Rincón feller, they'll kill dead as anyone once they're shot right. And I never miss."

Horace Tabor, who had been chewing thoughtfully on the stub of an unlit cigar, said: "I've got an idea that might keep anyone from getting killed."

Every eye turned expectantly to the balding man.

An evil grin crossed Tabor's face. "I'd say, if they like that mine so much, we make sure they stay there."

Jake Crabtree was obviously perplexed. "If I ain't mistaken, you're telling us to go ahead and let 'em do what they came here for."

Tabor couldn't suppress a chuckle at his cleverness. "Rincón McCutchan's an idiot and Galt is a gunfighter. All they're packing is pistols. If a few of us grab rifles and stay under cover, we can keep them pinned down."

A spark of realization glistened in Antrim's eyes. "Of course. They likely didn't even pack a lunch. They're gonna get plenty hungry right soon."

A burly miner spoke up. "It'd be something to tell my grandkids that I lobbed a few bullets at Great Man Galt."

"I'm with you!" another yelled.

"Don't go shooting them," Tabor ordered. "Just make sure they stay put."

More than two dozen determined hard-rock miners stormed out of the saloon to grab whatever rifle they owned and to take up a position at the mine.

"I'm betting that you can find a sharp lawyer who'll take your case for a slice of the pie," Tabor said to Jake. "I know of one who has a reputation of never losing. His name is Fred Johnson. Why don't you telegraph him?"

Jake wore an expression of bewilderment. "You know, Tabor, that pie you mention started out being all mine. If things keep going the way they have been, all I'm going to wind up with is some crumbs. The durndest part is, I ain't certain how it come about."

Cyrus T. Pettibone was feeling immensely proud of himself as he strolled down the main street of Baker City. His first order of business was the purchase of Jake Crabtree's note of indebtedness to the Virtue Bank. Once this matter was taken care of, he would have a wonderful club to use in the second bone of contention: The acquisition of Jake Crabtree's half interest. With a feeling of satisfaction the ponderous attorney swung open the ornate oak door of the bank and strode inside.

Otis A. McElroy regarded Pettibone's approach to the cashier's cage as he did all of his customers: He looked irritated at having been bothered.

"Good morning, sir," McElroy droned. "How may I be of service to you?"

"I believe the Virtue Bank has loaned a considerable sum of money to a Mister Jake Crabtree, using some mining claims owned by him as collateral."

The cashier shrugged. "We do not divulge our clients' business."

Cyrus T. Pettibone surreptitiously slid an eagle to the stoic clerk.

"Ah, yes," Otis McElroy said, palming the gold coin. "It comes to mind now that Crabtree *did* mortgage his mine at this establishment."

"And that is the purpose of my visit. I wish to purchase this indebtedness. And at an attractive premium, I might add."

"It can't be done," the cashier said sharply. "Good day, sir."

"Perhaps you could take a moment from your terribly busy schedule" — Pettibone made a point of scanning the empty bank — "and give me a brief explanation, or shall I pay Colonel Ruckle a visit."

"The colonel is away on business for several weeks. But I am certain he would love to visit with you upon his return. As to

286

the matter of Jake Crabtree's note, we cannot sell it to you because it has been paid in full."

Shock siphoned the blood from Pettibone's face. "Paid!" he exclaimed. "That can't be. You've made a mistake. I won't stand for this!"

Otis McElroy gave a shrug of indifference. "Notes are made here and notes are paid off here. This *is* a bank, my good man."

"Wh . . . wh . . . who, paid it?" the lawyer stammered.

"It was Miss MacNair. She cashed a draft *you* gave her, then she paid off Crabtree's indebtedness."

For the first time in his life, the brilliant courtroom orator and political hopeful, Cyrus Tiberius Pettibone, was speechless.

Jake Crabtree was in a funk. It had cost him the unbelievable sum of twelve dollars to send a telegraph to that mining lawyer. Perhaps, he mused, he shouldn't have used so many words to describe his plight. As Jake wandered from the telegraph office, a rumble deep in his belly reminded him that he hadn't eaten since last night. Galt and Rincón's antics had ripped him from the arms of feminine bliss to take care of business.

He headed for the hotel. A heaping platter of sourdough pancakes smothered with mounds of hot red chili and sweet onions beckoned. There was a lot of thinking that needed to be done, and a man's head always got muddled when he was hungry.

Jake's mouth fell open when he stepped inside the restaurant and saw Cecilia Mac-Nair sitting alone at a small table.

"Hello, Jake," the redhead said in a concerned voice. "I'm glad to see you. Please sit down and join me."

Jake wondered what had happened to Cecilia to make her act so nice. To be on the safe side, he made sure there weren't any empty whiskey bottles near her reach before taking the chair across from her.

"Gage always thought of you as one of his best friends. He mentioned a few times that you were somewhat . . . uh . . . eccentric, but that you were an honest and caring man who kept chasing dreams like a kid does a firefly."

Jake poured steaming coffee from his cup into the saucer to cool. Women being so blasted fickle about a man's choice of words, he decided it would be safer simply to smile and let her keep talking.

"There was no other way I could think of to fight than to sell my interest to raise money for our defense." Cecilia extracted a handful of papers from her handbag and laid them on the table.

"This is the mortgage the bank held on the mine. I paid it off in full. You found that gold and I couldn't desert you at a time when everything you worked for was falling apart. And I know Gage wouldn't have, either."

Jake Crabtree stared into his cooling saucer of coffee, his mind a tumble of confused thoughts and feelings. Then he remembered with a start that he had offered the lawyer, Johnson, half of his half interest if the attorney was successful in beating Hedgepath. That pie Tabor kept talking about was sure getting whittled down in a hurry. Jake felt it might be best to inform Cecilia of this development at some future date. He swallowed to clear his throat. "I . . . I'm telling you plain, whatever comes from all this, you've got half of it."

Cecilia said: "It's going to take a good lawyer. I did some research and found a man in Denver who is not only an attorney, but also a mining engineer. I've already sent him a retainer and he should be here tomorrow."

Jake was flabbergasted. "We could hold a convention for shysters here in Baker City. I sent a wire for a lawyer myself just before I came in for some grub."

Cecilia's reply was halted while the waitress set out Jake's food. When they were alone again, she said: "I suppose they could work together. It's said two heads are better than one, but Fred Johnson is supposed to be the best."

"You know," Jake said grabbing up his fork to dig into the mound of flapjacks and chili, "if I'd dropped in here first, I could have saved a whole twelve dollars."

CHAPTER TWENTY-FIVE

Another heavy caliber rifle bullet slammed into the wood head frame over the mine shaft and sent splinters flying. Great Man Galt and Rincón McCutchan scurried for cover back in the depths of the mine opening.

Rincón growled: "You sure seem to have 'em plenty scared. It does my heart good to watch an expert gunfighter in action."

"They weren't supposed to do this," Galt said with a whine. His fear of close spaces was playing tag with his worry over getting shot. "People are supposed to be afraid of me. They're supposed to run away."

"Well, go an' tell 'em that. Hedgepath didn't pay you to hide."

"I wasn't hired to get myself killed, either." Galt spat. "Those scallywags are out of pistol range and hiding behind trees, shooting at us."

Rincón frowned. "Looks like you got the

problem figgered out just fine." A knowing look crossed his face. "Horace Tabor's behind all this. I know he is. I wanted to shoot him in the worst way, but Hedgepath said no, we can't do that. Now look what went and happened."

Great Man Galt stuck his head from the shaft and peered cautiously about. "It'll be dark soon. Maybe then we can make a break for it."

"It's near to bein' a full moon out. I'd reckon we'd make for good target practice if we tried that."

Galt forced himself to swallow his bitter anger. He hated being made a fool of. The last thing he needed was an idiot like Rincón McCutchan irritating him. Never in his entire career had things gone so haywire.

Rincón spoke up. "I got some supplies in my saddlebags. Cover me."

With no further talk Rincón bolted from the shaft and ran toward where their horses were tethered by the creek. A fusillade of bullets marked his progress. Galt ventured a couple of feet from the hole and emptied his gun at the countryside. Then Rincón came running back packing a pair of leather saddlebags draped over his shoulder.

After taking a moment to catch his breath, Rincón said: "That bunch out there is toler-

292

able pissed at us. At least I got what I went for."

Galt couldn't suppress a groan when he watched McCutchan begin to unload bottles of whiskey. "We nearly got ourselves killed over some booze?"

Rincón grinned. "Didn't even break a single one. Things are lookin' up. Good thing I brought along ten quarts. Shucks, that'll keep us in great shape for a day or two."

Galt understood why Rincón walked around packing five lead slugs in his belly. A box of rocks held more intelligence than the man's head did. In all of his gunfighting years the albino had never been wounded. Neither had he killed anyone. Every opponent he'd come up against had run from the pink-eyed gunslinger. Galt's eyesight was now failing badly. Doctors had told him it was a hereditary condition due to his albinism. Thick eyeglasses allowed him to read when he was in private. A gunfighter wearing glasses wouldn't be taken seriously. But lately he even had difficulty negotiating stairs without falling. His bloody reputation had kept him employed simply because no one had ever stood up to him — then he had the misfortune to come to Slab Creek.

■ ■ ■ ■

Henry McCarty gave Tabor a puzzled look. "I thought that Great Man Galt was supposed to be the best there is. Shucks, Mister Tabor, I could have killed him a dozen times by now."

Tabor grinned. "Most gunmen aren't used to having folks stand up to them. About now I'd reckon he's stewing on how to get out of this pickle with that white hide of his intact. Rincón McCutchan's too stupid to worry."

Henry stared down the tree-covered slope at the mine and shook his head. "What I don't understand, sir, is how that lawyer figures on getting by with jumping this mine. The lawyer didn't find that gold. Jake Crabtree did. Why can't the sheriff just run them off? It seems to me the law shouldn't allow this to happen."

Tabor said after thinking for a moment: "I know sometimes the law seems to contradict common sense, but it is a system that works more times than not. Learn to curb your temper, Henry, or you may wind up in more trouble than you can handle."

Henry McCarty looked downcast. "The problem is, when I see someone getting picked on, I try to help them. I can't make myself look the other way."

"And you shouldn't. It just pays to give a situation a little thought before jumping in."

"Yes, sir, but I'll never turn my back on a friend."

Horace Tabor sighed. He realized now that the lad had a stubborn streak in him wider than a flooded river. He sincerely hoped the boy didn't wind up on the wrong end of a gun or rope, for above all he liked the kid.

"This is beautiful country," Cecilia said as she walked along the boardwalk close to Jake, while casting a glance at the distant, rugged mountain peaks. "I can see why living here is so uplifting. All you have to do is raise your eyes to realize just how insignificant your problems really are."

"Worrying on a matter never solves anything," Jake said. "I've got a mighty pretty lady by my side. A preacher might say that heaven's a tad better, but I've got my doubts."

"Jake Crabtree," Cecilia said with a feigned scowl, "you're incorrigible."

"Yes, ma'am, I reckon I am at that."

All too soon they came to the freight office. Jake, with a surprising display of manners, opened the door for her.

A lanky man sporting a beard streaked with rivulets of tobacco juice stood solemnly behind the ticket counter. "What'll you folks be needin'?"

Jake grinned and stepped close. "Three tickets for the afternoon stage to Slab Creek. Tell Packy Jackson to charge 'em against what he owes me. My name is Jake Crabtree."

The man spat a wad of tobacco contemptuously onto the plank floor. "I don't care if you're Ulysses S. Grant, it's gonna cost ya three bucks fer each of them tickets or you can go to blazes."

"Reckon you didn't hear me right," Jake said, his smile fading. "Packy knows me. If you'll fetch him, we can work this out while you still have a job."

The man behind the counter sneered. "That's gonna be plenty hard to do, considerin' the undertaker planted him some days ago. My name's Lucas Woolly. I bought the outfit off his widow. An' I ain't runnin' no charity."

The color drained from Jake's face. "Packy's dead? How did it happen?"

Lucas Woolly shrugged. "He weren't nothin' but a drunk. Fell into the river an' drowned."

Jake glared at the freighter. "Packy Jackson was a good man. It wouldn't hurt you to speak well of the dead."

Woolly spat another wad of tobacco. "You want them tickets or not? I'm a busy man."

"You're the one who can go to blazes," Jake growled. "Come on, Cecilia, we'll go rent a buggy from the livery stable."

Woolly growled: "That's fine with me. I'm gonna stop runnin' a stage up to that place. Only folks leavin' there pays me to make the run as it is."

Once they were outside, Cecilia slid her soft hand into Jake's. "I'm so sorry about your friend."

Jake focused his gaze on the same mountains Cecilia had been admiring earlier. "All I done was try to help Packy out, but for some reason I feel what happened to him is my fault."

"How could that be? Jake, giving a hand to a friend isn't wrong."

Jake said: "That gold has caused a passel of problems. I'm not any too sure that, if I hadn't found that mine, Packy might still be playing with his kids."

Cecilia MacNair blinked away a building tear. "Let's go rent that buggy. Fred Johnson will be here before long."

Jake took one last look at the freight office, then without a word escorted Cecilia along the creaking boardwalk to the livery stable.

Great Man Galt bit off a piece of moldy jerky. His back ached from squatting on a ladder all night. It galled the albino that McCutchan had drunk two quarts of rye, then curled up and snored contentedly until daybreak.

"Goat jerky's might tasty, ain't it?" Rincón said happily. "I sure like it better'n beef." He peered into the saddlebags. "Looks like I brought plenty."

"Friend," Galt said testily, "some of us would like water to drink. I'm dying of thirst."

Rincón held out an empty whiskey bottle. "There might be some water in the bottom of the shaft. Why don't you climb down and take a look?"

Galt shuddered at the thought of going deeper in the mine. "I think I'll check topside. Once word got out they are dealing with Great Man Galt, common sense may have prevailed."

After breathing the stale mine air, having his head out in God's open country was a blessing to Galt. Then a bullet struck a rock about two feet away and went singing off into the forest.

Rincón took a swig of whiskey. "Looks like those idiots out there still don't know who they're dealin' with."

Galt was too tired for an argument. "You mentioned there might be some water in the bottom of the mine. I'll keep a look-out if you'll take an empty whiskey bottle and go fill it up."

"Reckon I could do that," Rincón said agreeably. "While I'm down there, I'll take a gander at all that gold. Once Henry gets title to this mine, I've got a share coming."

"I'm *so* proud for you."

"Don't worry none," Rincón's voice faded as he receded into the depths. "I'll take care of our expensive gunfighter everyone's so scared of."

Great Man Galt slumped against a timber and looked skyward. He decided when — if — he got out of this fix, he would head south, possibly Arizona Territory. Once word of this shameful débâcle got bandied around, someone would call his bluff and shoot him for sure.

After what seemed an eternity, Rincón's boots could be heard grating on the wooden ladder rungs. With a grunt McCutchan tossed the obviously empty saddlebags onto the landing and sat to catch his breath.

"Did you get my water?" Galt asked.

Rincón McCutchan shook his head angrily and growled: "There ain't no blasted water, and worse'n that there ain't gold. This mine's been plumb worked out."

Great Man Galt lowered his chin to his chest and closed his eyes. "Well, give me a bottle of whiskey then. Likely as not there will still be a fight over this dirty hole, gold or no gold."

CHAPTER TWENTY-SIX

Henry Hayes Hedgepath stood in the sheriff's office in a red-faced fury. "I have men being held at gunpoint on my mining property and you refuse to help. Why, I'll form a recall and throw you out on your ear."

Sheriff Kingman said: "It's a civil matter."

"This is deplorable," Hedgepath growled. "I demand you do your job!"

Alton Kingman stared into his coffee cup. "Go ahead and demand all you want. Me and my deputy's staying right here."

"This is an outrage!" Hedgepath was screaming now. "I am an attorney, I'll have you know."

"Yep, reckon everybody knows that. While we're jawin' about the law, you hired Galt. If he shoots someone, I'll arrest *you* for bein' an accessory."

"Any blood shed shall be on your hands," Hedgepath spat.

The sheriff shrugged. "Don't let the door

hit your butt on your way out."

The glistening steam pump chugged along rhythmically, puffing and hissing like some mythical dragon. Seth Dugan wrestled another log into the firebox and slammed shut the heavy steel door. He glanced at the pressure gage, then turned to Lanny Payton. "We're holding real good at a hundred and ten pounds. There's enough wood in the boiler for a spell. I think I'll go eat dinner."

"Don't be too long," she ordered.

"I'll be back shortly," he told her.

"Don't fret none, Lanny, ol' girl," T. Greene Moss said. "That mine's gettin' dryer than a Baptist revival. With any decent luck we'll be able to hoist a little ore by tomorrow."

"We can start this evening," Lanny said firmly. "I don't see why the Dugans can't work a little harder."

"Everybody gets tuckered," T. Greene said. "I'll bet you ain't had two hours of decent shut-eye fer three whole days. Why don't you go stretch out and rest yer bones fer a spell."

Lanny reared her head in determination. "I'm staying at the mine. *Somebody* around here has to see this through."

Warm Stove Williams roused with a grunt and swung to sit on his cot. "By cracky, that heat's finally workin'. There ain't been a shiver strike fer hours."

"Glad ya finally got warm," T. Greene said, surprising Warm Stove that he didn't have some wisecrack to make.

"We got any vittles cooked up?" Warm Stove asked. "Not freezing to death has given me a powerful appetite."

"Seth Dugan's at the cabin eating dinner," Lanny said. "There's a big pot of pinto beans and side pork on the stove."

T. Greene shot a concerned glance at Lanny. "Why don't we all go have dinner together? I'd fancy you're half starved yourself."

"I'm not hungry," she answered staunchly.

Warm Stove and T. Greene exchanged knowing looks and began making their way to the cabin. Ever since the pumping had begun, there had been no reasoning with the increasingly cantankerous nurse.

Alone now, Lanny Payton contemplated the huge boiler and chugging pump as she would a critically ill patient. The up-and-down strokes of the engine she likened to a heartbeat. Every hiss and throb moved water from her rich vein of gold surely as a heart pumped blood through veins and arteries. Each movement insured life itself. Should the pulse slow or stop, it would mean death to her wonderful, rich mine.

The pump has slowed down. Lanny counted the strokes as she would a human pulse. Earlier, the pump had operated at sixty cycles per minute. Every nerve in her body turned raw. *Thirty-four beats in sixty seconds. This can't be. The water will flood my rich mine again.*

She quickly looked at the pressure gauge. *One hundred and ten pounds. At least there was a full head of steam. No need to go summon Seth Dugan from his meal.*

The large brass valve with a long handle controlled how much steam went to the engine. With determination engraved in her face, Lanny stepped over and opened the valve wide.

The huge cast iron flywheel gave a hard jerk as it built up speed. She left the boiler and ran over to where the steel discharge pipe gushed water into the gulch. It gratified her to see the stream increase in size.

Lanny sat down on a nearby log and listened contentedly as the heartbeat of the pump built to where it should have been all along. Then a heavy booming sound like a stick of dynamite had exploded resonated from the mine shaft, shaking the ground beneath where she sat. Lanny bolted upright, her face white with shock.

For some reason she couldn't comprehend, the engine and flywheel began running faster and faster. It quickly became a screaming machine, obviously out of control. Lanny rose to run and shut the steam valve. In the distance she saw T. Greene bolt from the cabin door only to become entangled in his canes and fall. Seth Dugan tripped over the fallen man and went sprawling into the dirt.

When Lanny was only a few feet away from the valve, it happened. The wildly throbbing engine blew apart. Huge pieces of the cast iron flywheel flew like shrapnel across the verdant countryside. One jagged piece that weighed at least two hundred pounds ripped open a gash in the side of the boiler. White clouds of steam blew from the rupture like the hiss of a thousand demons.

Then, suddenly as it had begun, silence reclaimed the mountain valley. Only the sibilant sound of water dripping from the ruined boiler into the red-hot ashes that were still smoldering in the bottom of the firebox remained to punctuate the moment. Lanny Payton stood frozen in dismay and horror at what had transpired.

"Are you OK, ma'am?" Seth Dugan yelled, running to her side.

The only thing Lanny could look at was the demolished pump. What remained of the once shiny engine leaned precariously over the mine shaft, threatening to drop into the opening at any moment.

"Wha . . . who . . . what happened?" she stammered. Lanny's only concern was the Golden Ruckus Mine. "How long will it take to fix it? We need to get on with the pumping you know."

Seth Dugan shook his head sadly. "Miss Payton, as far as fixing the pump . . . well, ma'am, it's plain destroyed . . . surely you can see that."

"We have to get back to pumping," Lanny said flatly, keeping her now vacant eyes on the shaft.

T. Greene leaned on one cane and placed his hand gently on her arm. "Why don't we all go to the cabin an' you can tell us all about it there."

"Yes," Lanny said without emotion. "I think I'd like that." She rolled her head to face Seth Dugan. "You keep on with the mining. We need another load of ore out by tomorrow. That vug's lined with pure gold, did you know that?"

Seth swallowed and nodded. "Yes, ma'am,

we'll take care of it."

Warm Stove Williams and the miner watched in silence as T. Greene and Lanny Payton slowly made their way to the cabin.

"She doesn't even realize what happened," Seth said. "I wonder if she ever will?"

"I reckon the bank'll take the mine over now," Warm Stove said as a tear ran from his right eye and trickled into his white beard. "My guess is the poor old gal will keep right on mining gold for the rest of her life. Even if it is just in her mind."

Seth said: "That's a sad thing."

Warm Stove said: "It surely is."

Fred Johnson turned out to be nothing like either Jake Crabtree or Cecilia had expected. He wore a ragged blue wool shirt and faded Levi's. His beard was scraggly and he badly needed a haircut.

Once his grip had been loaded onto the rented spring buggy, the mining specialist grinned, then chuckled. "I'm certain you're both wondering why I dress and travel like I do."

"The question has occurred," Jake said.

"Everyone expects me to look like an attorney or engineer. A man down on his luck can ask questions and get honest answers a lot easier than someone who looks like a shyster."

"I never heard a lawyer refer to himself as a shyster before," Jake said with a smile. "That's a mighty refreshing statement."

"Jake!" Cecilia scolded. "Mister Johnson's here to help us. Don't go insulting him."

"No offense taken. Even my wife teases me about being a lawyer. Please just call me Fred. My real forte lies in being a mining engineer. It just so happens that most rich mines wind up needing both a lawyer and an engineer to straighten out matters on occasion." He gave Cecilia an amused grin. "That's why I can get by with charging double."

Jake Crabtree was relieved to hear the engineer mention he had a wife. The way the man went out of his way to admire Cecilia's form was a peeve.

The engineer turned serious. "Tell me everything you can about this attorney, Henry Hayes Hedgepath. I've never had the pleasure of meeting him."

Jake snorted: "The pleasure would be kinda like stepping on a rusty nail." Then he proceeded to describe the bony lawyer and his so-called partner, Rincón McCutchan, omitting more picturesque terms for Cecilia's sake.

Fred Johnson then extracted a leather

folder from his traveling bag and spent the rest of the trip in silence, making notes and meticulously perusing a book on the mining laws of the state of Oregon.

Jake reined the buggy to a stop in front of the Mint Saloon. Horace Tabor, accompanied by Henry, stepped through the batwing doors. Tabor grabbed the traces while Henry McCarty stood staring at Cecilia like a puppy begging for a treat.

"Why, hello, Miss Cecilia," he said. "Everyone said you was headed back East."

The redhead flashed the boy a smile. "That was what I had to make everyone think. I hope you have been practicing your reading."

Henry studied his scuffed boots. "No, ma'am, I can't truthfully say that I have. There's some claim jumpers at the mine an' I've been keeping plenty busy shooting at them."

Cecilia scowled. "Henry, you're just a kid. You shouldn't be doing things like that."

Fred Johnson stepped forward and introduced himself to Tabor and Henry. Jake took a moment to peruse his town of Slab Creek. Smoke drifted lazily from the chimneys of only two cabins. "Folks shouldn't be leaving here."

"It gets a lot worse," Horace said, rolling

sad eyes to the upper story of the saloon.

Jake Crabtree looked dazed. "Tell me it ain't so."

Tabor clucked his tongue. "French Rita said to tell you she's sorry, but that a girl has to make a living."

Fred Johnson spoke up. "Let's get on with business."

"What's first on your list?" Jake asked.

"We're going to the mine and have a chat with Great Man Galt and Rincón Mc-Cutchan, that's what."

Horace Tabor and Jake Crabtree faced each other. "Oh, bugger," they said in unison.

Rincón McCutchan had a difficult time not staring at the third pink eye that had again manifested itself in the middle of Galt's pasty forehead. As irritable as the albino had become, Rincón thought it best to ignore the entire situation. It was too bad that they had run out of whiskey. Not only did the amber fluid keep Rincón's spooks at bay, it also worked wonders for Galt's chafing personality. After the gunfighter had drunk half of a bottle, his attitude turned downright decent. *No man should ever leave town with less than a case of whiskey,* Rincón mused.

Great Man Galt lovingly stroked the pearl handle of his revolver with long, dainty fingers. "I've never killed a lawyer before, but, once we get out of this fix, I'm gonna put so many holes in Hedgepath that a person could read a newspaper through him."

"At least wait until I get my net profits," Rincón said.

"*What* profits, you flaming idiot?" Galt fumed. "In case you forgot already, the mine's worthless."

Rincón frowned. "Now that you mention the fact, I'd suppose the profit off of nothing ain't a lot."

Galt groaned and continued stroking his pistol. After a long moment of scowling at Rincón, he mumbled: "We have no choice but to surrender."

Rincón kicked an empty whiskey bottle with his boot. "Not havin' anything to drink sure does pile on the agony."

A voice booming from the distance took their attention.

"Rincón . . . Rincón McCutchan. You and Galt come out and talk. We're not armed and no one's gonna get hurt."

Both recognized Jake Crabtree as the man doing the yelling.

Galt's grim smile returned. "Now that's

more like it."

Rincón shook his head sadly. "I'm bettin' they ain't here to give up."

Galt stood and shouted: "All right Crabtree, we're coming out! But don't forget who you're dealing with." Great Man Galt took up a gunfighter's stance and squinted his pink eyes. "This here's Hedgepath's property," he growled.

"Why don't you two just hightail it back to Baker City before someone gets shot?" Jake said calmly.

Galt could think of nothing but reclaiming his tarnished reputation. "You're not the ones who should be worrying. You are all in pistol range."

"Now hold on," Tabor snorted. "We come to parley. No one here has a gun."

That piece of news was all the albino needed to hear. His vision was so bad he couldn't tell if the men in front of him were armed or not. The famed gunfighter drew his pistol in less time than it took for an eye to blink and began firing at them.

Rincón McCutchan jumped back in horror and yelled at Galt: "You white-faced fool, there's a woman with them!"

Galt's pistol was already empty. Rincón's warning caused the gunfighter's legs to turn rubbery. Shooting a woman, even by accident, would certainly get him lynched. That was one thing a man could never hope to get by with in the West. He breathed a sigh of relief when he made out all four of the blurry forms scamper away into the trees.

A rifle shot rang out and Galt's black hat went flying.

"Get back in the mine, you idiot!" Rincón yelled, spinning to run. "We're sittin' ducks out here."

Two more lead bullets slammed into the ground as the pair dove back into the shelter of the mine.

Rincón glowered at the panting albino. "I don't know what you were tryin' to prove, scarin' those folks like you done." Then he thought on the matter. "You *weren't* tryin' to scare 'em. Galt, not one of those bullets of yours hit within ten feet of a soul out there. And I'll swear you were shootin' *at* 'em. Why, you're blind as a bat. You'd be lucky to hit your mouth with a fork full of food."

Great Man Galt sighed and began reloading his Colt. "But they *did* run away. As long as you keep your trap shut, I can keep on being a gunfighter."

Rincón snorted: "There's one thing you're forgettin'."

"And what might that be, *friend* Rincón?" Galt's melodious voice chimed.

"You went an' shot at a woman. They'll likely be comin' back in a tolerable pissed-off mood over that."

Galt swallowed hard. His blood turned cold when the gravity of his unforgivable action struck. He glanced up at the tripod over the shaft and shivered. The thing would make a wonderful gallows. For the first time in his gunfighting career, the famous man could visualize his own death.

Cecilia MacNair sat down shakily in the chair Fred Johnson had thoughtfully slid out for her. "I've never been shot at before," she said.

"That albino gunfighter's not only nuttier than an outhouse rat," Horace Tabor grumbled, "he's got to be the worst shot west of the Mississippi. That man's a fraud for sure. I can see now why him and Rincón are pals."

Fred sat down at the table. "I must say that I did not anticipate Great Man Galt's foolhardy move."

Cecilia's lower lip trembled. "That Galt looks like the angel of death. When he started shooting, I thought we were all going to die."

Henry McCarty walked over to the table and set down a bottle of whiskey. The youth's normally twinkling eyes flashed like silver lightning. "They shouldn't have shot at you, Miss Cecilia. To my way of thinking, neither of them has any reason to go on breathing."

Horace Tabor passed around the glasses. He hesitated when he came to Cecilia. "Miss, folks claim there's a time and place for everything. Right about now I'd say this is the time and this is the place."

The redhead stared at the empty glass and nodded. "Perhaps a small one will settle my nerves."

"That's the only reason I ever drink the stuff," Jake said with a grin as he poured her about an inch of rye. "It works mighty fine even if a person thinks they might get nervous later on."

Every eye watched as Cecilia belted down the drink in one gulp. She batted her eyelids. "May I have another? And don't be so stingy this time when you pour."

The mining engineer looked toward Cecilia with lowered eyes. "Miss MacNair, I wish to apologize again for my short-sightedness in allowing you to accompany us into a potentially dangerous situation."

"You assumed, as did I," she answered,

"that we were dealing with rational people."

Horace Tabor lit a cigar. "I'm the one who should have known better. I knew we were dealing with a maniac and an idiot. My only regret is, when I put those two slugs into Rincón's belly that time in Colorado, the bullets didn't take."

Cecilia and Fred stared at Tabor open-mouthed.

Tabor shrugged his shoulders indifferently. "Shucks, these things happen around mining claims."

Jake said: "Reckon we've pretty well figgered out what won't work. Let's put our heads to working on something that might."

"Dynamite's not a bad idea," Tabor said with a grin. "We could bundle up a dozen sticks or so and someone could run up and toss it down the shaft. That oughta get their attention."

"It would also blow up my mine," Jake growled. "Those two idiots ain't worth the cost of the dynamite, let alone wrecking the shaft."

Fred took a sip of whiskey. "By all rights, this problem concerns The Venture Corporation. I will go to town tomorrow and pay a call on the sheriff and Pettibone. Until I can get a court order removing Henry Hayes Hedgepath and his associates from the mine, pending the results of a lawsuit, I would suggest we allow those galoots to remain where they are."

Cecilia motioned to Horace Tabor with her empty glass. "We should have one more round." She smiled at Jake Crabtree. "And don't you go getting into a funk. Fred Johnson is the best man we could have on our side. There's no reason to believe the Merry Widow Mine won't still make a fortune."

"Let's all drink to that," Horace Tabor said as he refilled the glasses. "And the fact that Great Man Galt couldn't hit the side of a barn if he was shut inside it."

No one at the table noticed Henry strapping on his Colt. With a rifle carried in the crook of his arm, Henry slipped silently from the saloon and strode toward the mine with determination and anger etched into his youthful face.

"Well this sure is a fine kettle of fish," Rincón grumbled. "Here I wind up owning a big hunk of nothing. There's folks outside wantin' to ventilate me and I'm hiding in a mine with a gunfighter that can't shoot worth beans."

"At least we're still alive," Galt uttered.

Rincón blinked his eyes, trying to make

the myriad of rattlesnakes writhing behind the mine timbers go away. It didn't work. "I might just plain give up. After all, it wasn't me that went and shot at a woman."

Galt cleared his throat. "I wouldn't count on them being so forgiving. My guess is they're knotting *two* hang ropes as we speak."

"I need a drink. My head's hurtin' something fierce and I can't think."

"Whiskey clouds a man's judgment. I'm just as glad you don't have any. When we make our escape, your gun will make a difference."

"Just for grins, let's say we do get out of this mess with our hides intact. Where are we gonna go? The climate in Oregon ain't a healthy one. I'd also reckon that your gunfightin' reputation is worth about as much around these parts as my interest in this gold mine turned out to be."

Galt clucked his tongue. "Let's head south. There's been some rich strikes in the Southwest. Down there no one will have ever heard of us."

Rincón thought for a moment. "I've always had a hankerin' to rob a bank or maybe a train, like Jesse James. Seems to me robbin' dang' near anything would pay better than hidin' in a mine shaft."

"You do make a good point. I wonder just how much money we could make holding up a bank?"

"Why, there ain't likely one of them joints that don't have fifty thousand dollars on a bad day."

The thought of making big money brightened Galt. "OK, partner, when we get out of this mess, we'll make the James gang look like pikers."

"There you go. Now that we got us a plan, all we gotta do is stay alive to make it work."

"Great Man Galt!" a youthful voice yelled from near the mine opening. "This is Henry McCarty. I'm callin' you out, fair and square, to see who's the fastest."

Rincón sneered: "That's Antrim's boy. Shucks, I heard tell he's only seventeen."

Galt couldn't conceal his seething anger. "I can't run from a kid. I'd be the laughingstock of the entire Northwest if I did."

Rincón rolled his head and pointed upward to the wooden gallows frame. "Seems to me that'd be preferable to receivin' a suspended sentence."

The albino pursed his lips and sighed. "Well, let's go get this over with. The sooner we get to some place where no one has ever heard of me, the better I'll like it."

"Great Man Galt!" Henry yelled. "I'm

givin' you till the count of three."

"We're comin' out, kid!" Galt bellowed.

A moment later both Rincón and Galt stood fifty feet away from Henry McCarty. The boy kept his steely eyes fixed on their faces with a steady hand held over the handle of the Colt revolver.

"This is your last chance," Henry said icily. "You two either leave Slab Creek or die where you stand."

Great Man Galt bit his lip so hard a trickle of blood ran down his ghostly chin. "OK, you win. Rincón and I'll leave."

Henry didn't move a muscle. "With one hand, drop your gun belts, nice and slow. If either of you try anything, I'll drop *you*."

With a cross between a sob and a growl Galt slowly unbuckled his gun belt and let his holstered pistol with custom-made pearl handgrips drop into the dirt. "OK, kid," he spat, "you win . . . this time."

A cocky grin crossed Henry's face. "Then the next time, you *will* die."

"Let's get out of this place," Rincón said, dropping his gun belt and motioning to their horses.

Galt glared his pink eyes at the blurry form of the kid who had just disgraced him. The famous gunfighter bit his lip once

again, then joined Rincón in a dash to get
the hell out of Oregon.

Chapter Twenty-Seven

"Henry, that was a foolhardy thing you done." William Antrim's scowl couldn't mask his admiration. "You might have gotten killed. I nearly had a conniption when I saw what was going on."

Antrim failed to mention the fact that he had Great Man Galt in his rifle sights all the while.

"Shucks, sir, those two didn't have the backbone to face me fair. Why you should 'a' seen 'em turn tail and run. I even got their guns to remember them by."

Horace chewed on his cigar and regarded the beaming lad. "Now don't go fancy yourself a gunslinger, son."

"Yes, sir," Henry said. "But I actually backed down Great Man Galt. I reckon I must be tougher than I thought to get that job done without firin' a shot."

"The word is firing, Henry," Cecilia corrected. "We are all proud of what you did and are thankful that you were not hurt. Proper use of the English language, however, is still a necessity." She smiled at the youth. "Even for brave heroes like yourself."

Henry McCarty's cheeks turned crimson and he gazed at the plank floor. "Ah, shucks, ma'am, it weren't . . . was not anything."

Cecilia added: "Henry, I still think you are the bravest *man* I've ever known."

"I agree that Henry has spunk," Jake said. "But for Pete's sake, don't go ramblin' on or he'll likely become a lawyer or, even worse, go into politics."

"I have more hopes for him than that," Antrim said with a grin. "Having a lawyer in the family would be a terrible cross to bear."

Fred Johnson pried another chunk of white quartz loose from the vein with his small rock pick. The engineer grabbed the rock and took a small magnifying glass from his pocket and squinted as he closely studied the sample.

"Uhmmm," Johnson mumbled. For the entire two hours the group had spent in the dank, stifling, and cramped tunnels and shafts of the mine, an impassionate *"Uhmmm"* or a *"Harrumph!"* seemed to be the only words in the mining engineer's

vocabulary.

Fred Johnson spoke his first complete sentence since he had begun his examination of the Merry Widow Mine. "I think we ought to take time to gather a specimen or two for the lovely Miss MacNair. Then, I believe, we should adjourn to the saloon."

"I'm glad you're finally satisfied with my gold mine," Jake said.

The mining engineer nodded gravely. "Yes, Jake, I have completed a sufficient examination to come to a tentative conclusion."

Jake beamed. "Well, now that you're happy, let's go back to the saloon and have a drink. Then you can tell everyone just how rich the mine is."

Fred Johnson replied: "Yes, that is a good idea. Then, after we eat, I'll give you my professional opinion."

Only the mournful hooting of an owl perched in a nearby yellow pine broke the still silence of night in the Blue Mountains. A hint of early winter in the form of a chill breeze had caused Jake to shut the windows and door of the saloon. Heat from the massive cook stove radiated agreeably to where the group was just polishing off a delightful supper of venison stew and sourdough biscuits. Henry McCarty, to everyone's surprise, had spent his time cooking while the mine examination was under way.

"You're a remarkable lad," Fred Johnson said to Henry. "Not only can you face down a pair of gunslingers, you also make the fluffiest and tastiest biscuits I've ever eaten."

"The boy has a great future ahead of him," William Antrim said. "I'm very proud of my stepson, but I'm afraid that we need to be getting back to Silver City. We'll be leaving tomorrow on the afternoon stage . . . if it shows up."

Jake focused on Antrim with a look of worry. "Couldn't you stick around and run the mine until I can hire someone to replace you?"

Antrim sighed and turned to Fred Johnson. "I reckon it's time you came out with it."

Jake's brow furrowed. "Come out with what?"

The engineer helped himself to a cigar, lit it from the flame of the kerosene lamp on the table, then leaned back in his chair. "Jake, what Antrim is trying to tell you has been verified by my examination. There is no easy way to say this except to come straight to the point . . . there simply is no more gold left for anyone to mine."

Color drained from Jake's face. He blinked and stared at Antrim. "You buy this cock-and-bull story?"

Antrim replied softly: "I didn't think you would believe me if I told you."

Jake appeared dumbstruck when he turned to his friend. "Horace, is any of this true?"

Memories of his own gold mine playing out darkened Horace Tabor's eyes with despair. "A prospector told me once that when you take out the first shovel full of ore, you've begun to kill a mine. And, yes, I must say that from my experience, the Merry Widow is likely finished."

Cecilia appeared on the verge of tears. "Oh, Jake, I'm so sorry."

"Henry," Jake said, turning to the stone-faced boy who stood at the end of the bar, "is there any more whiskey left?"

"Yes, sir. I found a whole case of the stuff."

"Could you please bring me a bottle? This is one time I really *need* a snort."

Morbid silence hung in the saloon like a heavy fog while Jake sipped on his whiskey with a faraway expression. Several minutes passed before he spoke. "I reckon I'm not only poor as Job's turkey, I also owe Cecilia a passel of money." He rolled sad eyes toward the redhead. "If it takes me the rest of my life to do it, I'll pay you every penny . . . somehow."

Fred Johnson said with a sly grin: "I can't see where that should be any problem."

"Huh?" Jake grunted while Horace Tabor blinked in bafflement.

The engineer continued: "Jake, if you can accept the fact the mine's played out, then there's no problem."

"What do you mean 'no problem,' " Jake boomed. "Everybody and their dog are tellin' me the gold is gone!"

Fred's grin widened. "Let's all have a glass of that wonderful bourbon and I'll explain how money is *really* made in the mining business."

Rincón McCutchan tried hard to keep his eyes from Great Man Galt. The albino had sprouted two curved horns, one out of each side of his head. There was no doubt that Galt looked uncomfortably like the devil. The pair was riding south, following the Snake River. Partnering up with a pasty-faced gunfighter who couldn't hit a bull in the butt with a board was agony enough. Rincón felt the fact that Galt now looked like Satan to be very disquieting.

"I thought you was gonna shoot Hedge-path before we left," Rincón said, keeping his gaze straight ahead.

"With what?" Galt grumbled. "If you remember correctly that little squirt, Henry, took our guns."

Rincón's head felt like it had been whacked with a sledgehammer. "Oh, yeah, well, I wouldn't fret it any. He's a lawyer. Someone else will likely shoot him. I've been thinking. Most outlaws call themselves by a handle. It seems to spook folks considerable. How does McCutchan's Marauders strike you?"

Galt groaned. "I would say that since I am the man with the reputation of a gunfighter, Galt's Wild Bunch might garner more respect."

Rincón chuckled. "If they've heard about what happened in Oregon, they'll just take your gun away again." He shot a glance and noticed the albino's pink eyes had become slitted, like those of a goat or a demon. A cold chill trickled down his spine. "I'm only funnin' you. Why don't we think on it for a spell. Arizona's a far piece away."

"Yes," Galt said icily, "I simply can't wait until we get there."

"I feel the same way you do," Rincón said.

Both men spurred their horses into a faster gait. The sooner they robbed something, the happier at least *one* of them would be.

Cyrus Pettibone could scarcely believe his good fortune. Those elusive, gilded shares in The Venture Corporation seemed once again to be within his grasp. He folded his pudgy hands to form a tent and leaned forward over his cluttered desk.

"Now, Mister Crabtree," he said with crispness, "my understanding of the situation is" — he nodded to Fred Johnson who sat in a chair alongside Jake — "that your counsel has advised you to sell your interest in the Merry Widow Mine. I wish to commend my fellow barrister on his wise guidance."

Fred Johnson's face was unreadable. "I must inform you that The Venture Corporation . . . which I know is your client . . . is only one of many mining concerns that may wish to pursue the matter. I have already received one proposal that I believe to be of interest."

Pettibone's brow furrowed as those stock shares took flight again. "My good sir, Mister Sinrod is being most generous to offer thirty thousand dollars for your client's interest in an unproven property with a lawsuit clouding the title. Miss MacNair was quite happy to sell at that price."

"Yes, I'm certain she was," Fred said. "But *I* was not there to negotiate the sale. As you know, I have many connections in the business. My recommendations carry great credence in the industry."

Pettibone paled. "You have examined the mine?"

"I have," Johnson replied firmly. "And my client will not sell his interest for a mere thirty thousand dollars."

Cyrus squeezed his hands together so tightly the knuckles turned white.

Jake couldn't suppress a grin of satisfaction at the show. The question as to whether or not the mining engineer's scheme would actually work remained to be seen. Even if it didn't, Jake felt that Johnson was definitely earning his fee.

"Tut, tut, Cyrus," Fred said. "My sole reason for bringing Mister Crabtree by was to give your clients an opportunity to join in the bidding."

"Bidding! What do you mean bidding?"

"Why, Cyrus, you really should not get so emotional over business matters. It will upset your digestion."

Pettibone glared across his huge desk. "This is blackmail."

"Such a harsh term for negotiation." Fred leaned forward. "I will give you a price, which, if accepted within the frame of the next two hours, will purchase my client's interest. If the terms are not met, the price to The Venture Corporation will increase at the rate of one thousand dollars per hour or until certain *other* parties choose to exercise their option."

Cyrus T. Pettibone worried his lower lip with his tongue. "You did say you examined the mine?"

Fred Johnson nodded.

Pettibone sighed. "Tell me the price."

"Fifty thousand dollars by wire transfer to the Virtue Bank. Upon receipt of these funds, payable to Jacob Crabtree, he will execute a deed to The Venture Corporation or any other entity of your choosing."

"I must contact my client."

"Of course, Cyrus," Fred said. "The telegraph office is but a short walk. I know, for I have used their services several times this morning." He pulled a gold pocket watch from his jacket pocket and flipped open the cover. "Why, it's nearly noon already. Jake and I have a dinner date to see some friends off on a journey. We'll reconvene here at . . . say . . . two for your client's response? If the reply is negative, this will give me ample time to utilize the telegraph system myself."

"I shall attempt to contact Mister Sinrod," Cyrus said with a hint of defeat. "He is a very busy man."

Standing, Fred said: "At the rate of one thousand dollars an hour, I'm certain your client will find time for you. Enjoy your dinner, Cyrus."

Cecilia MacNair smiled at Henry McCarty across their table at the hotel. "I'm going to miss you very much, Henry," she said sadly. "Promise me that you'll keep up on your studies. Reading and writing are necessary skills these days."

"Yes, ma'am," Henry replied. "I surely will."

"We're grateful to all of you," Antrim said. "I'd reckon both of us will be plenty glad to see Catherine again."

"You know everyone hopes she gets better," Jake said.

Antrim said firmly: "Henry and I are going to see to her care."

Jake fidgeted with his mustache. "You two got money to get home on?"

William Antrim spoke up quickly before Henry could say anything: "Yes, sir, we're just fine. We only hope things go well for you, Mister Crabtree."

Fred Johnson said: "Oh, I believe they

will. Right about now I'll bet Pettibone is heating up the telegraph wires between here and San Francisco. Let's all walk to the train station. Jake and I have some time to kill before we go make a little killing of our own."

"You're mighty sure of yourself," Jake said. "I'd just be glad to get enough to pay Cecilia back."

Fred chuckled. "The mining business is like playing poker. We just called. Now it's up to Cyrus to convince his client to buy the mine before someone else does."

Jake bit his lip to keep quiet. He knew there was no one except Henry Hayes Hedgepath who wanted his mine, and Hedgepath surely wasn't going to pay money for it.

William Antrim said: "Well, folks, I hate to say it, but we have to get to the train."

Henry McCarty flashed sad eyes at Cecilia. "Ma'am, I'm surely gonna miss you."

Cecilia MacNair stood, walked to Henry's side, and offered her arm. "A handsome and brave gentleman like yourself should never want for feminine companionship."

Otis McElroy traipsed to his teller's cage at the Virtue Bank and met Jake Crabtree and Fred Johnson with his usual display of surly indifference. " 'Afternoon, gentlemen. How may I be of service?"

"We're here to get some money," Jake said. "I reckon you got a transfer for me from San Francisco."

"Ah, yes, we have received instructions from a certain Venture Corporation to that effect for the grand sum of fifty thousand dollars."

"Well, we're here for it," Jake said firmly.

"All of it?" McElroy said with a rare display of emotion. "Surely not in cash. Why, that is more than we have on hand."

Fred Johnson stepped forward. "Cashiers checks on this establishment will be acceptable."

"Yes, sir," the clerk said with obvious relief. "And how would Mister Crabtree wish these made out?"

Jake grinned broadly. "Eighteen thousand to Miss Cecilia MacNair and another for fifteen thousand dollars to Fred Johnson. I'll leave the rest here for a spell."

McElroy grumbled: "This will take a while. There are a great many book entries to be made."

"We'll wait," Jake said. "It'd be a shame if you broke the lead outta your pencil by hurryin'."

Otis McElroy gave a scowl and began

writing. "At least some people were lucky enough to make money at Slab Creek. This establishment is going to quit loaning money to that area. We are being forced to foreclose on a mining property up there as we speak."

Jake asked with concern. "Who's in dutch, anyway?"

McElroy sneered. "Oh, that cripple, T. Greene Moss and Doctor MacNair's nurse, Lanny Payton. I was obliging enough to risk bank funds and loan them money to buy a pump. Unfortunately the machine blew up and now there is no choice left to protect the bank's interest other than to foreclose on their mining property. I feel simply terrible about the bank's loss."

Jake said: "Don't go losin' any sleep over it. Just how much money do they owe this gyp joint anyway?"

The clerk cocked his head in thought. "The note was for five hundred dollars. Considering our reasonable charges and fees, I would estimate that approximately six hundred dollars would clear their indebtedness."

"While you're in the figgerin' business," Jake growled, "go ahead and add up their tab. I'll pay it off outta my account."

A rare smile crossed McElroy's bony face.

"How wonderful of you. Perhaps, after you have foreclosed on the property and run those people off, the investment might be a prudent one for a man of your judgment in mining."

Jake Crabtree's features turned into granite. "When I get that note marked 'paid in full,' I intend to burn it."

Shock washed across Otis McElroy's face. "Why . . . why in the world would you do something that foolish?"

"You'd never understand in a thousand years," Jake said.

A shrill blast from the brass whistle atop the black, huffing locomotive hooked to a half-dozen passenger cars warned that its departure was imminent. Jake Crabtree and a teary-eyed Cecilia MacNair faced Fred Johnson at the same boarding area where they had seen William Antrim and Henry McCarty off.

"I wish Horace Tabor could have been here to watch you operate," Jake said, "but he felt he should stay in Slab Creek and guard the whiskey supply. Reckon that's about the only thing up there outside of my tomcat that's worth anything. And I got my doubts about the cat."

"There's simply no way properly to thank

you, Fred," Cecilia said. "I don't know how you accomplished what you did, but you were wonderful."

Fred patted his jacket pocket and grinned. "Oh, I've been thanked very well." The lawyer snickered. "Don't worry any about the Venture people. They've already kited their stock on the news of buying your mine and sold some for enough to pay all expenses and make a tidy profit. Never feel sorry for stockbrokers." The mining engineer grew pensive. "Under the terms of our sale agreement you must be out of Slab Creek within ten days. Do you have any plans?"

Jake couldn't contain a smile of satisfaction when Cecilia grasped his hand. "We're going to talk about that," she replied. "When we get back to Slab Creek, there will be plenty of time to sort things out."

"Now that I know what gold looks like," Jake said with a huge grin, "I'd have to work hard at *not* gettin' rich."

CHAPTER TWENTY-EIGHT

Fluffy white snowflakes drifted lazily earthward from a pewter sky, giving little doubt that an early winter had begun to claim its icy grip on the rugged Blue Mountains of eastern Oregon. The interior of the Mint Saloon seemed vast and lonely to Cecilia and Jake as the last two people left in Slab Creek sat facing each other across a table. Ulysses was stretched out contentedly in front of the redhead who kept the sleek black tomcat purring loudly by gently stroking his ears.

"That was a decent thing you did," Cecilia said, "paying off the bank note for those poor old folks, then leaving them money at the bank. I'm sorry that Lanny Payton lost her mind like she did. It's a sad thing the way she sits in that rocking chair and stares out the window with those vacant eyes of hers. I hope someday she may snap out of it."

Jake poured two glasses of whiskey and slid one to Cecilia. "I'd reckon all anybody can do for her is hope."

She sighed. "Yes, I know." Then she asked: "Are you sure you want to leave your money with me? That is a great sum."

"It's likely a bunch safer with you than if I had it." He grinned. "I've still got a thousand dollars from that last ore shipment. Horace Tabor and me's going to meet up in Albuquerque after he sees to things in Oro City. Then we're going to head down to the area around Silver City. With Tabor and me working together, we can't help but get rich."

Cecilia's eyes were gentle and understanding. "I'm sure you will. I have decided to settle in Baker City. I've grown to love the town and the mountains. I may even buy a house. I've always wanted a place of my own."

Jake Crabtree worried his mustache as he carefully mulled his words. "Cecilia, I know I'm a little rough around the edges, but I've learned to recognize a good claim when I see one. Do you think we . . . you know . . . maybe we could make a go of it together?"

Cecilia blushed slightly, then took her hand off of Ulysses and reached across and softly touched Jake's cheek. "You're honest and generous. I like that in a man. Get the wanderlust out of your system, Jake, then we'll see. Go to New Mexico with Horace Tabor and chase a firefly or two. I'll be in Baker City whenever you catch one . . . or decide to let it go." She tried to laugh while wiping tears from her eyes. "Besides that, I know you'll show up again, because I'm going to keep your cat and your money to make sure you do."

"Oh, then I'll be back for sure," Jake said with feigned seriousness. "It'd pain me something fierce to lose that cat."

Cecilia stared out the window at the lessening snow and grew pensive. "It was quite a dream, wasn't it? Building a town here in the middle of a wilderness, then in a period of a brief summer have it fade into nothingness."

"It was worth everything that happened because I met you."

"You're not only honest and generous, but you're turning into a sweet-talker, too. Be careful, Jake Crabtree, or I may not let you go chasing fireflies."

Jake shuffled uneasily in his chair, then suddenly he stared out the window, his eyes wide with astonishment. An opening in the gray clouds had let a shaft of sunlight peek though. Cecilia gasped when she saw what held Jake's attention. It was the sunbeam reflecting off the distant metal sign that marked her brother's final resting place.

"We oughta give him a toast," Jake said with a cracking voice. "That man there is who really found the gold."

Tears welled in her emerald eyes. Cecilia knew she wouldn't be able to speak without crying, so she raised her glass in silence and clicked it to Jake's.

Very soon the only resident of the town of Slab Creek would be Dr. Gage MacNair and, like the sign said, his office was upstairs.

ACKNOWLEDGMENTS

I would like to give heartfelt thanks to Jon Tuska and Vicki Piekarski of Golden West Literary Agency for making it happen. Kudos to Hazel Rumney and Russell Davis at Thorndike Press and, last but not least, to Myron C. Woodley of Sumpter, Oregon for sharing the rich lode of mining lore of the majestic Blue Mountains with me.